KILLING TIME

A DCI REECE THRILLER

LIAM HANSON

Copyright © 2022 by Liam Hanson

All rights reserved.

No part of this publication may be reproduced, distributed, or transmitted in any form or by any means, including photocopying, recording, or other electronic or mechanical methods, without the prior written permission of the publisher, except as permitted by U.K. copyright law. For permission requests, contact author.

The story, all names, characters, and incidents portrayed in this production are fictitious. No identification with actual persons, living or deceased, is intended or should be inferred.

Cover: Photo by Ales Krivec © on Unsplash

Published by CRIME PRINTS

An Imprint of Liam Hanson Media

ISBN-13 : 979-8401895226

For my wife and children

Current books in the series:
_____

DEADLY MOTIVE
COLD GROUND
KILLING TIME
CHASING SHADOWS
DEVIL'S BREAD

KILLING TIME

Chapter 1

RADYR, CARDIFF. DECEMBER 22nd 1989.

Dai Kosh didn't intend to take the left-hand side of the other man's head off. He hadn't intended to shoot and kill him at all. It just happened that way when both angry farmers wrestled for possession of the same loaded shotgun.

One second, Old Man Jasper was standing there—head 'n' all—swearing like a sailor and pulling at the gun with gloved hands and gritted teeth. The next, he was wobbling on unsteady legs. Blood spraying skywards in a fan-like pattern. His jaw and a fair amount of cheek and frontal bone landing a good ten to fifteen feet behind him. He grimaced at the onlookers through what was one eye and half a face, before falling to the floor like a felled oak.

He didn't reach out in front of him when he went down.

LIAM HANSON

Didn't object, nor issue verbal threats of retribution against the other man.

He did little at all as the remaining contents of his shattered skull spilled into the powdery snow like the yolk from a soft-boiled egg.

And it all happened quicker than the time it took for the loud bang to stop chasing itself across the nearby hills.

The cause of the violent fracas was one the farmers had previously thrashed out umpteen times or more. Namely: land boundaries. Whose family owned what. And since when.

It always started the same way. With words, threats, and the occasional push and pull. A bloodied nose on Jasper's part a few months earlier. But never before today had it finished with a twitching corpse.

'Fucking hell, Dad!' The boy was no older than eight or nine years, and was the colour of the winter landscape surrounding them. 'You've killed him.'

Kosh swiped at the youngster with an open hand. A glancing blow that impacted only the fold-over of a woolly cap. 'Mind your foul tongue or I'll take my belt to you.' He spoke in the Welsh language, but meant the same.

The child backed away and pointed a trembling finger. 'You killed Old Man Jasper.'

'Jasper killed himself.' Kosh retrieved the fallen shotgun and brushed snow off its stock and barrel with his ungloved hand. '*He* had hold of the trigger, not me.'

The boy stared at the mess, and until then, had managed to hold back the tears. 'But—'

Kosh pinched his son's quivering chin and didn't let go until he was good and ready. 'Shall I have Mam put you in a girls' dress for school after the holidays?' He laughed, though only he found humour in the situation.

The boy shook his head when free of his father's grip and used both hands to wipe his eyes. He blinked several times, composing himself. 'No. Don't do that.'

Kosh turned away and let the second cartridge off into a cloud base that hung ominously low over a wide expanse of land. Then he cocked the smoking gun and took it back to a beaten-up Land Rover Defender. To the cowering boy, he said: 'This didn't happen. Old Man Jasper was never here. Not in our fields.'

The youngster swallowed and went through another round of intense blinking and eye wiping before answering with a barely audible, 'Okay.'

Kosh slammed shut the rear door and loomed over the boy with the thumb of his right hand resting behind the buckle of his leather belt. With the other hand, he straightened a flat cap that carried a dusting of fresh snow. 'If I ever find out you broke your word . . .' He pulled at the buckle for added effect. Done with threats, he told the boy to get in the waiting vehicle.

The Defender started on the second attempt and moved away with a short-lived wheelspin.

LIAM HANSON

The boy turned to look through the rear window. He wouldn't have been able to see much from where he was, but tried all the same.

Kosh gave him a firm nudge. 'I told you to leave be. I'll be back later tonight to sort it out.'

True to his word, Kosh returned after little more than an hour, accompanied by a pair of loyal farmhands. Young John was at home. Left to deal with a terrible secret and a steaming bowl of lamb cawl. He'd been silent on their journey back to the farmhouse and hadn't stopped shaking the entire way there.

A cloak of darkness had fallen over the farm and neighbouring land, the ghostly silhouettes of outbuildings and agricultural equipment melding into unified blobs of indistinct grey.

It didn't matter any, Kosh had made the same trip out to that field a thousand times or more. At night. Day. In the worst of storms nature could throw at him. The Defender inched its way towards the gated field, the heavy grunt of its diesel engine and whir of worn wiper-blades the only thing audible for miles around. The headlights were on, for what it was worth, the snow falling like silver-tipped arrows unleashed by a marauding foe.

Kosh was sucking on a roll-your-own cigarette. Blowing smoke and spitting flecks of tobacco from the tip of his tongue. He pulled the vehicle to a full stop and turned to the man sitting next to him. 'Go open it.'

Flint got out, waving an ineffective hand at the onslaught, sinking until the level of snow almost matched the tops of his wellies for height. He used his other hand to pull at a metal gate. It snow-ploughed a good pile in front of it before getting stuck. He rounded the thing, digging here and there with his heel. After checking the gap was wide enough for further passage, he got out of the weather, blowing on his hands while the Defender rocked side-to-side on its way through.

Jasper's body was lying somewhere on the brow of the field. In an area before the ground fell steeply towards a wood and a frozen stream. They couldn't see him. Not even with full beams selected. The fresh snowfall had covered his corpse and hidden it from view. Fortunate for the moment, but not once the thaw came.

Kosh knew every inch of his land. He'd farmed it, man and boy. His father and grandfather before him. There was enough reflected light to make out a few distinctive landmarks, and if he wasn't very much mistaken, the body of Old Man Jasper should be little more than a hundred yards further on.

Chapter 2

THE DRUID INN IN the quiet village of Radyr was playing host to its usual gathering of customers. Farmers, farriers, and veterinary surgeons, mostly. The place was as cosy as it was popular. Low beamed ceilings, stone walls, and a flagstone floor giving it the look of the medieval tavern it once was. Inside, the air was thick with tobacco smoke and sweet-smelling wood sap from a roaring log fire. Lying on a rug in front of it was Lola, the resident Welsh Collie, her nose tuned to the tantalising aroma of offerings coming from the busy kitchen.

'You don't think they've killed each other at long last?' As pub landlord, Badger was positioned behind the bar, drying pint pots with a clean towel. So nicknamed because of a distinctive flash of white running through his jet-black hair, he leaned an elbow on the counter and whispered: 'They've been going at it like a pair of fighting cocks lately. Coming close to getting themselves barred.' He separated a finger and thumb by a small amount. 'This close.'

'It wouldn't surprise me if they have,' a local said from behind a veil of thick smoke. 'One of them's likely to be burying the other in a shallow grave as we speak.'

Kosh wasn't burying the other man. He was busy gutting a dead sheep they'd taken with them. The sharp blade cut through thick fur and tight abdomen with little resistance. He knelt and reached inside the animal's carcass, spilling lengths of small bowel and liver into the snow. He made a few jagged passes at the neck. 'I'm making it look like a dog attack,' he told the other men, and shifted his attention to the mound concealing Old Man Jasper's body.

There, under the light of December's Cold Moon, he scraped at the snow with both hands. Kept going until the colour of it changed from white to something significantly darker. His fingers burned, stung, and itched all at the same time. He put them to his mouth and blew warm air on them.

With a semblance of sensation returning to his fingertips, he went at it again. Hunched over with his arms held out in front of him, clawing at the snow like an animal sensing a free feast. Something sliced through the flesh of his middle finger. He withdrew his hand with a quick-fire foul mouth, shaking blood spots all around him.

The culprit was a jagged piece of jawbone. The half not removed by the powerful blast of gunshot.

Old Man Jasper stared at his killer through his remaining eye. He looked grotesque. Unnerving in his temporary grave. 'Don't just stand there,' Kosh told the other men, and licked his bloody wound, sheep mess and all.

Flint caught hold of the dead man's ankles. Pulled, but couldn't get him moving. It was as though Jasper was fastened to the floor by something unseen. Something that claimed ownership rights. 'He's stuck.' Flint gave up.

Hodges went over to the Defender, lowering his head to a wind that whipped across the exposed land like an arctic chill. Returning with a loop of thick wire, he fastened it to Jasper's ankles before starting up the winch at the rear of the vehicle. The mechanism made quick work of the job, dragging the corpse close enough for the three of them to each take a hold and heave it into the back of the Land Rover. It helped that the body was frozen stiff and not floppy and falling about as it would have been at any other time of year.

Kosh stood with one arm bent, leaning on the cold metal of the Defender's rear wing. He caught his breath and wiped his brow while surveying the macabre scene. In the moonlight, he saw the rust-coloured area where Jasper's remains had lain. The trough where the man's dead body had been dragged the better part of twenty feet. 'There's more snow to come. They said so on the farming forecast.' He spat on the ground once he'd finished coughing. 'It's likely to be a proper white Christmas, by all accounts.' The two other men watched as he pointed to the trough in the ground. 'This'll soon be filled in, don't you worry.'

Hodges nodded.

Flint was struck by a sudden and unnerving thought. 'What happens when spring comes?'

Hodges frowned. 'It'll be washed away. Blood and all.'

'That bit of his head won't. If someone comes up here and finds it before the animals do, there'll be questions to answer.'

Kosh had seen Jasper's face and underlying structures tear off and fly into the distance. Where they were stood was only a stone's throw from a public access footpath, and people often strayed off it for one reason or the other. Flint had a fair point. 'We need a story. An alibi, just in case.'

'You're not sticking with the dog attack?' Flint asked.

Kosh slammed shut the Defender's rear door. 'Let's get down the Druid's. I always think better with a pint in my hand.'

'Here's one of them now,' Badger announced over the rumble of pub chatter and festive music. The landlord was a big man, with a torso almost as round as the casks of real ale stacked head-high behind him. He wore a black apron over jeans and a red checked shirt, and made a show of noting the time on a weighty-looking wristwatch. 'We were about to send out a search party to look for you.'

Dai Kosh stood framed in the pub doorway. He kicked snow off his boots and was a menacing sight dressed in several layers of outdoor clobber. There were calls from the nearest customers for the new arrivals to close the door, though none were foolish enough to make much of a fuss.

Kosh had a reputation in the village as someone to stay on the right side of unless you fancied a split lip and chest full of slack ribs. Flint and Hodges came behind, patiently waiting for their employer to move out of the way.

Badger took a few steps to his right behind the polished oak bar, angling his head to see past the decorated branches of a squat Christmas tree. 'Jasper not with you? I thought you might have given him a lift over here?' The landlord laughed. Boomed described it better. 'It *is* Christmas after all.'

Despite the comment being innocent banter, Badger wasn't too far off the mark. The trio had given *most* of Jasper a lift to the pub. The bit not lost to the snow was lying under an oily tarpaulin in the back of the Land Rover.

'I don't get you?' Kosh said, letting one of the others shut the door behind them. His boots left wet marks on the flagstone floor as he stomped his way to the bar.

Badger took a pint-pot hanging from a hook in a thick overhead beam and filled it from a tap hammered into the front of a wooden cask. 'Jasper's not been in tonight. Some of us thought the two of you might have got into a serious scrap this time.'

Kosh held the pint-pot against a closed mouth. Not drinking. Not putting it down. He stared at the landlord. After what seemed like an age, he gulped half his pint and twisted at the waist to see who else was there. His eyes settled on each of them in turn. The veterinary surgeons smoking thick cigars and drinking expensive whisky. Farmers puffing on pipes and shaking their heads while exchanging tales of woe. The village folk who'd ventured out for a traditional pre-Christmas drink.

And then there was the loner. Sitting in a dark corner of his own. Minding his business while sketching what looked to be a butterfly on a beer mat he'd peeled the surface off.

Baines was the man's name. Arvel Baines. The vagrant. The weirdo. His beaten-up caravan trespassing in Dai Kosh's woods. The farmer downed the rest of his pint and shook the empty pot at Badger. 'Fill that up and meet me in the back room.'

Chapter 3

THEY HATCHED AN EVIL plan in that back room. Men who were not shy in the company of lies and dark dealings. One made over bowls of steaming cawl and several pints of frothing ale.

Dai Kosh had two specific problems. The most pressing, but easier of them, was getting rid of Old Man Jasper's thawing corpse. Given the amount of land Kosh owned—most of it off limits to the public—that shouldn't prove to be much of an issue.

The second was more troubling. Worrying even. There were many years of witnessed bad blood between the two farmers. When it came to motive, it was no secret that Kosh had plenty.

It was Badger who'd highlighted a third problem, together with a neat solution to all three.

Arvel Baines had, some months previously, appeared in the woods from who knew where. In a caravan towed by a beaten up Ford Sierra. He wore multi-coloured waistcoats and black eyeliner, and could often be found prancing about the place with a butterfly net. He even collected wild plants and petals, leading some villagers to speculate that he was mixing potions with the intention of poisoning them.

They wanted him gone.

Children were warned to stay clear.

Baines refused to leave when asked, resorting to not opening the caravan door when Kosh hammered his fists against it. He'd then put up a good fight when the angry farmer brought a tractor and a few men to help pull the temporary home apart.

The police refused to get involved. Their stance being: it was a matter for the courts, not them. Though that wasn't strictly true in law, it was the approach they took all the same.

Baines was going nowhere, and lived off the land—Dai Kosh's land—helping himself to apples and rabbits whenever he saw fit. Pissing and bathing, often simultaneously, in the nearby stream.

Dai Kosh's stream.

'This is your chance to get rid of him for good,' Badger said. Each man, including Kosh, nodded in agreement. 'And you won't get a better one to sort out this mess you've got yourself into.'

With conversation and refreshments done with, Kosh left the portly landlord with strict instructions to keep Baines occupied for as long as he could, estimating they'd need at least an hour, given the worsening weather.

The ageing Land Rover skirted the edge of a frozen stream, spewing thick clouds of black smoke whenever it lost its grip on the ice lurking beneath the snow. When it entered the woods, it rocked violently. The overhanging branches of old oaks slapped at it as though it were *running the gauntlet*.

'There it is.' Flint pointed towards a lopsided caravan; its front end supported on a large rock. To the rear was the rusting Sierra. There was no light on inside the caravan. Its sole occupant was detained elsewhere.

Hodges looked deeply concerned. 'What about our tyre tracks and footprints?'

'Only Baines will see them,' Kosh said. 'And he won't have a clue what's going on until Badger gets the police to call round in the morning.'

Flint watched the snow falling on the other side of his window. 'And by then, they'll mostly be covered over.'

That didn't settle Hodges. 'Not the ones in the wood.' It was true. Despite the continued onslaught, the trees and unprotected land were copping for most of the snowfall.

'Shush with your whining,' Kosh told him. 'We'll see to them when the time comes.'

Hodges knew better than to argue. He let it go, but wore a nervous expression as tightly as he did his black woollen hat.

'You two go find somewhere to put him.' Kosh indicated he meant the corpse. He reached behind his seat and took hold of Old Man Jasper's shotgun. 'I'll deal with this.' He got out and trudged towards the caravan, finding its ill-fitting door unlocked when he got there. The latch was cold in his hand. He pulled at it and put his head inside. It was no warmer. His right boot hovered only inches above the mat. To go in, or not to go in? He decided on the latter and shut the door. The key to success was to not make it look too obvious. Baines would have hidden the shotgun after killing Jasper, not left it to be found so easily.

Kosh negotiated the slippery steps and went round to the other side of the caravan. He dropped to his knees and crawled underneath, wishing he'd sent the younger and more nimble Hodges to do it.

There was a long, flat ledge welded to the rusting chassis. One barely wide enough to accommodate the shotgun without too much of it being on show. He checked from all sides. Stretched his neck in front and back of the wheel. The weapon couldn't be seen unless a person was specifically looking for it. And that's exactly what the police would be doing the very next morning.

'Dai.' It was Flint. He came towards the farmer, twirling something on the end of a gloved finger. As the object spun, it caught the light on two points of each rotation. 'Best chuck this in there as well. It'll make it look all the more convincing.'

Kosh took the gold bracelet from the farmhand and knew from previous sight of it that it had Jasper's name engraved on a plate anchored between a dozen chunky links. He gave it back. 'Put it with the gun.' He clapped his hands. 'It's time we got back to the Druid's. There's an alibi to sort out.'

Chapter 4

ARVEL BAINES SLOWED HIS pace when the Defender went spluttering by. Although it was travelling in the opposite direction to him, he had no desire to have it stop for its Neanderthal occupants to beat him up again.

Dai Kosh wanted him off his land. Most farmers did. There was nothing new or surprising about that. But this particular farmer was a nasty piece of work and his threats carried a believable level of menace. Kosh had promised that it was only a matter of time before he succeeded in getting rid of him, and the hired help would do just about anything asked of them, should they wish to remain in the farmer's employment.

Baines had already decided to move on once the snow had thawed. He'd pack up and disappear before anything serious happened between them. There was a popular market town in mid-Wales where he could get himself set up for spring. Wait for summer and make potent herbal teas well away from the raging bully that was Dai Kosh.

Baines pressed himself almost as close to the stone wall as the climbing ivy that clung to the open joints of its crumbling mortar. He waited until the red taillights of the Land Rover were gone. Then a touch longer for its engine noise to disappear from earshot.

He'd earlier that evening seen all three of the vehicle's occupants at the Druid Inn, talking with the landlord before disappearing into the back room to do who knew what. Nothing good. Not if his prior interaction with the group was anything to go by.

When he entered the woods, his pace slowed for a second time. There were tyre tracks in the snow. Some of it churned up enough to reveal dark streaks of frozen earth beneath. That's when he first noticed the footprints leading towards the door of his caravan. He broke into a comedic trot, his knees rising high to lift his boots clear of the snow that weighed him down.

With a hand on the latch, he paused before opening it.

What if there was someone inside waiting to cut his throat? He'd seen Kosh and both farmhands only twenty minutes earlier, travelling in the direction of the village. Might they have rigged the door to an improvised incendiary device? Their intention being to blow him to smithereens – blaming it on a dodgy gas cannister.

Baines put all such thoughts away and went inside with his breath held somewhere in the depths of his chest.

On first inspection, everything looked the same as it had done when he'd left some hours earlier. The place wasn't trashed, thankfully. There was nothing of any real value in there to steal. When at last he exhaled, the escaping moisture rose to feed islands of black mould spots on the low ceiling. After opening a few internal doors, drawers, and cupboards, he'd more or less satisfied himself that no one else had been in there.

Why then had someone come up the steps but chosen not to venture inside? The caravan was unlocked. Couldn't be locked. Its mechanism was good for little, like the van itself. They'd have realised straight away.

Had they simply knocked and then left again? Unlikely. The amount of churned snow around the outside of the caravan suggested otherwise.

He took to the steps, a small torch in hand, its weak puddle of light dancing ahead of him. Crouching once he'd contacted solid ground, he swung the beam under the caravan, checking behind the nearside wheel. For what exactly, he didn't know. He stretched an arm and ran a hand along the axle, his skin almost welding itself to the frigid metal.

He went round the other side of the caravan and repeated the process, his shoulder denting the flimsy panelling when he leaned against it. There was a deep gouge in the snow a bit further on, similar to the one he'd made himself. Somebody had been under there – their trailing leg used as an anchor-point for leverage.

There had been an obvious effort made to hide the gouge from sight. But not nearly enough to be effective when viewed from Baines's current vantage point.

He got down on his belly, pushing his toes into the ground, forcing himself into the narrow gap between the underside of the caravan and the wet grass.

He swung the torch beam in all directions and saw what looked to be a long length of metal that was far shinier than any of the rusting parts surrounding it. When he closed his hand over both barrels, he knew exactly what it was.

Someone was up to no good. It wasn't too difficult to imagine who that might be.

Dai Kosh was propping up the bar at the Druid's. Holding his back to it while making conversation with a couple of veterinary surgeons. 'Dogs, I reckon,' Kosh said, recounting the attack on the ewe. 'A fox wouldn't have taken her down like that.'

'If she was already injured,' one vet suggested, 'then it might have done.'

The farmer looked unconvinced, his gaze zig-zagging the full length and breadth of the smoky room. The pub was quieter than it had been earlier in the evening. Most of the clientele had long since begun their journeys home. 'Where's the weirdo?' he asked when he couldn't find Arvel Baines.

'He left when you were out the back,' the same vet said between a few puffs on a cigar. 'What were you doing, leaving Badger to play darts with the man?'

Kosh turned to face the landlord. 'Darts? Me and the boys out the garage fixing the gearbox on your four-by-four, and that's how you repay us.'

Badger shrugged his shoulders. He held a wet glass in one hand. A dry cloth in the other. 'I've a business to run. Besides, you've no proof of him being a criminal.'

'Not true!' Kosh hammered a fist onto the wooden surface of the bar. 'He's trespassing on my land. Littering and helping himself to just about anything he fancies.'

'I suppose.'

'No supposing about it. He's a bad egg. You mark my words.' Kosh winked and downed the remainder of his pint.

They sounded convincing. An alibi produced in developing layers of loud banter.

'Did you finish the job?' the vet asked. 'I might get you to look at mine when you have the time.'

Kosh put his empty beer pot down. 'That gearbox is working like a Swiss watch,' he said, shoving his hands in their faces. 'And those there are the cuts 'n' bruises to show for it.'

Chapter 5

NEXT MORNING

Radyr Police Station was little more than a double-fronted, stone-built house on a sharp bend in the main road. It had been there since the end of the First World War.

Entry was off the flagstone pavement, up three wide steps and through a black door onto linoleum flooring the colour of ox-blood. In places—the area in front of the main desk particularly—the linoleum had worn away to reveal a dull grey base colour.

Above the exterior lintel-piece of the building was a plaque reminding villagers they were under the jurisdiction of the South Wales Police.

Detective Inspector Idris Roberts was sitting behind his cluttered desk, smoking a Players No.6 down to its stained filter while reading the back page of the previous evening's newspaper. 'Lost two nil,' he said, his eyes screwed shut, teeth clenched onto what was left of the smouldering cigarette. He lifted his back end and noisily broke wind. 'At home an' all, can you believe?' He peeked round a tower of case files raised between himself and his junior. 'Pardon me. Shouldn't have had that second helping of baked beans this morning.' He flapped at the air and pulled a face. 'Toxic, that one.'

'Puts them mid-table at best after that performance.' Brân Reece, his young detective constable finished whatever it was he'd been typing and went rooting through his desk drawers until he straightened with a five-and-a-quarter inch floppy disk in hand. Pushing the black disk into a slot at the front of the machine, he sat back and listened while the thing whirred and clicked into life.

'I know where they are.' Roberts slapped the folded newspaper onto the desk, sending a pot of pens sprawling just about everywhere. He made no attempt to get up and retrieve them, and pushed one out of the way with his foot. 'Mid-table, and only just above Wimbledon, for God's sake.' He was already reaching for his next cigarette.

'I fancy Arsenal, myself'. Reece slurped a mouthful of sweet coffee, a homemade Welshcake with a half-moon bitten out of it, held in his other hand. 'Liverpool for runners-up, if you ask me.'

'I didn't.' Roberts tossed a white envelope and its contents across the room, watching it cut through the air like the rotors of a helicopter.

'What's this?' Reece caught the envelope in two clumsy attempts. 'My Christmas bonus?'

'You wish.'

The newbie read the handwritten name from the facing side of it: **Brân.** The writing was deliberate and very neat. A woman's, no doubt about it.

Roberts stared at him. 'It's a Christmas card from Anwen. She said I was to give it to you.'

'*Anwen?*' Reece looked horrified. 'But she's only thirteen.'

'And don't you forget it,' Roberts said with a serious voice. 'The girl's got it in her head that the pair of you are gonna get married and live in a country cottage someday.'

Reece lowered his head and put the card to one side without opening it. 'I'm twenty-five next birthday.'

Roberts clicked his fingers. 'It's just a . . . *Oh*, what do you call something when it's only a fad?' He closed his eyes as though that might help him remember. It didn't.

Reece ejected the disk and put it back in its clear pocket. 'A phase, you mean?' He dropped the pocket into an open drawer and shoved Anwen's envelope in there with it.

'That's the one,' Roberts said. 'It's a phase she's going through at the minute. Trying to be all grown up before her time. She'll be through it soon enough.'

Reece looked relieved to hear it. He'd never been much good with women, and a lovestruck teenager chasing after him wasn't going to improve his chances, any.

Roberts finished his tea with a noisy slurp and another escape of noxious wind. This time, he didn't own up, silent as it was. 'I suppose we'd better go speak with Elgan Collins. The man claims he's got something important to tell us. *'Serious'* was the word he used.'

Reece stood and went over to one of a pair of panelled windows. He wiped a circle of condensation from its thin pane and peered through the wet swirl. He used the other hand to give the glass a second going-over.

There were a couple of young kids making a snowman on the otherwise deserted pavement outside. Dressed in woollen hats and scarfs, their coats were fastened over so many layers of clothing, it made it almost impossible for them to raise their arms above shoulder level. When they turned, it was by twisting awkwardly from the ankles.

'In *this?*' Reece came away from the window looking none too keen.

Roberts was buttoning his coat with a cigarette dangling loosely from his lips. 'We've been stuck inside for days. Come on, get your things.'

Reece followed his boss through the dingy foyer. Past the grinning desk sergeant who made a show of warming his hands on a steaming mug of Bovril. Down the outer steps they went, onto a pavement covered with several inches of snow.

'Cut that out.' Roberts crossed the road, his loud reprimand directed at the two young boys who were now ramping up to a good argument.

'I never,' one of them said to the other and got a heavy shove in the chest for his rebuttal.

'Leave it!' Roberts said before the disagreement could degenerate into a full-blown fist fight. 'What's up with you two, anyway?'

The boy in the red bobble-hat and matching scarf pointed at the other kid. 'It's him. He's a right miserable git today.'

John Kosh tried to pull himself free of the detective's grip. 'Piss off. All of you.'

Roberts gave him a swift clip round the ear. 'What do you think your old man would say if he got wind of this?' Despite his question, Roberts had a fair idea. Dai Kosh would expect his son to pummel his opponent. If not, he'd earn himself another good hiding when he got home. He let go of the boy's collar only when the youngster had stopped struggling. 'That's better. Why the face like a slapped arse?'

'He's been like it since yesterday,' Bobble-hat said before Kosh could answer for himself. 'He won't tell me what's wrong.' Bobble-hat nodded at the detectives. 'Something's up. I know it is. He always gets like this when he's hiding something from me.'

'That true?' Roberts asked. 'You up to no good?'

Kosh neither admitted nor denied the accusation and stood kicking the toe of his boot into the compacted snow.

Reece circled the snowman, admiring it as though it had been chiselled from the finest marble. 'Did you make this?'

'Yeah.' Kosh didn't look up and carried on kicking at the ground. 'He helped a bit.'

'A bit?' Bobble-hat's eyes opened wide.

'I did most of it,' Kosh said, his voice rising louder than it needed to be.

'You didn't.'

Roberts pulled them apart for a second time.

Reece straightened the carrot nose and pressed a finger against a stone eye that was at risk of falling to the floor. 'You should be proud of yourselves. It's a pretty good effort.' The boys stared at one-another in silence. Reece reached into his pocket and handed over some loose change. 'Go get yourselves a packet of sweets and stop playing silly buggers.' To Kosh, he said: 'And you're sure there's nothing you want to get off your chest?'

With a firm shake of his head, the two boys were gone. Trudging up the middle of the road like the best of friends.

Idris Roberts clucked his tongue. 'Maybe you should be a community bobby instead of a detective?' He walked off. 'You've definitely got a way with the youngsters.'

Reece looked worried and followed like Bambi on ice. 'You're not serious, are you, boss? A detective is what I want to be.'

'It's still early days.' Roberts led the way around the side of the building, towards the car park. 'I haven't made my mind up about you as yet.'

Chapter 6

THEY USED THE STATION Land Rover for the journey to the Druid Inn, Reece at the wheel, Roberts chain-smoking next to a part-open window. When the vehicle could travel no further, they got out and trudged a good half-mile through shin-deep snow.

'It's bloody freezing.' Reece had fallen over for the second time and looked like a stranded turtle struggling to get moving again.

Roberts stopped to offer the younger man help. He held a glowing cigarette at arm's length. 'There you go, take a drag on that. It'll warm your cockles.'

Reece was beating himself down. Grabbing handfuls of snow trapped between his collar and skin. 'I don't smoke.'

'Take it.' Roberts waved the No.6 at him. 'It'll put hairs on your chest.'

Reece took a tentative drag and quickly descended into fits of coughing and spitting. He handed it back, looking like he might throw up at any moment. 'No more,' he croaked.

Roberts pinched the end of the unwanted cigarette and put it away in his coat pocket for later. 'I'll do the talking,' he said, leading the way inside the pub.

They found Elgan Collins stood watching a wall-mounted television screen with eight empty pint glasses clenched between the fingers of both his hands. They knew it was him. Bulk aside, the wide flash of white hair against black gave his identity away in an instant.

'Gone with the Wind,' Roberts said, rubbing warmth into his cold hands. 'Now there's a classic.' He turned to Reece. 'None of that *Star Wars* crap your generation is into.'

Reece frowned. 'I've never seen *Star Wars*.'

Badger turned to face them, the glasses clinking in time with his movement. 'You got my message,' he said, depositing the empties on a cleared section of the bar. He dried his hands on a cloth he'd only moments earlier had draped over a shoulder. When done, he tossed it into an aluminium sink. 'We had a bit of a late one last night.' He put a hand over his mouth so only Roberts could hear. 'Feel free to join us whenever you want.'

'You said your call was urgent,' Roberts reminded him, making no mention of the landlord's invitation to the regular lock-ins held at the Druid's. 'Something about you witnessing a serious assault?'

Badger pulled an apologetic face. 'Ah, yeah . . . that.'

It had taken the best part of an hour for them to get out there and Roberts was in no mood for being messed about. 'You don't sound so sure now?'

The landlord squeezed past and took his place on the other side of the bar. 'What if I get you boys a drink before we get started?'

Roberts ordered for both of them. 'Brandy for me. Lemonade for him.'

Reece's eyes narrowed. 'Why do I get pop?'

'Because you're driving and you don't want me nicking you.'

Reece sighed. 'Can't I have a coffee to warm me up?'

Roberts shook his head. *Toughen up*, is what you need to do.' He turned to the landlord. 'Always moaning, this one. If it's not about the canteen food, it's the weather.'

'I've got the same problem with the bar staff,' Badger said, tapping one of the glasses he'd collected. 'These should have been cleared away last night. There's no get-up-and-go in them these days.'

Roberts gave Reece a damning look. 'Traffic is where he's headed if he doesn't get his arse in gear.'

'I'll get us a seat,' the young detective constable said, wandering off in a sulk.

'Not *there!*' Roberts raised his hands above his head. 'Jesus Christ. Don't you listen to a word I've told you? We sit with our backs to the wall.' He pinched the bridge of his nose. 'I don't know where we're getting them these days.'

Badger shook his head. 'I'll put a double in yours, shall I?'

'You best do that.' Roberts went to the other side of the room and sat down. He took the half-smoked cigarette from his pocket and lit it.

Reece waited until he was listening. 'You didn't mean what you said about sending me to traffic, did you, boss?'

Roberts blew smoke at him. 'CID isn't for everyone. It takes a certain sort of person to see and do the things we get lumbered with.'

Reece leaned on his elbows. 'Give me a chance to show you what I can do. I know I've got what it takes.'

Roberts watched the landlord, who was still busy on the other side of the bar. 'We'll see.'

It didn't take Badger long to return with the drinks. He'd brought an extra coffee for himself. 'There you go, boys.'

Roberts took a sip and looked suitably pleased with the ratio of brandy to coffee. 'So, tell me I didn't come all the way out here for this,' he said, holding the glass mug up in front of him. 'Young Scott of the Antarctic here would never forgive me.'

Reece rolled his eyes in silence.

For a moment Badger looked as though he was wrestling with his conscience. His performance was polished and deserving of a wider audience. 'It's probably nothing, but Old Man Jasper didn't come in last night.'

'What of it?'

'That never happens. Not in all the years I've owned this place.'

Roberts shrugged. 'Maybe the weather put him off.' He thumped Reece on the upper arm. 'You weren't keen, were you?'

Reece rubbed his burning triceps and shifted a few inches further away.

'Start writing something down instead of playing with yourself.' Roberts tapped the table with a clubbed fingernail. 'In your pocketbook.'

Reece stretched his arm a few times to get blood flowing through the muscle. He took the top off his Biro and committed the date, time and location to paper. 'There's nothing else to write,' he said in response to Roberts staring at the nib hovering above the paper.

'Brân's right,' the DI told Badger. 'You'd better get on with it.'

A log cracked in the open fireplace, sending sparkles of orange fireflies into the hearth as it broke in two. There was an acrid smell of burning in the room. Badger got up and pressed his foot to a smouldering edge of rug. 'I think Old Man Jasper's been done in.'

Roberts lowered his mug, milk froth sticking to his moustachioed top lip. He wiped it with the back of his hand. 'What makes you say that?'

Badger checked over his shoulder – loose-mouthed landlords getting a bad press and all that. 'We've had a traveller in here lately. Bit of a thief, by all accounts.' He leaned across the table and kept his voice low. 'Arvel Baines is his name.'

Chapter 7

Reece clung two-handed from a pull-bar welded to the side of a blue tractor, worrying it was a long way down to the road should he fall. He screwed his eyes shut and made a decision to journey back to the station on foot when the time came.

DI Roberts had enlisted the help of Dai Kosh and a couple of grumpy farmhands on Badger's suggestion.

There being shepherd's pie on the menu back at the works' canteen meant Roberts was nowhere to be seen. He'd promised to keep the newbie a portion. Chips, garden peas and gravy to go with it.

As the convoy travelled along country lanes thick with snow, uniformed officers rode the outside of the vehicles like weary soldiers hitching a lift home from war. The tractors' engines made loud clackety-clack sounds, their vertical exhaust pipes spewing copious amounts of black soot into the crisp morning air. At the steering wheels were Flint and Hodges.

'Over there,' Hodges shouted, bringing his vehicle to a halt with a short skid. 'There,' he repeated, and stuck an arm out of the window, pointing to a clearing in the wood. Moments later, he was climbing out of the cab, leaving its engine running.

Kosh got out of the same tractor and joined Hodges on the ground. 'Baines,' he shouted. '*Baines!*'

'Get back from there,' Reece told the farmer when he strayed too close to the caravan. 'You're trampling through potential evidence if this turns out to be a crime scene.'

'We'll flush him like the sewer rat he is,' Kosh said, taking no notice. He used hand signals and a series of whistles to direct Flint and Hodges to the front and back of the caravan. 'When I tell you, boys.'

Reece was off the tractor and grabbing handfuls of Kosh's coat. His legs were wobbly from the journey. 'I told you to wait.' The headbutt was unexpected and caught him square on the nose, knocking him to the ground.

'In yer go,' Kosh shouted to his men. One of the uniforms came forward and caught hold of him. 'Get out of it!' Kosh yelled, yanking his arm free of the police officer's grip.

Flint went bounding up the steps. Hodges in close pursuit. Both entering the caravan without invitation to do so. Both reversing out of there only a moment later, their hands held in an open-palmed surrender. 'Whoa,' Flint said. 'Take it easy with that thing.'

Hodges's mouth opened and closed in silence.

Reece wiped blood from his nose and got up off the ground to witness a man brandishing both barrels of a shotgun at them. He produced his warrant card. 'Mr Baines, I'm Detective Constable Brân Reece. Put the gun down.'

Arvel Baines swung the weapon left and right. 'What's going on?'

'We're here to talk.' Reece's eyes were watering and obscuring his vision. He blinked a few times, marginally improving things. 'Old Man Jasper from the next farm along – did you see him at all yesterday?'

Baines shook his head. He looked flighty and unpredictable. 'Why should I have done?'

Kosh turned to one of the uniforms. 'That's Jasper's shotgun. There'll be a small brass plate screwed to the stock. His initials are on it.'

'Is that true?' Reece asked. 'Is that Jasper's gun?'

'I found it last night. Under the caravan.' Baines lowered his head and simultaneously let go of the weapon. It caught the bottom step and somersaulted a short distance away.

Kosh was the first of them to respond, Reece screaming at him to leave the shotgun where it was. 'There you go,' Kosh said, rubbing snow off the brass plate. 'It's Jasper's, right enough.'

'Put it down,' Reece insisted. 'You're getting your prints all over it.' He ordered a uniform to confiscate the shotgun; the officer putting it away in an evidence bag for safekeeping.

Baines shoved a hand in his pocket. 'And there's this,' he said, dangling what looked to be a gold bracelet.

'Well, would you look at that.' Kosh yelled. 'Ol' Arvel's been helping himself to a nice bit of bounty.'

Chapter 8

THE WALLS OF INTERVIEW Room 1 were painted in two-tone shades of shitty-brown; the darker variant sinking below waist level. There was cigarette smoke in the air. Lots of it. An overhead strip light provided the room's only escape from darkness, its four-foot-long electrical element buzzing in cycles that went through mildly annoying to something quieter, then back again.

Silent, it never was.

Detective Inspector Idris Roberts reached sideways in his seat to press the red *Rec* button on a tape recorder device, puffing on a seemingly endless supply of cigarettes. He ran through the *'those present in the room'* spiel. 'Confirm your name and current address for the tape,' he said, once most of the preliminaries were out of the way.

Baines was positioned opposite. His clothing had been bagged and sent to Cardiff for forensic analysis. He wore a grey sweatshirt with matching joggers. 'Arvel Baines. I currently live on Dai Kosh's land – you'd know that already.' His tone was tinged with sarcasm.

'I need more detail,' Roberts told him. 'A fixed abode for the benefit of the tape.'

Baines helped himself to a No.6 poking out of a packet on the desk between them. 'You don't mind?' He got no answer and lit it with a cheap plastic lighter that didn't belong to him. 'It's a caravan,' he said, waving smoke from his line of sight. 'I can't be any more specific than that.' When he exhaled, it was with his head raised to the underside of the yellowed ceiling.

Roberts squinted through his own veil of smoke. 'Describe it.'

'It's small. Rectangular. Had two wheels and a couple of drafty windows last time I looked.' Baines brought his shoulders up to meet a pair of ears that were a size too small for his head. He spread his arms wide. 'They all look the same to me.'

'You using it to store and supply drugs?'

Baines's hand, together with the burning cigarette, hovered a few inches short of his mouth. 'Nobody said anything about drugs.'

'We found jars of white powder.' Roberts took another cigarette and lit it from the one he'd only just finished. 'We've sent them to Cardiff,' he said, placing the pack and lighter out of the other man's reach.

'Those aren't drugs. Not the sort you mean. I specialise in herbal remedies. Can't get a decent kip without them.'

'Sleeping potions?'

'If you like. And some other stuff.'

'Such as?'

'Powders and teas to calm nerves. Settle stomach upsets. That sort of thing.'

Roberts took a deep drag on his cigarette. 'We'll know soon enough if you're telling the truth.'

Baines folded his arms and pushed back in the chair. 'If you'd asked, I could have spared you the time and expense.'

Roberts lifted the bagged shotgun from an area of floor next to his chair. He put it on the table with a thud, then reached into his pocket and dropped a smaller evidence bag alongside it. 'Let's talk about these.'

'I've been through that already.' Baines nodded at Reece. 'With *him*.'

'And now you're going to do it with me.'

Baines straightened with a weariness befitting the situation and spoke in clipped sentences. 'I found them last night. Under my caravan. It's a fit up. Has to be.'

'Found them, you say?' Roberts forced a thin-lipped smile. 'That old chestnut.'

'Afraid so.'

Roberts tapped cigarette ash on the floor. 'Who'd do such a thing? Who'd want to stitch you up?'

Baines crossed his arms and slid lower in the chair; his legs stretched out in front of him. 'As if you couldn't make that connection yourselves.'

'If you want to play games,' Roberts waved a hand dismissively, 'I've got all day.'

'Kosh has had it in for me ever since I arrived in this poxy village.'

'Because you're trespassing on his land.'

'I wasn't doing anything destructive. Just minding my own business.'

'You were helping yourself to whatever you fancied. To things that didn't belong to you.'

'Apples. Nuts. The odd rabbit here and there. They're wild, and fair game.'

'Dai wouldn't have seen it that way.'

'Exactly.'

They sat in silence for a while. Baines staring at the table. Roberts staring at Baines. Reece alternating his attention between them both. 'Did Jasper also *have it in for you?*' Roberts asked.

'I hardly ever saw him.'

'But you would have done from time to time?'

'Once or twice.'

'Did he say something that pissed you off?'

'We never spoke.'

'You saw that gold bracelet of his and fancied it for yourself?'

'Bullshit.'

Roberts took the smaller of the two evidence bags and weighed it in his hand. 'There must be a couple of hundred quidsworth there. What do you say, Brân?' He passed it to his junior. 'Enough to kill for, do you think?' Reece got no opportunity to comment.

Baines was on his feet with his hands pressed flat against the surface of the table. 'None of this is anything to do with me. The shotgun. The gold bracelet. Whatever you found by that stream.' He shook his head. 'None of it.'

'Sit down.'

Baines lowered himself and turned to Reece. 'You believe me, don't you?'

'He believes whatever I tell him to,' Roberts said. He squeezed the young constable's knee. 'Ain't that right?'

Reece grimaced and withdrew his leg. He neither confirmed nor denied the claim.

Roberts lit a cigarette from a nip held between his finger and thumb. He inhaled deeply, smoke escaping from just about everywhere except his ears. 'Let's cut through the bullshit. Did you kill Old Man Jasper?'

'No.'

'I don't believe you.' Roberts banged the table, making Reece jump. 'There's no point in you looking at Brân, here. I already told you, he believes whatever I do.'

'I didn't kill anyone.'

'I say you did.'

'You're wrong.'

'If it wasn't you, then who was it?'

Baines scoffed. 'The same man who set me up, of course. That thug, Kosh.'

'Why would Dai do such a thing?'

'You said yourself: I was on his land and he wanted me off.'

'You're saying Dai Kosh killed Jasper and framed you for it?'

'Got it in one.' Baines leaned his head across the table and spoke calmly. 'I've heard the talk in that pub. It's no secret those two hated each other.'

Roberts balanced a blue folder on his lap and went rifling through it with one eye closed and the cigarette hanging from the corner of his mouth. 'I hope you didn't eat before coming here.' He tossed a Polaroid onto the table. 'Not looking his best, is he?'

Baines threw up immediately. Some of the splatter caught Reece's raised arm and cheek.

'Better out than in,' Roberts said, getting to his feet. He pointed a finger when Baines got up. 'You stay put.' Reece used his sleeve to wipe his face. 'Elgan Collins saw blood under your fingernails when the pair of you were playing darts yesterday. How did that get there?' Roberts asked.

Baines used the collar of his sweatshirt to clean his lips and front teeth. He looked for somewhere to spit, but swallowed when nothing was forthcoming. 'Rabbits. I'd been skinning rabbits by the stream.'

Roberts sat down and extinguished his cigarette in an expanding puddle of watery vomit. 'Is that when Jasper came along and the two of you got into an argument?'

'He wouldn't have been there,' Baines said. 'That bit of field belonged to Kosh.'

'That depends on who you believe,' Roberts told Reece. 'It's like *no man's land*: both farmers fighting for ownership of a stretch of worthless mud.'

'That could give Dai Kosh motive,' Reece said, moving his knee from under a drip of Baines's stomach contents. 'If Kosh thought Jasper was up to no good, then—'

Roberts nudged him with an elbow. 'Who put you in charge?'

Reece rubbed his ribs. 'I was only—'

'Getting above your station is what you were doing.'

'He's right,' Baines said. 'Kosh and those farmhands are the ones you need to be talking to. I saw them last night. Driving home from the woods.'

Roberts glared at Reece. 'See what's happened now you've started giving him ideas?'

Chapter 9

Arvel Baines had been taken back to his cell to await his fate.

Roberts and Reece were in the staff canteen—it was more of a lean-to attached to the rear of the building—waiting for the first of the lab reports to come back from Cardiff.

Reece was staring at his shepherd's pie and trimmings. He puffed his cheeks and pushed the plate away.

'I'm not surprised you've no stomach for it,' Roberts said. 'Not after matey boy's yodelling display in the interview room. The place reeks of strong cheese.'

'Don't.' Reece looked away and then back at his DI. 'Boss, do you always have to—'

'Waste not, want not,' Roberts said, dragging the plate towards him. He loaded the fork and filled his mouth, chasing the pie down with a loud slurp of lukewarm tea. 'You were saying?'

'It doesn't matter.' Reece took a swig from a can of Coke and burped into a clenched fist. 'What do you think about Baines seeing Kosh and his farmhands last night?'

'You mean three thirsty fellas driving from work to the pub?' Roberts speared a garden pea and looked up from his plate. 'I don't see a problem there.'

Reece took another drink and burped again. He apologised, though Roberts didn't seem to care. 'You didn't see how Kosh and his boys trashed the area around that caravan. It was like they were doing it on purpose.'

Roberts started on the cake and custard next. He dipped the spoon and licked it like it was a lollipop. 'Dai's a farmer, for Christ's sake, not a scene of crime expert.' Roberts shook his head. 'And you can stop fiddling with that nose of yours.'

Reece pinched its bridge and opened and closed his mouth like a fish out of water. 'I want him done for assault.'

'A coming together of heads is what Dai said.' Roberts scraped the last bits of custard off the sides of the bowl. 'He got a bit excited, that's all.'

'And you'd take his word over mine?'

Roberts put the spoon down and tapped his pockets in search of another pack of No.6s. He pushed his back against the upright of his seat. 'Let me tell you something,' he said, thumbing the wheel of a lighter. 'Being a detective is all about getting results.' He raised a finger to shut Reece up. 'Those results are often a bugger to come by. Other times, they hop along and hand themselves to you on a plate. Like in this case, for instance.' Roberts stood once he'd got the cigarette going. 'If you want to stay long enough to let me get to know you, then you'd better learn fast not to rock the boat.'

Roberts waited in front of the custody sergeant's desk while someone went to fetch Arvel Baines from his cell. Reece stood reading from a flyer pinned to a corkboard on the corridor wall. He moved to his right and read another. The theme was the same. Theft. From houses, garden sheds, and offices. There was a thief suited to every one of them.

Baines shuffled along the corridor with his hands cuffed in front of him. He had the look of someone who already knew he was in for an outing. He stopped in front of Reece and gave him a quick up and down. 'I hoped you'd be different. My bad. You're just like the rest of them.'

Reece shook his head and looked like he might say something.

'That's enough.' Roberts put a swift end to the chitchat and had Baines brought across to the custody desk. The DI and sergeant exchanged a few brief sentences, after which the charge of murder was read out.

Chapter 10

BUTETOWN, CARDIFF. PRESENT DAY.

Detective Chief Inspector Brân Reece woke to the sound of a telephone ringing somewhere in the dark living room. It was an annoying chirping noise that refused to shush until he gave in and interacted with it.

At first, he couldn't locate the thing. He opened both eyes and swept a hand along the carpeted floor. That didn't help any.

Wedged side-on in an armchair that gripped him like an ageing aunt, he rolled his stiff neck, grimacing when what sounded like bits of loose grit made scraping sounds where his spine formed a joint with the base of his skull.

He was getting old and didn't he know it. Aches and pains were the early symptoms. Still to come—but no time soon, he hoped—was memory loss. Then incontinence when lifting anything heavier than a newspaper. He'd always said he wanted to be vaporised the very first time that happened. He hadn't changed his mind.

The phone kept calling to him like a toddler demanding to be picked up and comforted.

'I'm hunting for you!' He had no clue what time it was, though the makings of light outside suggested morning had already arrived. He'd missed his run for the first time since taking it up after his wife's murder, miraculously sleeping through the night without a single bad dream to contend with. Progress at last.

He closed his fingers around the handset, which, incidentally, had been under the cushion behind him all along. He brought the phone to his ear and confirmed his name.

'Boss, it's Jenkins.' His work partner and very capable detective sergeant.

Reece wedged the handset between his shoulder and chin and went over to the window to open the curtains. Craning his neck skywards, he saw no whale of a cloud lumbering by.

Progress indeed.

'It's Jenkins,' she repeated when he didn't reply the first time.

'There's two of you now?'

'Huh?' She was momentarily thrown by his use of flippant sarcasm, though shouldn't have been.

'Never mind,' he said with a deep sigh. 'What do you want?' Pacing in front of the window, he gave his whiskered chin a good scratch and watched the street outside. It was dry for once, with the promise of sunshine if the scattered patches of pastel blue were anything to go by.

'We've found a body.'

Reece lowered himself onto the low bay windowsill, a porcelain vase tapping against the glass behind him. He twisted at the waist and moved it out of harm's way. 'I'm listening.'

'This one has the hallmarks of a gangland killing.'

That got Reece's attention quicker than most things. 'Billy *Creed*.' He lengthened the surname, his heart rate changing up a gear with the anticipation of a chase.

'I didn't say that, boss.'

'You didn't have to.' He slid off the windowsill and headed for the shower. 'Text me the address. I'm on my way.'

The battered Peugeot 205 started on the second attempt and with a fair amount of pumping action from Reece's right foot. It had been doing that a lot lately, as well as idling roughly and missing.

His best mate, Yanto, had told him it was blowing blue smoke from the exhaust. That meant a faulty PCV valve or a screwed engine was to blame. Either way, "*The thing's just about fucked,*" Yanto had so eloquently informed him.

Reece stretched over the gearstick and worn fabric of the front passenger seat, reaching for the trusty Stubby screwdriver he kept in the glovebox. Knocking a few empty crisp packets into the wheel well, he straightened and thrust the Stubby into a hole in the front of the radio, above which read: *Channel Select.*

The radio spat and hissed as he turned the screwdriver, first one way, and then the opposite. It spoke in the Russian language for a second or two. Then with the accent of the people of the coastal regions of north-western Europe.

It went totally silent next.

Reece was about to give up trying when he accidentally hit on the sound of Ritchie Blackmore's guitar. He recognised the instrumental ballad instantly. *'Maybe Next Time,'* he said, pulling away into the traffic. 'I can't argue with that.'

Chapter 11

THE JOURNEY FROM REECE'S main home in Llandaff to Trellick House, Butetown, took him little more than fifteen minutes.

The Peugeot came to a halt with an ear-piercing squeal of its brakes and a lurch of its front suspension; the radio changing stations without help from the Stubby screwdriver. Through the dirty windscreen he saw blue and white crime scene tape trailing from one lamppost to the next.

A crowd of onlookers gathered in huddles on the other side of it, busy sharing every development to their social media platforms. Reece wondered how they'd react if it was one of their family up there on the seventh floor, bound to a chair with their kneecaps drilled by some unhinged maniac.

He saw no one he recognised from the press, but knew they wouldn't be too far away. Like sharks sensing blood from miles off, they'd already be en route.

He locked the car and went round to the other side of the perimeter railings, counting fifteen floors above ground level. Red brick. Painted cladding. Row-upon-row of white uPVC windows. Some had curtains. Others, netting or blinds. One or two sported half-inch plyboard and screws.

There was no getting away from it; this was the tough end of town.

Crime scene investigators were busy with a grey wheelie bin. One of those large top-loader types mostly found at the rear of pubs and restaurants. There was somebody in the bin: a woman dressed in white hooded coveralls and facemask, visible only from mid-chest level, upwards. She was handing something out to a CSI holding an evidence bag at arm's length. Reece recognised the woman despite her *disguise* and went over to join her.

'Sioned, what've you got?'

Sioned Williams was the crime scene manager. 'Morning to you too,' she said, fighting to stay upright on top of the rubbish.

Reece mumbled a belated greeting. 'Is that any better?'

'You've made my day,' she told him with a wide smile that showed even from behind her facemask. She pointed at a bagged exhibit on the ground next to the bin. 'That's what did it, if I'm not mistaken.'

'Is it okay to pick it up?' Reece asked.

Williams checked with one of her team, making sure the evidence bag was properly sealed and labelled. 'Be my guest.'

Reece squatted over the cordless drill. It was yellow and black, with a **DEWALT** manufacturer's name stamped along the side of it. On closer inspection, it was obvious the barrel of the tool was contaminated with blood. He put the drill back where he'd found it and stood. He didn't speak. Just puffed his cheeks and let it out with a shake of his head.

Williams rested her elbows on the lip of the bin, leaning like a neighbour chatting over a garden fence. 'This is a nasty one. Cara Frost's up there with Jenkins.' She leaned a bit closer and whispered. 'Are those two still an item?'

Reece pulled a face. 'How should I know?'

'You must have an idea. You're with Elan all day.'

He shrugged and made his way towards the main entrance of the building, stopping to shout before going in: 'If they are, then at least this one hasn't tried killing her yet.'

'*Brân!*'

It smelled of stale urine inside Trellick House, and not all of it belonging to the resident tomcat. The metal door slammed shut behind Reece, a loud bang echoing like a gunshot off the bare concrete walls of the dingy foyer.

Overhead was a strip light that buzzed inside a metal cage. Two of its rusted fasteners were twisted to one side, the rectangular cage hanging free from the end furthest away from him.

Abstract patterns of colourful graffiti decorated what would otherwise have been dull grey walls. Where there was writing, it was mostly crude and vulgar. Threats. Promises. Nothing hopeful.

The single lift had a door that was painted black. Scratched to the bare metal like pockmarked skin. In places, there wasn't enough space to put anything wider than a fingertip between the etchings of hearts, guns, and knives. The once-polished metal surround was dented. Loose along its left-hand edge.

Reece took the steps to the seventh floor, all the while thankful the killer hadn't disposed of his victim in the loft. He met no one on the way, the smell of pee getting no better the higher he went.

There was music pounding through the building, the early hour not registering with at least one of Trellick House's tenants. Or maybe it had, and the person didn't give a shit who they disturbed. It was one of those places. Somewhere people knew better than to voice a complaint.

Rounding off on the seventh floor, Reece pushed on a heavy fire door and made his way along a narrow walkway, exposed to the elements. It was like entering a wind tunnel that sucked and blew cold air in turns.

The pee smell was mostly replaced by the cloying odour of damp. Someone was frying bacon. Reece's stomach rumbled. He'd had no time for breakfast and was regretting it.

A uniform stepped away from the doorway as he approached. 'Sir.'

'Relax,' he told the man. 'I'm not royalty.'

In the eyes of many of the *rank and file* at the Cardiff Bay station, Reece wasn't far off. 'Sorry, sir.'

'This one, is it?' There was no need for the question, given the level of activity in and around the flat. Taking a clipboard from the uniform, he scribbled his name, rank, and time of entry on a sheet of paper. He handed it back and went through the process of donning a paper suit and overshoes.

'You're here, boss.'

Reece recognised the voice and wobbled on one leg. He put out an arm and steadied himself against the wall. 'Obviously.'

Jenkins knew better than to object when the DCI was in this type of mood. 'The victim's not a pretty sight,' she said, leading the way inside. 'Must have really pissed someone off for them to have done this to him.'

'What's his name?'

'Diric Ali.' Jenkins stopped in the main living room to expand on her initial response. 'Twenty-three. Somalian heritage. We're not getting much help from the neighbours either.'

Reece wasn't surprised.

Diric Ali was positioned on a wooden chair with a clear plastic bag draped over his head and taped securely to his neck. His facial features were distorted. Lips retracted in a yellow-toothed grimace that made no secret of the pain he'd experienced prior to a death that couldn't have come quickly enough.

'He was trying to chew a hole in it.' Dr Cara Frost, Home Office Forensic Pathologist, reached into her bag for something she didn't find. 'Suffocation and resultant heart failure would be my best guess prior to taking a proper look inside him.'

Reece's attention had since moved to a pair of reddish-brown patches on Ali's knees. There were longer streaks of a similar colour extending down the shins of his tan corduroy trousers. More again on the white socks and matching training shoes. His groin was soiled with what Reece could only assume was urine, or worse.

Frost was closing her bag and getting ready to leave.

Jenkins said she'd see her later that evening and would pick up a takeaway on the way home. She turned to Reece: 'What are you thinking, boss?'

'That I know what to tell Sioned Williams on the way out of here.' He ignored the look of confusion. 'Come on. There's work to do.'

Chapter 12

Reece used a Biro to tap out a beat on his knee while he ended what had been a very brief case outline.

Chief Superintendent Cable held her head in her hands and rocked back and forth in her chair. 'Are you trying to put me in an early grave?'

Reece brought the drumming to an abrupt end. 'You didn't see the crime scene, ma'am. Diric Ali's death was a gangland killing. No doubt about it.'

'That, I don't doubt. But it doesn't automatically mean Billy Creed's to blame.'

Reece tossed the pen onto the desk. It pinged off the chief super's half-empty cup of tea and rolled towards her. 'It does in my book.'

She lowered her hands and sat up straight. 'Brân. I wanted to—'

'Here it comes again. The *leave him be* speech.'

'Meaning?'

'It's always the same where Creed is concerned. No wonder nothing we ever pin on him sticks.'

Cable's eyes widened. 'If you're suggesting—'

'You wouldn't be the first,' Reece said, not looking away. 'There's plenty round these parts, and others further afield, who'd have good reason to turn a blind eye to Creed's antics.'

Cable swatted the idle Biro with the back of her hand and flew out of her chair, leaning all five feet three inches of herself towards him. 'Did you come here looking for a fight? Because if you did, I'm happy to give you one.'

'I'm just saying how it looks.'

She sat down again and patted both lapels of her regulation blouse in turn. She looked away and took a moment to calm herself. 'I want to see the evidence before you do anything else.'

'The evidence is chilling in the city morgue.' Reece pointed over his left shoulder. 'You're welcome to go take a peek any time you want.'

Cable searched through the top drawer of her desk, closing it once she had a bottle of aspirin on her lap. She tapped two white tablets out onto her palm and swallowed them dry. '*Evidence*. You're to do nothing before then.'

Reece stood and handed her his unopened bottle of water. 'I'll get you plenty. Don't you worry about that.'

He pulled away from the lights, crossing two lanes of busy traffic to set up correctly for the approach to the roundabout. Several other drivers beeped their horns at him. For once, he chose not to respond in kind. The engine got a heavy revving as they waited at the *Give Way* point; thick clouds of blue smoke creeping ominously alongside the battered Peugeot.

Elan Jenkins was sitting side-on to him, oblivious to the silent newcomer at her window. 'And you're sure that's what Cable said? She's on board with this?'

Reece wobbled a flat hand of uncertainty above the steering wheel. 'Of a fashion, yes.'

Jenkins stared at him. 'What's that supposed to mean?'

The car momentarily lost all power. Reece ground the gears and floored the clutch and accelerator pedals simultaneously. They lurched forward in their seats as the vehicle somehow recovered from its failed attempt to die. 'It means . . . *sort of*.'

'Sort of.' It was almost a whisper. Jenkins shook her head. 'You do remember I'm on a final written warning? One cock-up short of getting myself booted out of here.'

Reece sighed. 'I've told you a hundred times already, those things are good for wiping your arse on and nothing else. Forget about it. It's no big deal.'

'Not for you, maybe. But *I've* supposedly still got the makings of a career in front of me.' She pressed a hand against the dashboard when they slowed with the traffic. 'That's if I do nothing else to screw it up.'

Reece rolled his eyes. 'Stay in the car if this is such a big deal.'

'I don't want to stay in the car.'

'Shut up then and stop moaning.'

Chapter 13

Reece walked straight into the office without waiting to be invited. 'Afternoon.'

'Don't they teach you lot to knock at Copper School?' Creed took his leg off a low footrest and rubbed his knee. He made eyes at Jimmy Chin, swearing under his breath as he struggled to get the limb comfortably positioned.

Chin took the hint and scooped handfuls of fifty-pound notes into a canvass kitbag balanced across his thighs.

'And they say crime doesn't pay.' Reece left the door open for Jenkins. She was zig-zagging through the maze of snooker tables in the other room. He took a seat opposite Creed with his hands clasped together and resting between his open knees.

'Who does?' The initial look of surprise at the detectives' unexpected arrival was gone from Creed's tattooed face. 'Not anybody I know.' He pushed his back against the plastic chair, no longer fiddling with his injury. 'What about you, Jimmy? You ever hear anyone say that?'

'Nope.' Chin pulled the bag's zipper closed before putting it away under the table.

'He's not in much of a talking mood today,' Creed said, nodding towards the hired muscle. 'Didn't get his full quota of beauty sleep last night.'

'Doing a spot of DIY, was he?'

Creed's eyes narrowed. 'Too much on his mind.' He pointed a finger at Chin. 'He's a thinking man. Ain't you, Jimmy?'

Reece craned his neck to get a better look at the kitbag. 'You boys saving up for a new drill?' He raised his eyes to the level of the gangster's. 'Those branded types don't come cheap, I bet? Not when you leave them behind on the latest job.'

Creed was about to reply, but stopped himself when Jenkins appeared in the doorway. 'You must be here for the pole dancing audition?' He laughed. Then coughed. 'You can take your kit off in the corner there. Jimmy won't look.'

Jenkins leaned against the door frame with her arms folded across her chest. 'Sod off, creep.'

'You can't be smacking her hard enough.' Creed lit a cigar and took a few quick puffs to get it going. 'The woman doesn't know her place.'

Jenkins scowled. 'Maybe *this* woman's place is to come over there and slap that thing down your throat.'

Reece swivelled. 'I thought you were waiting in the car?' He got one of her *don't you dare* looks in part reply.

'I wouldn't miss this for the world,' she said, alternating her attention between Creed and Jimmy Chin. 'It's been a while since I went to the zoo. Can't say the apes are up to much in this one.'

Creed shrugged. All signs of humour quickly gone. 'Okay, Copper, let's cut to the chase. What brings you sniffing round my door?'

Reece turned to the front. 'Where were you both last night?'

Creed looked to the ceiling. Then towards his partner in crime. 'Playing five-a-side football, weren't we, Jimmy?' Laughing at his own humour, he pointed to his duff knee and added: 'Goes without saying, *I* was in goals.'

'Really?'

'You should join us,' Creed said, getting the cigar going again. 'There's always room for one more.'

'Wrong shaped ball,' Reece told him. 'Besides, I can't stand all that rolling about on the floor nonsense.'

'I heard you're a running man,' Creed said. 'Can be a dangerous thing that – never knowing who or what's coming round the next bend.'

Jenkins stepped further into the room and stood with her hands on her hips. 'Is that a threat?'

Reece told her to let it go. 'Does the name Diric Ali mean anything to you?'

Creed shook his head. 'Local, is it?' he asked, descending into fits of laughter. '*Alley*. Get it?'

Jimmy Chin copied him. 'Nice one.'

Reece got to his feet—ready to leave—and gave the closest edge of Creed's footstool a good tap. 'My bad,' he said, squeezing past. When he got to the doorway, he stopped next to Jenkins. 'You're mine, Billy. This time it's over.'

Creed rubbed his knee. '*Door!*' he screamed after them.

Reece led the way back to the car. 'Fancy a bag of chips?' He slowed as they passed the open door of a place advertising itself as *Sam's Fish Bar*.

Jenkins checked her watch. 'Sorry but I can't.'

Reece retraced his footsteps and waited in the open doorway, sniffing the air. 'Share a bag with me then, if you can't eat one of your own.'

Jenkins looked embarrassed when she answered. 'I'm going to the gym with Ffion.'

'Reece bent at the waist, blowing wind through his lips. '*You?* Gym?'

Jenkins's eyes narrowed. 'What's so bloody funny?'

'With Ffion?'

'Yeah.'

'Why?'

'Why what?' She followed when he stepped into the chip shop, chuckling to himself. 'Come on. Tell me.'

'A large bag of chips for me,' Reece said to the man serving behind the counter. When he turned to Jenkins, he started laughing again. 'What time's the weigh-in?'

She mouthed the words '*sod off*' and ordered herself a piece of chicken. 'Microwaved, not deep fried.'

Reece leaned against the flat of the countertop, enjoying the heat of the metalwork on his back. 'I thought you were allergic to exercise?' He rolled his eyes at the fish fryer. 'As well as alcohol.'

The man shook the fat off a basket of freshly cooked chips. The look of warning from Jenkins was presumably why he didn't respond to Reece's comment.

Jenkins was naturally slight in stature and rarely did she entertain getting physical just for the fun of it. Exercise was, she'd said on more than one occasion, 'for people with fat round their middles and too much time on their hands.' Or something like that. 'Ffion's worried about me,' she said. 'That thing with Belle Gillighan was the start of it. Doctor Death happening only a short while later has made her go all mumsy.'

Almost a year earlier, Jenkins had unwittingly allowed a serial killer into her private life. The whole thing had been a complete mess. A colleague was dead. Billy Creed lost a knee. And Reece had taken a bullet to the chest and shoulder, spending close to a week in a local intensive care unit. Not her finest moment, for sure. And the reason her personal record was blotted with a final written warning.

Reece collected his chips and added lashings of salt and vinegar to them. 'So, you're going to learn how to fight?'

'It's not *fighting*,' Jenkins said, nibbling at the chicken. She blew on it and tried again. 'Ffion reckons it's more of a keep fit sort of thing.'

Chapter 14

Jenkins sprawled on all fours in the corner of the room, gasping for breath and burping repeatedly. '*Jesus*, Ffion. What were you thinking?' She grabbed a towel and draped it over her head. Then collapsed onto her side with a heavy thud. Someone went over to her, asking if she was all right. She waved them away, unable to speak in full sentences. She lifted the towel only enough to look out from under it. 'I paid good money for this shit.'

Morgan spat her gumshield into a gloved hand and moved side-to-side on the balls of her feet. 'You not enjoying it?'

Jenkins rolled onto her back, knees raised, her feet flat to the floor. The room was spinning. Kaleidoscopic flashes of light interrupting her true vision. 'I've been beaten up since the minute we got here.'

She dug a thumb beneath the Velcro wristband of her boxing glove, loosening it. 'Fucking maniacs, the lot of them.' She pointed at a teenager wearing white gloves emblazoned with orange goldfish. 'Especially that one. She's gotta know I'm a copper.' Jenkins's eyes narrowed. 'Do you recognise her from anywhere?'

'Only from here.' Morgan couldn't stop laughing. 'This is what they call sparring. Next time we're going to be—'

'I don't give a toss what it's called.' Jenkins used the wall to get onto her feet again. 'That's it for me. No more.'

Morgan's smile slipped away. 'You've only been once.'

'And that's only because you kept on at me until I gave in.' She threw the loose glove into a pile of equipment on the floor at the front of the gym. She picked at the wristband of the other one. 'You didn't mention any of this bollocks, did you?'

'You've come close to getting yourself killed twice already this year.' Morgan held up a gloved fist. 'This *bollocks*, as you call it, is going to help keep you safe.'

'*Safe!*' Jenkins squealed the word. 'I can't walk. Look,' she said, throwing a leg out in front of her. 'It's like I've shit myself.'

Morgan watched the others finish their short break and take their positions for the rest of the class. 'Will you please stop swearing. You'll get us barred.'

'I fucking hope so.' Jenkins waved at the instructor. 'We've been called back to work,' she said, crossing in front of the class with her hand held to the base of her spine like a pregnant mother. She glared at the smirking teenager, committing her face to memory.

Morgan went several shades of red and apologised before following her limping colleague out of the room. 'You didn't give it a proper try,' she said while the lift climbed two floors. Its doors opened with a clunk and judder. 'Once you get the hang of it, you'll . . .'

Jenkins didn't catch the rest. She pushed on the door to the changing room, mumbling to herself.

Morgan wasn't letting up. 'We could go running instead?'

Jenkins pressed her head against the cold metal of a locker door. 'Firing range. Now that's something I'd be willing to give a go.'

'Guns?'

'Yep.'

'Why?' Morgan had undressed and was on her way to the showers with a white towel wrapped around her middle-section.

'Because I could shoot that little shit downstairs.' Jenkins held her nose and gently wobbled it from side to side. 'Are you sure we haven't nicked her in the past?' She followed Morgan into the shower area, adjusting the taps until she got the water temperature right. 'Hey, I asked you a question.'

'Huh?' Morgan was suddenly preoccupied, her hand pressed flat to her left breast.

'The girl downstairs. Have we . . .' Jenkins didn't finish. She leaned closer. 'What's the matter?'

Morgan wrapped the towel tight to her body and headed back to the locker room. 'It's nothing. Nothing at all.'

Chapter 15

Reece needed to run every day. And today more than most. Having earlier spent time with Billy Creed and his heavily jawed crone, he felt physically sick. The greasy chips, though appetising at the time, were doing little to settle his stomach.

As he pounded the dark streets of Llandaff, he wondered if Jenkins had turned up to her first kickboxing session. He'd never known her shy away from anything and guessed she'd have given it a go at the very least. She was a competent detective. *Wasted* on the Cardiff Murder Squad? Reece didn't think so. But some might. Those upstairs, for example. The pen-pushers. Force politicians. The people who didn't know their arse from their elbows.

Assistant Chief Constable Harris for one.

Cable too? Reece was still reserving judgement where that one was concerned. She might turn out to be okay in the long run, though usually her type didn't. Not once they'd risen above a certain level of command.

The road ahead began a gradual climb for a couple of hundred metres. Nothing to make him slow his pace any. His thoughts returned to Jenkins. She'd shown an interest in offender profiling, though had no real training in it to date. A one-day taster session with the Met some eighteen months previously being her only experience.

Reece had promised to consider a secondment. Somewhere in the United States, probably. But to lose an officer of Jenkins's ability, if only for six months, had been reason enough for him to put it on the back burner for a while longer.

Rounding off at the top of the hill, he passed a jeweller's shop. The one from which he and Anwen had bought their wedding rings almost two years earlier. He swallowed hard. Nothing to do with the exertion of the run. Had it really been that long since his beautiful wife had been fatally stabbed on their honeymoon in Rome?

He'd been looking at guitars in a sidestreet music shop when it happened. Talking with the store's owner about the influence of American blues on the British bands of the sixties. About the downward decline of today's offerings. Music that required no playing of instruments. Voices sent through an array of technological wizardry until it came out the other end, sterile and *meh* at best. And don't get him started on modern-day lyrics. He couldn't understand half of what they were going on about most of the time.

Where was the next Bob Dylan, Neil Young, or Jackson Browne? Reece feared the world would never again hear the likes of them.

It was the not being with Anwen at her time of greatest need that haunted him most. As a husband, he'd vowed to protect her, but hadn't. He'd let her down with the gravest of consequences. Instead of chewing the cud with the shop owner, he should have been out there on the street.

Ready to protect her.

There to pull that thieving bastard off the scooter before the man had a chance to use his knife.

Failing that, *he* should have been the one to die, not Anwen. It was a thought that crushed him every day. One that frequently had him consider ending it all beneath a bus, lorry, or train. Walking fully clothed into a fast-flowing river, or the sea at high tide. Cutting his wrists in a steaming hot bath, or gorging on a menu of spirits and pills.

Had it not been for a promise made to Idris Roberts—his old boss and Anwen's father—Reece wouldn't have hesitated to do so. Only a couple of months previously, he'd stood above the huge sluice gates of the Cardiff Bay barrage system, ready to let go of the railings and plummet into the icy torrent of seawater gushing below.

But Anwen had *spoken* to him. An apparition in a lightning storm raging high above the Norwegian Church on the waterfront. Telling him to go home. There to keep him safe.

Their roles had been reversed. He loathed himself, believing he was undeserving of walking the same streets as other men.

The pavement ahead sank with the downward slope of the road. It had started raining. In Reece's mind, the droplets on his face represented Anwen's tears. The wind on his neck, her breath, encouraging him to carry on.

He lengthened his stride and ran into the night, alone and bereft.

Chapter 16

'Did I tell either of you to kill him?' Billy Creed was in the basement of the Midnight Club, dance music pounding through the concrete ceiling above him. Taped to the wall opposite, and to sections of the floor and ceiling, was a clear plastic dust sheet. 'How do you expect me to get my money back from a stiff?'

Stood on the sheet was a naked man, his hands cupped over his groin. His entire body shook like a wet mongrel. 'We didn't mean to, Billy. He just went blue and croaked.'

Creed lifted a revolver from the shelf next to him and used the thumb of his other hand to press a single shell into the cylinder, spinning it when done. 'Stand still,' he said when the cowering man shifted position. 'My aim ain't what it used to be.'

'Billy—'

'Shut it.' The gangster brandished the loaded gun, whipping the air before extending his arm out in front of him. 'You weren't supposed to leave the bag on his head.'

The target ducked, as though that might help, both hands now clasped to the sides of his head. '*Fuck!*'

'Keep still.' Creed aimed. 'You're making it more difficult for me to hit you.'

The man swivelled left, then right, his head still tucked away in his hands. He lifted a leg. Then put it down. And lifted it again in a curious routine he repeated several times over.

'There's six holes in this cylinder.' Creed counted them out loud for the other man's benefit. 'One bullet,' he said, spinning the cylinder for a second time. 'That means you've got a five-to-one chance of making it out of here alive.'

'Them's good odds,' Jimmy Chin said from his position behind Creed. 'I'd take them.'

'Give me my stick so I can steady myself.' Creed reached and took it, wincing with the twisting motion. He rested his left hand on it for balance. The other, he held out in front of him. 'I'm going to ask you three questions, after which, you may or may not still be in the world of the living. Ready?'

'*Billy!*' The man started up with his dance again, and on this occasion, might also have been crying.

'Question one: What's thicker than pig shit?'

The man's hands flapped about in front of his face, as though he was trying to say something.

'Time's up.' Creed pulled the trigger. *CLICK*. He tutted and spun the cylinder. 'The correct answer was: '*I* am. You should kill me, Billy.' Repositioning himself with a good deal of grunting, he moved on to question two. 'What was the answer to question one?'

This time, the man did say something. 'I am.' Leaving it at that, he lowered his head and stood surprisingly still for someone who must have known he was about to die.

Again, the cylinder spun, making a satisfying clicking sound as it rotated to a full stop. 'And the rest.' Creed nodded, prompting the man. 'You missed the last bit.'

'Billy?'

Creed pulled the trigger three times before the first shot went off, throwing the man hard against the wall. His flailing arms took a moment to catch up with the rest of him. When he bounced off the solid concrete, the second shot rang out as loudly as the first, spraying blood over the plastic sheeting. He was slumped on the floor and very much dead when the third bullet tore through his chest.

Creed stared at the smoking gun. Chin took his fingers out of his ears. 'There must have been two in there already,' the gangster said with a deep-throated chuckle. 'Get him out of here.' He turned on the walking stick, ominously serious. 'And give Nicky Zala a few hard slaps for his part in this fuck up. Let him know how lucky he is not to be leaking claret like his mate over there.'

Chapter 17

CARDIFF PRISON

Arvel Baines put his hands behind his head, closed his eyes and let the familiar assortment of sounds and smells of the prison wing wash over him one last time.

It was release day.

A new beginning.

Thirty years had come and gone. A period that represented half a lifetime for many people.

For him too, perhaps. Only time would tell. It usually did. Time was like that. If you stuck around long enough to let it do its thing, then it usually divulged its secrets – the rough and the smooth.

There were numerous occasions along the way when he'd doubted his ability to see it through to the end of his sentence – convinced he'd succumb to taking his own life like so many others before him.

Or that he'd be spared the awful burden of committing the act himself, and instead, have another inmate do it on his behalf. In the shower block or exercise yard. Over an argument to do with a television channel, or the size of the dollop of mashed potato spooned onto a person's plate.

Absurd in any normal environment, but then again, prison was anything but. Prison was a zoo crammed to bursting with fucked-up people with only one thing on their minds. *Survival.*

Not all succeeded. Not all survived. The secrets of time, not theirs to hear.

Prison officers—PO's. Screws—tried to quash trouble before it escalated into anything more dangerous. But escalate, it often did.

Shanking—stabbing or slashing someone with an improvised blade—was as vicious as it was common. Baines had once seen a man sat on an open toilet with a fistful of yellow omentum protruding through a gaping slit in his upper abdomen. Preoccupied, and using a couple of fingers to push the apron-like fold of innards back inside himself, his attacker had then targeted an undefended neck.

The man had died there on a cold floor stained with his own blood, urine, and excrement. Bled out at the scene while his attacker was dragged away, kicking and screaming.

The dead man was one of many to experience such a grisly end. The public blissfully ignorant, or simply in a state of, *I don't give a shit about those animals.*

The improvised weapons of choice varied enormously in construction. Toothbrushes filed to sharp points, or decorated with razor blades pressed into plastic softened under the heat of a match. The leading edge of a food tray was good for smashing teeth, or opening the vascular flesh above a man's eye.

Boiling water and dissolved sugar was a particular favourite. Known as *napalming,* when emptied onto a victim's back, it caused the skin beneath the soggy mixture to bubble and peel away in ragged sheets.

The list of possibilities was almost endless. A person could be harmed or killed with just about anything if a hater put his mind to it. A fact that hadn't gone unnoticed by Arvel Baines.

Baines had never been shy of violence. Expelled from school for frequent bouts of fighting, he'd later been charged for a serious assault when only a teenager.

His intention had been to break into a grotty bedsit on the cheap side of the city, to *steal* back a watch that had rightfully belonged to his late father. The police had done sod all about apprehending the thief, even though he'd provided them with the squatter's identity and temporary location. He couldn't be blamed then for going over there to sort it out for himself.

But when the drugged-up thief lunged out of the darkness, spitting threats and swinging a claw hammer, Baines's immediate reaction had been to hit back with his head, fists, and just about anything else he could get his hands on.

Including the hammer.

The court had been lenient. The circumstances of why Baines had gone to the bedsit in the first place, together with the age difference between himself and the victim, finding in his favour.

He thought it totally absurd that the thief should be labelled a *victim*. The man had broken into the Baines family home, trashed the place, and taken whatever he fancied. Had Arvel Baines not defended himself, then *he* might have been the one admitted to a neurosurgical ward, and not the other man.

But that experience came nowhere close to highlighting the failings of the justice system, as the Old Man Jasper case did.

The judge had taken the presented facts—an oxymoron if ever there was one—and delivered a summing-up that left the jury with no alternative other than to find Baines guilty of murder.

Predictably, just about everyone he knew in life disowned him from that day onward. Not that they totalled many in number. Baines had always preferred to remain something of a loner. Chasing and drawing butterflies. Experimenting with his herbal remedies.

What did hurt, and surprise him, was his mother's decision to not make prison visits. She'd also treated his letters home with the same apparent contempt she'd developed for him as a son.

Baines sighed, the sound of yet another argument on one of the landings temporarily breaking his train of thought. There was the clatter of boots on metal and plenty of raised voices. Clapping and cheering. Nothing he hadn't heard a thousand times before. He lay there waiting for things to settle down before returning to his daydream.

On reflection, prison had been good to him in many ways. He'd learnt more inside its claustrophobic walls than he'd ever done at school. His mother would have been amazed if only she'd given a damn.

He'd successfully completed two university degrees. Had also been educated in the darker dealings of life. He'd seen power struggles succeed and fail. Bloodthirsty vendettas acted out. His mind was crammed full of newfound knowledge.

Baines had learned more in prison than he could ever have imagined, becoming something of an expert in the construct of revenge.

And in all his years there, never once had he gone hungry. For three decades, he'd had a roof over his head. Remained dry. Electricity on tap, though annoyingly, someone else controlled the all-important switch.

He opened his eyes, wanting to view the basic contents of the cell one last time. The double bunk. The table set against the opposite wall; its chair having one leg shorter than the other three. He'd measured them using a strand of hair as a ruler. His suspicion confirmed. If he hadn't known better, he'd say the screws had done it on purpose. Cut a bit off the bottom just to piss him off.

And piss him off, it had.

There was a metal toilet and wash basin over in the corner. He couldn't call it the *far* corner. There was nothing in the cell that could ever be described as far away. Not even by the most enterprising of estate agents.

A selection of calender girls winked at him from their pride of place on the scratched walls. Positioned among the girls were sketches of butterflies. Some coloured in. Most in charcoal grey and white.

They'd not let him dabble with herbs during his sentence; no doubt fearful of the illicit uses he might find for them.

'I was worried you were going to sleep through and miss your big day.'

Baines drew his eyes away from the voluptuous curves of his favourite girl—a ponytailed blonde wearing a big smile and little else—and saw Sykes, his pungent cellmate. The man stood in the doorway with his hands planted firmly against the frame on both sides. He was on one leg, the foot of the other wrapped tightly around his calf. It gave him the appearance of a pelican. A beaked nose and matching chin, only adding to the unfortunate likeness.

The man was a lifer. A serial offender who'd quickly progressed from episodes of petty crime to the needless killing of a postmaster in a job gone horribly wrong. To compound his error, Sykes had then shot dead the only witness: a twelve-year-old girl who'd ventured into the corner shop to post a letter for her grandmother. When the emergency services arrived a few minutes too late, the girl was still clutching her money and chocolate bar.

Apprehended the same day, and with a little over three-hundred quid to show for his efforts, Sykes had been incarcerated ever since.

'You almost ready to go?'

Baines nodded at the bag hanging lopsidedly off the back of the chair. 'Yep.' It wasn't much to show for a lifetime. A toothbrush, shaving gear and a few items of clothing making up the bulk of it. 'Just having a quiet minute before I make a move.'

There was no such thing in prison, but Sykes nodded as though he understood the deeper meaning. He picked at the flaking paintwork and cursed when some of it broke away, stabbing under a fingernail. 'Be sure to leave the detective 'till last,' he said, nibbling at the offending sliver of green paint. 'Or they'll hound you down like a fox in a Sunday hunt.'

Baines had always been careful with the information he divulged to his cellmate. Prisoners talked. Sold knowledge. The screws, too. Word of his murderous intentions could easily get out and find the ears of the wrong people. Ruined before he'd had a proper chance to get them going.

Baines had once told Sykes that Detective Constable Brân Reece was on his list. That the officer would be getting a visit from him. But that was a long while ago, and well before Baines had studied his own case as part of a law degree.

Reece had, if case transcripts could be believed, questioned the integrity of the Crown's evidence. He'd also fingered Dai Kosh for the killing of Old Man Jasper. Pity then no one else at the Radyr police station thought the same. Not only had the young detective's protests fallen on deaf ears, they'd also earned him a right royal bollocking for his noble efforts.

Those facts alone would spare the detective the same level of harm due to the others.

The older man—DI Idris Roberts—should count his blessings that lung cancer had already cut him down.

Chapter 18

The day outside had some spring warmth to it, but only when the sun peaked from behind a cloud. Arvel Baines jumped, startled by the main door to the building slamming shut behind him, the locks clunking noisily into position.

He was no longer in his cell. Nor in any sort of confinement block.

The wonder of being stood out in the open street after so many years of his world measuring little more than the distance between two arms stretched in opposite directions, was immediately overwhelming. The space was vast. His eyes able to wander several hundred metres in any direction with little obstruction other than traffic or another human being. And those humans were Joe Public, not cons or screws.

Baines put a hand against the stone wall and steadied himself, wondering if this was how sailors first reacted to walking on dry land after a long and arduous voyage at sea. He took a few deep breaths and let go of the rough stonework, taking his first tentative steps of freedom.

Nobody spoke to him as they walked on by. No acknowledgement of his existence. All heads held in a downward position, their owners mostly staring into the elongated screens of mobile phones. He knew what the devices were, obviously—prison was chock full of them—but rarely were they used so overtly. And rarer still were they such modern looking handsets.

He watched a Tesla Model 3 glide by, the only sound it made coming from the friction between its rubber tyres and the tarmac beneath it. Elon Musk couldn't be blamed for that, Baines decided. He'd read about electric vehicles in newspapers and magazines. It was the stuff of childhood fantasies. And now he was getting to see them in the flesh, so to speak.

Turning a full one-hundred and eighty degrees, he followed the Tesla, not blinking until it was out of sight. Then came a second. Only moments later. This one also in white paint. He'd have it in black. Was that an option? He'd ask when the time came.

Every vehicle that passed by was a far cry from his father's Ford Sierra. Even the ones that were barely bigger than a shoe box.

He scratched his chin, his eyes narrowing. There was a man in a dress heading towards him. He knew it was a man only because of the neat beard. The rest of him . . . *her* . . . Baines wasn't at all sure which, was heavily made up. There was even a pink bow tied in the person's hair.

Their; them; they; were the proper terms if memory served him correctly. Pronouns, wasn't it? Again, he'd only ever read of such things and had no real-world experience.

Still, he wouldn't judge—having himself fallen victim to similar bias in the good old days—and went on his way without provoking a scene.

He stopped for a moment to admire a patch of grass. It wouldn't have caught the eye of the casual observer, but to him, the greenness of it was mind-blowing. It was as though he was on an acid trip. Every colour popping vividly.

The speed of life on the outside was supercharged. Everybody racing about and paying little attention to anyone else. So different to his time spent in the *Big House*, where the pace of the day was interminably slow, and inmates' actions constantly scrutinised.

There was somewhere different to eat, almost everywhere he looked. Burger bars. Sandwich bars. Places with names that confused him. He stared at the sign next to one particular door. What the hell was a Wagamama?

Baines was so completely absorbed by the unfamiliar sights, smells, and sounds of the environment that he was blind to the existence of the heavy-chinned man following only a stone's throw behind him.

Chapter 19

CYNCOED, CARDIFF. ONE MONTH LATER.

There was blood.

Lots of blood.

Lukewarm and sticky.

On John Kosh's hands, clothing, and face. He woke up lying on his back, his head pressed against a tiled floor, staring at a semi-circle of chrome downlighters recessed in what was a recently painted ceiling. His blurred gaze travelled from left to right along the expanse, stopping only when it came across an explosion of red dots next to one of the polished light units.

He had no idea what those red dots were, or how they might have got all the way up there on his ceiling.

Not for the moment, anyway.

He had fuzzy memories of being at a party earlier that evening. But whose, or where it was, he didn't know.

Had he got drunk? Taken drugs, perhaps? Every question drew the same fat blank.

When he moved his arm, it slid through a puddle of something slimy, before coming to rest against what felt like the thin material of an evening dress. His head lolled to one side, leaving him looking into the glazed eyes of the woman next to him. He listened for sounds that might escape the gaping hole at the front of her long, slim neck, but heard none. She was dead and staring way off into the distance beyond him.

Kosh's brain struggled to compute what was going on, all cogs turning with a slow grinding motion that neither helped nor hindered his cause.

And then it caught up—his brain—moving through the gears with a fluid motion. First through to fifth in little more than an instant.

The dead woman was his wife.

This was his house.

His kitchen.

Where were the partygoers?

'*Helen!*' The effort of screaming that one word tore at Kosh's dry throat. Swallowing against the searing pain and breathing in shallow gasps, he rolled onto his side and groaned. It was a deep and guttural sound, summoned from the very depths of his tortured soul. '*Isla!*' Kosh scoured every inch of the kitchen floor for his daughter. All four corners of the room and every recess within it. The sixteen-year-old was nowhere to be seen. Maybe she'd arrived home in the middle of whatever this was and made a run for it?

Kosh instinctively knew that hadn't happened. Isla would never have left her mother all alone. Not like this.

She'd gone to get help. That's what she'd done. Knocked next door. Alerted a neighbour. Phoned the emergency services.

But Isla's phone was on the kitchen counter next to her green paisley Chilly water bottle. She wouldn't have forgotten to take the handset with her. Not even in a state of panic.

Unless, that was, she hadn't been able to get to it without putting her own life in jeopardy. The killer must have been standing in her way.

What else might that person have done? John Kosh didn't dare give the thought an airing. He drew his knees under him and used the corner of the kitchen cupboard to steady himself. Groaning, he got to his feet and counted the ragged puncture marks in Helen's yellow dress. There were five he could see. Each surrounded by widening patches of bright red blood. There was possibly a sixth stab wound above his wife's left hip, but that was wedged against a cabinet door, preventing him from getting a proper look.

He vomited onto the black, polished floor tiles; a mix of brown fluid and flecks of stomach lining. Only when he raised his right hand to his soiled lips was he aware of the object gripped in its clenched fist. He brought the hand up to his eyeline and couldn't imagine why it was he'd be holding a carving knife smeared with fresh blood.

Audible through the dividing wall to the adjoining property was the dull *thud-thud* of music, the sounds of laughter, and the occasional squeal of an overexcited woman.

The party.

Only then did Kosh remember being next door. Helen too. Dancing, drinking, then feeling decidedly unwell and needing to come straight home. He recalled precious little else after that.

How long ago was it? An hour or two was his best guess.

'Tut, tut. What *have* you done?'

John Kosh was startled and searched for the owner of the voice. For a fleeting moment, he wondered if it had originated from within his own aching head. But then it spoke again. This time loud and clear, and from somewhere off to his left.

The stranger wore a black balaclava, with a hoodie and matching jogging bottoms, and stepped out of the adjoining utility room. He was careful to keep well out of reach of the knife and not encroach upon the expanding puddle of blood and shards of broken glass. His bushy eyebrows shifted in greeting, then calmly, he said: 'You killed her. Murdered your own wife.'

'*No!*' Kosh spat the word, his gaze drawn from the stranger's hidden face, to the blade, and back again. Kosh couldn't place him. The eyes and surrounding skin had the appearance of belonging to someone who was beyond middle-age. Pasty, as though the man didn't get out much in natural sunlight. His toned physique, however, suggested someone half that number of years.

The stranger's eyes narrowed. 'You're the one holding the murder weapon. I'd argue you did.'

Kosh lowered his head and took in the horrific scene. When he looked up again, there was a snap to his voice. 'Who the fuck are you?'

A chuckle. 'I'm a nightmare that's only just beginning.'

Kosh took a step closer, his fist tightening. '*You* did this. Not me.'

'Uh-uh.' The stranger's eyes were fixed on the knife now that it was angled towards him. 'Not if you ever again want to see that pretty little daughter of yours.'

Kosh felt his bladder relax and clenched in the nick of time. He rechecked every inch of the kitchen. Each corner in turn. Isla wasn't there. Not cowering behind the floor-to-ceiling curtains over by the patio doors. 'What have you done with her?' Kosh had never been so frightened in anticipation of an answer. 'Is she alive?'

The stranger barely nodded. 'For the time being, at least.'

'Don't hurt her.' Kosh was crying. His body convulsing with a mix of shock and grief. 'Please, I beg you.' He opened a cupboard door and removed a brandy glass stuffed with folded twenty-pound notes. 'There must be close to two-hundred quid there,' he said, offering the lot. 'I can get more from the bank if you need it? Won't take me long.'

'This isn't about money.' The stranger sounded offended by the remark.

Kosh used the cuff of his shirt to wipe scum from his dry lips. 'What then?'

The stranger clasped both gloved hands together, his thumbs turning in circles. 'How's life been for you, John?' There were granite work surfaces in the kitchen. An expensive brand of coffee machine and an American-style fridge-freezer. Even a dead woman leaking blood and other stuff on the tiled floor. 'Better before now, I'm guessing?'

Kosh went to lunge. Stopped himself in time. Images of his young daughter locked up somewhere dark and cold, flooding his mind. 'What do you want?'

'You're going to help me with something I've been planning for a very long time.'

'Fuck you!'

'Have it your own way.' The stranger disappeared into the utility room. 'I'll let Isla know before she dies that Daddy gave up on her.'

Kosh went after him and got there before he'd opened the back door. Grabbing a handful of the hoodie's material, he held the knife to the man's throat. 'You won't be going anywhere near my daughter.'

'Then what? You'll never find her. Not before the rats get there first.'

Kosh's mind was racing. 'Dogs. We'll use dogs to track Isla's scent.' The blade was poised to strike. 'Yeah, that's what we'll do.' He was growing in confidence and ready to draw the knife across the man's scrawny neck in punishment for what he'd done to Helen.

'There's someone waiting with her, John.' The stranger's voice was calm. Dignified. 'Someone who's expecting me back within the hour.'

The blade bit, drawing blood. 'You're bullshitting.'

'Are you willing to take the chance?'

Kosh steadied his breathing. It made sense. The man was unlikely to be working alone. 'Prove it.'

'I don't have to.'

Kosh closed his eyes, his grip tightening on the handle of the knife. It was now or never. A decision screaming to be made.

The stranger kept still. 'Kill me and you kill your daughter.'

Kosh's grip on the hoodie loosened. He went back to crying as a coping mechanism and took two steps rearwards.

'Put the knife away. It won't do you or Isla any good.'

'When will I see her? Where is she?'

The stranger steered him back into the kitchen. 'Patience, we're only just getting started here.' He pointed to a stool next to an impressive island unit in the middle of the room. 'Sit down. I need to explain something to you.'

Chapter 20

NEXT MORNING

REECE MARCHED DOUBLE-TIME ALONG the busy hospital corridor. Jenkins did her best to keep up. Cycling through a walk-trot-and fast walk again.

The DCI was in a particularly sour mood. News of a fatally stabbed woman doing nothing to lift his spirits. A missing teenager only served to make matters worse.

The previous night's sleep hadn't been that bad, all things considered. Not when compared with those of even a couple of months ago. The awful nightmares were definitely less frequent. Less vivid, too.

On occasions, he would reach Anwen in time, wrestling her attackers off the scooter, disarming and apprehending them. He was at last able to save his wife the indignity of bleeding to death on a cobbled road in Rome. But whenever he woke up, the bed was always empty on Anwen's side. Dreams. Only dreams.

Still, he was making progress.

There *was* one positive to come out of the previous night's murder: the bastard responsible was lying cuffed to a hospital trolley in the Emergency Department downstairs. 'Keep up,' Reece told the flagging Jenkins.

'I'm trying, boss, but my legs are shorter than yours.'

'Swing 'em faster then. Works for me, every time.' He didn't let up with the pace. Like a drill sergeant, he pounded on ahead.

Jenkins broke into another trot. 'They haven't been right since Ffion got me beaten up.'

Reece stopped to stare at her. 'That was ages ago.'

'I don't care. They still hurt.'

He started up again and spoke over his shoulder. 'Your problem, not mine.'

Jenkins swung her legs faster, but still lagged behind. 'I didn't say it was anything to do with you.'

'Hurry up,' Reece said, pulling on a locked door. It didn't budge.

Jenkins came alongside. She was out of breath. 'I think someone needs to swipe us through. Everything in this place works with security key cards.'

Reece put his forehead to the glass and rapped on the wood surround with his knuckles. 'Come on, open it,' he called to a uniform stood on the other side. The young constable came away from the nurse he was quite obviously chatting up and made several attempts to unlock the door. He pressed buttons on a wall-mounted panel like he was playing piano. Regardless of what the man tried, the door refused to unlock and let them through.

Reece swore under his breath. 'They get thicker every intake. Look at him – a bloody chimp would have had it open by now.'

Jenkins caught the uniform's eye and pointed behind him. 'Get one of the staff to open it. *Her*. That one there.'

A few moments later and they were in, the officer apologising as they went past. 'Where is he?' Reece wanted to know.

The uniform led the way behind a curtain that was, until then, pulled shut. 'Here he is, sir.'

On the other side was a dark-haired man lying in a head-up tilt on a trolley. His non-cuffed hand was held to his face. He didn't lower it. Not even when Reece spoke. 'Are you John Kosh?'

'Yes.' The answer was barely audible and delivered through a fan of spreading fingers.

'DCI Reece.' The introduction was straight to the point and absent of any pleasantries.

'I did it,' Kosh said almost immediately. 'I killed my wife.'

Reece stopped him. 'Keep that for the station. Where's your daughter, Isla?'

Kosh went back to crying, the handcuffs rattling against the raised side of the trolley. 'No comment.'

Reece leaned and put his face to Kosh's ear. 'Did you hurt her? Is Isla dead?' The tears didn't let up. 'Come on, John.' Reece pushed away from the trolley. 'You can't change what's happened to your wife, but for Isla's sake—'

Kosh lurched forward as far as the short tether would allow. 'No comment!'

'Please yourself.' Reece turned to the uniform. 'Leave the nurses alone and stay in here with him until a doctor tells you he's fit to leave.' To John Kosh, Reece said: 'I'm not known for my patience. You'd better be ready to talk next time we meet.'

Chapter 21

ON HIS ARRIVAL AT the crime scene, Reece signed the log with the scene guard at the front door, passing the clipboard to Jenkins, who did likewise. With that out of the way, they both stepped into white hooded coveralls that came with matching overshoes, then went inside.

The narrow hallway was lit up with bright artificial lighting that contrasted with crimson smears on the otherwise white walls. There was a sweet, familiar smell that years of working as police detectives told them was recently spilled blood.

Further along was an area of increased activity. A crime scene investigator, dressed like Reece and Jenkins, was busy photographing bloody handprints on the wall at the foot of the stairs. The click of the man's camera tapped out a staccato beat as he recorded the gruesome artwork from every conceivable angle.

Someone else was moving about the house with a video camera.

They waited for a natural break in the recording process before squeezing past into the living room, where the blood splatter analyst was studying something on the arm of a cream leather sofa. 'Is the pathologist here yet?' Reece asked.

The woman didn't look up from what she was doing. 'In the kitchen with the victim.'

Using metal stepping plates, and being careful not to compromise evidence, Reece led the way into a room full of more flashing lights and intense activity. 'Morning, Cara.' He still hadn't yet come to terms with the retirement of Dr Twm Pryce, his friend and colleague of many years. Pryce's replacement would have to go some to fill her predecessor's boots.

Dr Cara Frost turned on the balls of her feet. 'Messy one,' she said, pulling the mask away from her face to make herself better heard. 'Any news on the missing girl?'

'Not yet.' Reece stared at the woman lying in a puddle of her own blood. Much of it had congealed, resting by her corpse like the leftovers of a raspberry jelly. There was a smashed glass not too far away from the body, a clear fluid drying in the joints of the tiled floor. A puddle of vomit stank next to that. 'How many times was she stabbed?'

'Six, including the one at the front of her neck.' Frost got up. 'Any one of them could have been fatal in their own right.'

Jenkins took in the full extent of the grisly scene. 'No half measures, then.'

Sioned Williams, crime scene manager, entered the kitchen using the same stepping plates, her paper coverall rustling like a crisp packet until she came to a halt alongside the detectives. She pointed to a large wooden knife block next to a stainless-steel kettle and said: 'He used one of those.'

Reece counted from five back to zero, just as his counsellor had advised on such occasions. He hadn't gone running outside. Not yet. Wasn't ripping at his collar and gasping for air. Those who knew him well enough would be expecting him to do so anytime soon. He started at five for a second time, working backwards and slowing his breathing until able to speak. 'Did the husband have the knife with him when the first responders arrived?'

'Yep,' Williams said. 'And there are plenty of good prints on it.'

Reece was happy to hear that.

The dead woman was lying on her back with her eyes open. A stiff arm rested against a cabinet door, pointing at the ceiling. That's how it looked to Reece. He raised his head and checked. There was little to see except for a shower of browning blood spots next to one of the light fittings.

Sioned Williams must have read his thoughts. 'The girl's bedroom is right above us. I think the mother was trying to send help straight up there when it arrived.'

Reece couldn't begin to imagine what terror the woman must have suffered lying there, mortally injured, while God only knew what was going on upstairs. He closed his eyes and counted.

'Why?' Jenkins said, looking around. There was a silver photo frame on one of the units, three smiling faces staring out at them. The kitchen was expensive. The address, well out of her own affordable price bracket. 'John Kosh looks like he had it all. Why destroy that and then wait here to hand himself in?'

'The wife might have been playing away?' Williams suggested. 'He could have killed her in a fit of rage?'

'I guess everything's on the table at the minute,' Jenkins said, putting the photo frame back. 'And the daughter: what do you think happened there?'

Reece was still staring at the dead woman. 'I want you to find out everything there is to know about this Kosh character.' He wrestled his gaze away. 'Talk to work colleagues. Friends. Neighbours. Was there ever any indication something like this might happen? Get Ginge to check cautions for improper behaviour while you're at it.'

Jenkins stopped what she was doing. 'You don't think he tried it on with his own daughter, do you? Got caught, then this.'

Reece subscribed to the belief that all sex pests should be skinned alive and rolled in rock salt. 'He wouldn't be the first. And it would give him plenty of motive to want to shut them both up.'

'You know it's likely the girl's already dead?' Jenkins said. 'If the father's been interfering with her from a young age, then there's nothing to be gained by keeping her locked up somewhere. Not now he's done this to the mother.'

Something was bothering Reece. 'Why didn't he flee the scene and make out someone else was to blame?'

'Shock maybe?'

'But he phoned it in and stayed put until uniform arrived.' Reece took in the scene again, searching for that golden nugget he might have missed. 'John Kosh admits to killing his wife, but refuses to tell us where his daughter is. Why? What's he got to gain from that?'

'The upper hand?' Jenkins suggested. 'He'll be wanting to keep control of at least something now his life's unravelling.'

'You mean he intends to string us along?'

'It's all up to him now. Tell us. Don't tell us. The ball is in Kosh's court.'

Reece was aware of the pathologist's presence. 'What's your guess?'

'Death was sometime before midnight last night,' Frost said. 'That's the best I can do for now.'

'Why wait until morning to report it?' Reece was talking to himself. 'If that's what he was going to do, then why not make the phone call immediately?'

'I doubt he was thinking straight,' Frost answered. 'And who can blame him after this?'

'And he'd need time to move the daughter someplace else,' Jenkins said. 'Dispose of her body, or lock her up somewhere. Then he'd have to get back here and contact us. That would take time.'

Sioned Williams disagreed with the first bit. 'We've given both cars a once over already. We'll get a better look back at base, obviously, but given the mess, I'd have expected there to be visible signs of blood or a struggle in at least one of the family vehicles.'

'Give the local car rental firms a ring,' Reece told Jenkins. 'And find out if Kosh gets use of a works' vehicle.' With his order acknowledged, he went and tapped on the kitchen wall. It didn't have the feel of something overly thick. 'Did the neighbours hear anything?'

There was a uniform hovering in the background, a pocketbook held open in his left hand. Reading from it, he said: 'There was a housewarming party there last night, sir.'

'Any of the guests go for a smoke in the garden?' Reece asked. 'Or stand on the front doorstep for fresh air, or a sly snog?'

The uniform said he didn't know. 'The owners are still a bit hungover, sir, but I've got names and contact numbers for everyone they remember inviting.' He looked up. 'The thing is though, with them being new to the area, it was more of an open-door invite. A *bring a bottle and walk right in*, sort of thing.'

'Great,' Reece said with more than a hint of sarcasm. 'Just about every waif and stray in the village is likely to have wandered in and out unchallenged.'

'There'd be few waifs and strays in this area,' Jenkins reminded him.

Reece took the pocketbook from the young officer and skim-read, vocalising only three names from a list of what must have totalled close to twenty. *John, Helen, and Isla, next door.* He handed it back. 'Make sure you get that photocopied at the station. I want everyone ID'd and interviewed. And ask all of them if they dished out any invites of their own to friends.'

'Yes, sir.' The uniform was already on his way towards the front door, visibly eager to be free of the dead woman's company.

Reece called after him: 'And ask the hosts what excuse, if any, John Kosh gave for not going.'

The uniform about-turned and walked a few steps back towards them. 'The couple did go, sir. Then left again after only an hour or two. Something to do with Mr Kosh being unwell.'

Chapter 22

Isla Kosh's bedroom looked like any other teenage girl's. As a detective, Reece had visited his fair share over the years, and always under the same sombre circumstances.

Some girls had been reported missing.

Others already found dead.

A few were on the run with boyfriends twice their age.

He'd seen them all, and it never got any easier.

There was an expensive acoustic guitar propped against the wall in the far corner of the room, its hard carrycase poking out from beneath the bed. Under different circumstances, Reece might have picked up the Taylor and tried it out. But not these.

He counted fourteen light bulbs bordering the frame of a rectangular mirror that might easily have been borrowed from a movie star's dressing room. Or bought from any budget furniture store for that matter.

There were books and journals. Pots of pens and the usual things that went with school and homework.

A picture collage took up space on the far wall – photographs of Isla and what must have been friends of hers. Some of the photographs were taken in the schoolyard. Others on a beach. And several, by the looks of it, from a trip to Disneyland Paris.

Leaving the collage to safeguard its happier memories, Reece opened a drawer in the nearest piece of bedroom furniture. Underwear. He closed it again and moved onto the next one down. Socks. Folded T-shirts in the bottom drawer.

There was nothing to suggest there'd been a struggle. As with the cars outside, there was no visible blood contamination of anything in the room. Sioned Williams and her team would take a proper look just as soon as they were finished downstairs.

'Bag the journals and get Ginge to go through them,' Reece said.

Jenkins stood on the other side of the bed. 'Looking for what, specifically?'

'Anything. Hints that Isla was being abused or bullied. Names of friends. Boyfriend, if she has one.'

Jenkins must have picked up on the DCI's use of present tense. 'You think there's a possibility she's still alive?'

Reece scratched his bearded chin. 'I've a feeling this one's gonna throw up a heap of surprises.'

Chapter 23

Reece sat alongside Jenkins in one of the station's interview rooms. John Kosh and the duty solicitor mirrored their positions on the opposite side of the table. 'Are you sure you don't want to call your own brief?' Reece asked. 'I'd imagine you're able to afford a decent one.' He gave the duty solicitor a wink. 'No offence meant.'

'None taken.' A poker face and lack of eye contact from the man told a different story.

'I don't want anyone at all,' Kosh said. 'I'm guilty as charged.'

The solicitor looked somewhat bewildered. 'Are you telling me to leave?'

'Yes.' It didn't sound at all convincing. 'I want you to go. Right now.'

The solicitor got to his feet, his legs not quite straightening fully. 'What if I just sit here and take notes?' He lowered himself a few inches, his backside hovering above the seat of the plastic chair.

'I told you to go.' Kosh's quivering voice was barely audible. 'Will you do that for me? Please.'

The man didn't answer and marched out without so much as a backward glance. The door to the interview room remained open in his absence, the uniform propping himself up against the nearby wall having to unfold his arms to go and close it.

Reece informed the Digital Interview Recording device [DIR] of the change of circumstances, before checking the suspect understood the potential implications of such an unusual instruction on his part.

'I just want to get this over with.' Kosh lowered his head and picked fluff off the thighs of his joggers. 'I'm willing to sign anything you want me to.'

Reece watched him in silence before speaking again. 'What happened last night between you and your wife?'

Kosh didn't look up, his quivering fingers working overtime. 'Helen and I came back from the party. We argued. I killed her.' He sniffed and left it at that.

'Argued about what?'

'I felt unwell when we were next door. Helen thought I'd had too much to drink. I told her I hadn't and got pissed off at her for having a go at me.' Kosh shrugged. 'That's when we left.'

'And then you killed her?'

'Yeah.'

'Just like that?'

A pause. 'Yeah.'

'That seems a tad extreme, if you don't mind me saying.' Reece folded his arms. 'Are you normally a violent man?'

'No.' Kosh lifted his head only momentarily. 'But it's what happened yesterday.'

'You lost your temper? For the benefit of the tape, Mr Kosh is nodding,' Reece said. 'That's when you killed Helen?'

There was a brief delay. 'Yes.'

Reece pressed his back into the upright of the plastic chair and stared at the ceiling. It wasn't often a murder case got wound up as easily. Something about this one still nagged him. As yet, he had no idea what that was, but the troubling doubt was there all the same. 'Let's rewind a bit. Tell us about yesterday. Everything you remember prior to the party.'

John Kosh reached to lift a plastic cup of water from the table, his hand trembling enough to spill some before it reached his mouth. He pulled the cuff of his sweatshirt over his fingers and dabbed at the spillage. 'I got up around six-thirty, had breakfast, showered and went to work as normal.'

'Where?' It could be important and therefore warranted Reece's question.

'I own the butcher's shop in our village. The one on the corner by the lights.'

'*That* Kosh. Of course.' Reece made the connection and wondered why he hadn't done so any earlier. 'Kosh's Farm, right? Christ, I haven't clapped eyes on you since you were a kid.' He raised an arm to the approximate height of a nine or ten-year-old. 'About that big, you were.'

Kosh stared back. 'I recognise you now. You look—'

'Older?' Reece interrupted. 'I'd have been in my early to mid-twenties at the time.'

There was no verbal response. Only a shrug of the shoulders.

'I heard your dad passed away a couple of years ago.' Reece was building a rapport. Getting the suspect to engage in conversation. Basic skills utilised by a senior detective well versed in the practice of interviewing. 'I'm sorry about that.'

'A heart attack got him in the end. All those cigarettes, I suppose.' Kosh took a sip of water, this time avoiding a repeat mishap. 'I hear lung cancer got Idris. It's always one or the other with smokers, isn't it?'

Mention of his father-in-law caught Reece unawares. 'It usually is.'

Kosh was opening up. 'I remember Idris being a tough old so-and-so. Never afraid to give us a good clip round the ear whenever we stepped out of line.'

'Remember the snowman?' Reece asked. 'You and that other kid fighting in the street.'

There was almost a smile from Kosh. 'Idris kicked our arses. You gave us money for sweets. Good cop: bad cop.'

'You never did tell us what you were squabbling over that day.' Kosh lowered his head and didn't answer. Reece moved the conversation on. 'Who looks after the farm when you're busy at the butcher's shop?'

Kosh's chin remained glued to his chest. 'I had no stomach for that place.'

'Really? That was a good bit of land you had there.'

'My father was a bully, as you well know.' Kosh took a deep breath and let it out quickly. 'It wasn't only the farmhands who got a thump whenever he was pissed off.'

'Bad memories?'

'More than you'll ever know.'

'Is that why you sold the place?'

'With dad gone, I was able to start over. And with no brothers or sisters, selling seemed like the right thing to do.'

'So, you bought yourself a house and ploughed most of what was left into the new business?'

'Yeah.'

'And that's where you were working yesterday?'

'That's right.'

'Until what time?' Reece asked.

'We close at five. I locked up and left no more than half an hour later. I was back at the house some time before six.'

'Where were Isla and Helen when you got in?'

Kosh paused to think. 'Isla wasn't home from school yet.' He swallowed and put a fist to his mouth, shaking. 'I thought she must have gone round to a friend's house. Millie Scott's usually.'

Reece made sure Jenkins took the name. 'What time *did* Isla get in?'

Kosh stopped chewing his knuckles. 'She didn't.'

'We found her phone in the kitchen.' There was no need for Reece to elaborate.

'She must have come back when Helen and I were next door at the party. Then went out again.'

'Leaving her phone at home?' Reece thought it extremely unlikely. He turned to Jenkins. 'How many teenagers do you know would go anywhere without their phone?'

'I can't think of many, boss.'

'And that's the conundrum, John. Isla missing. Her phone not.'

Kosh shrugged. 'Maybe she was in a rush over something.'

'Where is she? Where's Isla?'

'I don't know.'

Reece slapped his hand against the table top, Kosh and Jenkins jumping in sync. 'You killed your wife. Your daughter's missing. You must realise how that looks?'

There was no response from the other man. Only the sound of grinding teeth.

'Isla came home when you were there, didn't she?'

'No.'

'Came in and caught you.'

'I said no.'

'Saw you with the knife in your hand.'

Kosh dropped his head against the desk with a loud thud. '*No!*'

'She caught you red-handed and was about to call the police.'

Kosh sat up straight. '*I* called the police and confessed to what I'd done. What would be the point in me harming Isla if I was going to hand myself in, anyway? And why wasn't she found on the floor next to her mother?'

Not knowing the answer to those questions was the main source of Reece's doubt. 'I'll ask again. Where is your daughter?'

Kosh stared at him through red-raw eyes. 'No comment.'

Chapter 24

It was mid-afternoon and Reece was pacing the incident room with a mug of sweet coffee in hand. Behind him on the evidence board were photographs of John Kosh and his dead wife, Helen. One of Isla was wedged between and below those of her parents. 'This girl is our priority now,' he said, tapping a finger alongside the smiling face. 'Every minute that passes decreases our chances of finding her alive.' He searched the crowded room for Ginge. 'Did you find anything on that phone of hers?'

The lanky detective constable towered over just about everyone else there. 'Isla was texting a friend early in the evening.'

Reece put his coffee down and spoke to Jenkins. 'What was the girl's name Kosh gave us?' He took a marker pen from a pot of several, its nib marking the surface of the board while he waited.

Jenkins read from her pocketbook. 'Millie Scott.'

'That's her,' Ginge said. 'And from the texts I've read so far, she was expecting Isla to go round there.'

Reece frowned. 'And not to the party?'

Ginge rechecked. 'According to this, the parents were going without her.'

Reece wrote Millie Scott's name on the far side of the evidence board, then hunted for the uniform who'd interviewed the party hosts. 'What did the neighbours say when you went back and asked? Did the parents go alone like John Kosh said they did?'

The uniform looked like he wanted a hole in the ground to appear and swallow him up. 'I haven't been back yet, sir. I was photocopying my notes like you told me to.'

Reece's eyes closed. 'Give me strength.' He pointed to the door. 'Get over there and find out.' His angry stare swept over all others remaining. 'Anyone else been sucking their thumbs?' He waited a few awkward seconds before continuing. 'Carry on Ginge.'

The young constable read through the remaining texts. 'If this here is anything to go by, then I'd say Isla went to neither.'

'How come?'

'Well, you've got the mother texting Isla, telling her to have a good time at Millie's. While Millie teases Isla for going out with her parents.'

Reece looked confused. 'So what was going on?'

Jenkins took a step forward. 'It could mean someone else was using Isla's phone. Making it look like she was alive and active.'

'When she'd already been abducted and . . .' Reece chewed on the possibility. 'What about the mother's phone?'

'That hasn't been found,' Ginge said.

Reece rested a buttock on the edge of a desk and scratched his head. 'What the hell is going on in this case?'

It was Jenkins who responded first. 'What if John Kosh picked his daughter up after school and abducted her under false pretences? She wouldn't have struggled, or known anything was wrong until they got someplace remote, by which time it would have been too late. He could have locked her up. Or killed her. Then gone home with her phone and played the mother and friend with a few texts. He goes to the party like nothing's happened, feigns illness, leaves early and kills the wife.' Jenkins waited for a response.

Reece stayed where he was on the edge of the desk. 'But then he contacts the police and does sod all else. Why not kill the girl along with her mother, if he's going to plead guilty?'

Jenkins didn't have an answer to that and admitted as much.

'And we've already checked with the other businesses in that area,' Ginge said. 'The butcher's was open until five. At least two of those owners report seeing him there.'

'Okay then,' Jenkins said. 'What about this for another angle: Isla kills her mother and Kosh takes the blame to protect her? The girl hasn't been abducted, or killed. She's on the run?'

Reece stared. '*Why?*'

Jenkins dropped onto her seat, her facial expression acknowledging defeat. 'God knows.'

'And what husband would cop for something like that?' Ginge asked.

Jenkins raised her hands in surrender. 'I already said I don't know. I was just putting it out there.'

'And you're right to.' Reece looked at the rest of the team. 'Anyone else?'

A few threw their theories at him, none of which were any more convincing than Jenkins's offerings. 'I want uniform knocking on doors. Trawling through the usual CCTV images,' Reece said once they'd exhausted the possibilities. 'We might catch sight of Isla, on foot, or getting on a bus.' He glanced at Jenkins. 'Check with border control, in case she *is* doing a runner.' He clapped his hands twice. 'Chop, chop. What are you all waiting for?'

They left with the rumble of chit-chat and shifting chairs. Ffion Morgan was pushing through the crowd, travelling in the opposite direction.

Jenkins went over to her. 'You're looking a bit pale. Everything all right?'

Morgan lifted her fringe and took Jenkins's hand. She pressed it to the swelling at her temple. 'I'm going to start wearing a helmet,' she said, searching for somewhere to sit down. Once seated, she left an inch gap between her finger and thumb. 'I'm this bloody close to having them line the mortuary floor with soft-play mats.' She closed her eyes and opened her coat, fanning herself with a flap of its material. 'Third time I've gone spark-out in front of the same technician. I even puked on the poor sod today.' She exhaled loudly and pinched the bridge of her nose. 'They're gonna ban me from the morgue if I keep this up.' Her eyes opened wide. 'Why didn't I think of that before? Get myself banned. Yeah, that's what I'll do.'

'Aw, Ffion, give us a cwtch.' Jenkins leaned over and gave her colleague a big hug. 'You're a real trooper.'

Morgan wriggled herself free. 'How do they get out of bed in the morning?' She went over to her own desk, took off her coat and draped it over the back of her seat. 'Seriously though, how do those people even eat?'

Reece laughed. 'Go and get some proper fresh air. Talk to Millie Scott. Jenkins will fill you in on the way.'

'And what will you be up to?' Jenkins asked.

Reece raised his eyes to the underside of the polystyrene ceiling tiles. 'I'll be upstairs. The chief super wants to see me.'

Chapter 25

Millie Scott wiped her eyes with the back of her hand. Jenkins offered a fold of paper tissues from her jacket pocket. 'They're clean. Take them. This must be very difficult for you,' she said. They were huddled around a glass table at the far end of a busily decorated living room. There to find out what, if anything, the missing girl's best friend knew. 'Do you have any idea where Isla might have gone after school yesterday?'

Millie twisted in her chair and reached to the windowsill behind her. 'I've got some here, thank you.' She turned to face the front again and dropped a squat yellow box of tissues onto the table. She pulled one free and blew her nose. 'No idea.'

Morgan leaned forward in her chair, its thin wooden legs creaking beneath her. 'Was Isla having any hassle in school?'

Millie scrunched the soiled tissue in her fist. A length of blonde hair, previously tucked neatly behind her ear, had come loose and hidden the left side of her face. She tucked it back, ignoring the bit that immediately broke free again. 'Not as far as I know.'

'And you'd be the one to know if she was?' Morgan paused. 'Because you're her best friend?'

Millie nodded. 'We tell each other everything.'

Jenkins removed her jacket and lowered it to the carpeted floor next to her. The girl's mother stood in the kitchen doorway looking understandably anxious. Jenkins nodded at her. It was a simple enough gesture, meant to reassure the woman. Mrs Scott returned the nod before going back to whatever it was she'd been doing. 'What about boyfriend issues?'

Millie's chin lifted, her eyes flicking between the two detectives before settling on Jenkins. 'Isla doesn't have one.'

'Has she had one?'

Millie pulled another tissue. Several others spewed out of the top of the box behind it. She tucked the unwanted ones back inside before answering. 'Not for a while, and even then, it was nothing serious.'

'Who broke up with who?' Morgan asked, poised to record the name in her pocketbook.

'It wasn't like that. Daniel's parents emigrated about a year ago. Dubai, I think. His dad was a pilot or something.'

They took the boyfriend's name for what it was worth, Jenkins telling Morgan to check with passport control when the teenager had last entered the UK. 'Were you aware of any problems at home?'

Millie looked confused.

Treading carefully, Jenkins rephrased her question. 'Did Isla have a good relationship with her parents?'

A frown. 'Of course she did.'

'No issues with her dad?'

The frown deepened. 'What are you saying?' Millie put a hand to her open mouth. 'Oh, my God. That's sick!'

Morgan rested her pen on the table top and reached for the girl's hand. 'I know it seems wrong, but we have to ask.'

'You're miles off the mark, if that's what you're thinking. Isla and her dad were close, but not in *that* way.'

'And you're sure you've no idea where she might have gone? No secret hiding place she uses whenever she's angry with someone?'

'Isla wasn't angry. I was with her all day at school. Even texted her afterwards. She was fine.' Millie didn't look at the detectives. 'You think she's dead, don't you?' The question brought another flood of tears.

Jenkins stood and circled to the other side of the table. She put an arm around the sobbing girl's shoulders and pulled her close. 'Listen to me. Our boss is the best there is in this business. If anyone can find Isla, it's him.'

Chapter 26

Reece waited for Chief Superintendent Cable's personal assistant to tell him it was okay to go in. He had his back to her desk and was staring out of the window.

On the street below was a young woman pushing a pram with three other kids in tow. Like kittens, each of them made off in different directions every time she let go of their coats. She'd travelled no more than ten to fifteen metres in the minutes Reece had been watching.

He found himself wondering about Isla Kosh. Where she was. Whether she'd survive to have kids of her own. She deserved to be given the option. Allowed to decide for herself. That was every woman's right.

His thoughts wandered further. To Rome, as they did several times a day. More so during the night. Anwen had been given no choice regarding motherhood. That opportunity had been taken away from her in a flash, by some drug-fuelled thug who'd later killed himself in custody, rather than endure a life-sentence in jail.

He dragged himself out of the daydream. The woman with the pram had got no further than she was the last time he looked. What was he doing wasting time inside, staring through windows and judging people? He should be out there in the streets, fields, or wherever else, hunting for Isla Kosh. He was about to leave when the PA called his name.

'You can go in now, Chief Inspector.'

'Wish me luck,' he said, passing the PA's desk, and got little more than a polite smile in reply.

Cable offered him tea as he closed the door. She tapped a spoon on the rim of her cup before resting it alongside a steaming tea bag. 'Or can I get you a coffee instead?'

'Neither, thanks. I haven't long had one.'

She indicated that he should take a seat on the other side of her desk. 'I wanted a quick catch up. Don't look so nervous.'

'John Kosh has—'

'Wait, wait.' Cable put the cup down. 'Diric Ali, first. Where are we on that one?'

Reece had been expecting as much. He was surprised it had taken this long before the chief super was put under pressure to discuss the matter more formally. 'Harris worried someone's about to play the racial card, is he?'

Cable stiffened. 'It's been a month without progress. What do you expect?'

Reece didn't like admitting they'd made no inroads on that one. But what could he have done differently? The deceased man was a foreign national, travelling on a false passport. And there had been a complete lack of witnesses in and around Trellick House. 'There might be something to report soon, ma'am.' He knew he was being hopeful at best. 'One or two items recovered from the crime scene got *mislaid* during processing.'

Cable dragged a hand across her forehead. 'Meaning?'

'They've turned up again now.' He looked apologetic, but didn't know why. It wasn't a cock up linked to a member of *his* team. 'Sioned's got some newbie in training. You know how it is?'

'Keep me posted.' Cable leaned forward in her chair and took another sip of tea. 'I hear you paid Billy Creed a visit.'

Reece had wondered on his way up the stairs if this was going to be another of those annoying tellings off. He shifted position, preparing for a few rounds of verbal sparring. 'Diric Ali was bound to a chair with Gaffer tape. A polythene bag stuck over his head. Several holes drilled into the bone of each knee . . .' He left it there. Round one, his.

'And that has to mean Creed's somehow involved?' Cable was playing him at his own game. Second round, hers.

'Who else can you think of?'

Cable didn't reply on the matter. She was staring at him. 'I'm on your side. Even if at times it doesn't appear that way.' Sneaky move. A draw.

Reece wondered what the purpose of such a comment was. He kept his guard raised, not wishing to get chinned this late in the contest. He managed something of a grunt in response.

Cable's eyes shifted to another point in the room. 'Let's move on to this awful domestic business.'

He told her everything he knew so far, including the bits that bothered him most. 'I don't think I've ever come across anything quite like it.'

Cable finished her tea and pushed the cup and saucer to one side of the desk, planting her elbows in the space left by the absent crockery. She nibbled at a thumbnail. 'Is there anything to suggest the husband is innocent?'

'Nothing that would hold up to any real scrutiny.' While Jenkins had been right to raise the possibility of Isla killing her mother before going AWOL, Reece remained unconvinced on that front.

'You've charged him?'

'I had no choice. Kosh insists he killed his wife, and there's nothing we've found so far to contradict that.'

'So why the doubt on your part?'

Reece didn't know the answer to that. His good shoulder rose and fell. 'Something doesn't ring true on this one.' He shrugged for a second time.

Cable lowered her arms flat to the table. 'Any sightings of the missing daughter?'

'None, ma'am.'

'When is John Kosh at magistrates' court?'

'First thing in the morning.'

'You're doing the right thing, Brân.' Reece wasn't so sure and got up, ready to leave. Cable pointed at the vacant chair. 'Sit down. There's something else I've been meaning to talk to you about.'

Reece's radar pinged an *incoming* warning. Hooking a thumb over his shoulder, he said: 'I told Jenkins I'd be back in a few minutes.'

'This won't take long.'

He sat down with a loud sigh and folded his arms in a defensive pose. 'Come on then, hit me with it.'

'Your counselling sessions . . .'

Reece's head flopped forward. He screwed both eyes shut. 'Not that again.' He opened one eye and squinted. 'I'm better.'

Cable puckered her lips but remained silent.

'It's true.' There was some truth to that. He wasn't crying as often, and it had been a while since he'd last put a fist through a panel door or plasterboard wall.

'Complaints made against you are at an all-time low. I'll give you that.'

'Well, then?'

'Miranda Beven won't be returning to work until next month at the very earliest, and between you and me, I'm surprised she's returning that soon.'

'She's obviously made of tough stuff.'

'But still would have died if it wasn't for your actions.'

Reece wasn't one for wallowing in compliments. In fact, he regarded them as being utterly cringeworthy. 'What's your point?'

'I'm going to send you to see someone else while Miranda is recuperating.'

Reece shook his head with some force. 'I'm not starting over with another shrink.' He got to his feet and opened the office door. 'Besides, I've already arranged to see her later this week.'

Chapter 27

John Kosh had awoken early—not that he'd got much sleep—ready for a 9am showing at the local magistrates' court. The custody officers had checked on him several times overnight, the metal flap on his cell door clattering like a letterbox caught in a storm.

He'd promised not to *top* himself. Gave them his word for what it was worth. They'd strip searched him regardless, looking for items capable of doing harm to himself or others.

They'd also taken and bagged his clothes. Dressed him head to toe in light grey joggers and matching sweatshirt. He looked like he should be selling drugs on a street corner.

Kosh demanded to know the purpose of their latest search. Given that all others had failed to find anything he shouldn't have had in his possession, did they think he was going to magic-up something dangerous from the confines of his own cell?

The *purpose*, he decided when they refused to tell him, was to piss him off and make clear who was boss. And that was only the beginning of the mental games. They were giving him a taste of what was to come in prison. Preparing him for a hell on Earth.

At court, he was to plead guilty to murdering his wife. There was no alternative, Helen's killer making it perfectly clear that it was the only way he'd ever again get to see Isla. The mere thought of his beautiful daughter brought tears to his eyes. He swallowed, and wiped them, determined not to let his captors witness his mounting fragility.

Kosh knew the importance of never looking like a victim or soft touch.

Ever.

He'd better start practising that mantra ready for when he went down, because *down* he was going. Like a helter-skelter rider hurtling from top to bottom without the safety rails in place.

'Turn to face the other way,' the custody officer said, before opening the cell door. It was an order, not a request. Every sentence the man uttered was clipped and to the point.

There was no chit-chat.

That suited Kosh.

The cell door hit against something that might have been the wall; the sound echoing like a gunshot.

'Hands behind your back.'

Kosh did as he was told. There were no prizes for being a dick. He flinched when the handcuffs snapped closed over his wrists. 'They're too tight,' he complained.

The custody officer gave no response to the protest, other than to steer him out of the cell in reverse gear. They stopped briefly at the sergeant's desk, the burly man sitting behind it, taking his time to check the paperwork for the correct dates and signatures. With that done, he sent them out of the building via the back door.

The security vehicle for the journey to court resembled a squat Portakabin on wheels. Plain white with a black window high up in the rear panel. Another smaller window was set below and to the right of it. When the side door opened, John Kosh was shepherded into a cage like an animal changing zoos.

There would be no chewy toffees and driving music to enjoy on this trip. No stopping at the motorway services to stretch his legs and buy an overpriced coffee and sugary bun.

When the vehicle pulled out of the station courtyard, it wasn't to loud sirens, screams, or angry shouts of retribution from onlookers. It was to an almost total silence.

Chapter 28

Reece took the middle position at a long table in the press room. On his left was Chief Superintendent Cable. To his delight, there was no Harris – the ACC being away on a week-long visit to New York, exploring alternative methods of policing local communities. Reece closed his eyes and swore under his breath. Cardiff. New York. Perfectly paired. He swore again, only this time louder.

Cable double-took. 'What did you say?'

Reece opened his eyes and stared straight ahead at the comings and goings. 'Nothing.'

'Don't give me that. Out with it.'

'It wasn't meant for your ears.'

'Whose then?'

'Nobody you know.'

She gave him a look of warning. 'Not today.'

He twisted at the waist to face her. 'What do you mean by that?'

'You know very well what I mean,' she said with a glare that might have reduced others to quivering wrecks. But not Reece.

Before he could launch into an all-out war of words, his attention was drawn to Jenkins on his right. 'Stop swinging on your chair.' He sounded like he meant it.

She used her teeth to take the lid off a bottle of water. 'We haven't started yet.' She gulped and coughed, spraying it just about everywhere.

Reece wiped wet spots off the sleeve of his suit jacket. 'It's like sitting next to a ten-year-old.' He snatched the bottle from her grip and put it out of harm's way. 'Leave it,' he said when she reached across him. She looked away, sulking.

Cable leaned in close and spoke through clenched teeth. 'What the hell's wrong with you?'

'*Me?*' Reece squealed the word. He was interrupted by a woman from one of the local news stations. She stopped in front of their table and said something to Cable, who nodded an answer. The woman went away and spoke with one of the camera operators.

There were several journalists in the audience. Maggie Kavanagh from the South Wales Herald, sitting in the front row like a mother at a school play. She gave Reece a wave that wasn't reciprocated. Another when he checked to see if she was still there.

Cable got a thumbs up from a man carrying a clipboard and called the room to order. 'It's time we got started,' she said. 'It looks like we're all here.'

Not ten minutes later, Reece was almost finished with his appeal for witnesses. He'd presented a condensed version of what the investigative team knew of Isla Kosh's abduction. There were details he'd left out. Facts not yet shared with a wider audience. This was about finding the missing schoolgirl alive and well.

He looked into the nearest television camera. 'Anything. No matter how insignificant it might have seemed at the time. Did you see Isla walking home from school on Tuesday afternoon? Or maybe later? She might have been alone. Could have had someone with her. Did she get into a car or taxi? Take a bus? Have another look at this,' he said, holding up a colour photograph for the cameraman to zoom in on. 'No detail is too small. If you think you saw something, then ring it in. Isla Kosh's young life might very well depend on it.'

One journalist at the back of the room shot to his feet and shouted a question before he could be stopped. 'Only this morning, the father pleaded guilty to killing his wife. What makes you so sure he didn't kill Isla while he was at it?'

The journalist was risking undermining everything Reece had said. If the watching public thought Isla was already dead, they'd be less engaged with the case. 'Isla's alive,' he told the people at home.

'But you've no proof of that.' Same reporter. Same idiot.

Reece contemplated dragging him out of there by his ears. 'Isla's alive,' he repeated. 'And we need your help in finding her.'

'Where should people search?' The question came from the front of the room.

Reece nodded in thanks for getting the appeal back on track. Maggie Kavanagh was smaller than the chief super. Heavily made up, with a gingery beehive hairstyle adding some extra inches to her diminutive frame. She wasn't smoking on this occasion, but would have been were it not banned indoors. A Columbo-style raincoat lay folded over a crossed leg.

'Anywhere and everywhere,' Reece said. 'Isla might be hidden away in someone's house or garage. Possibly somewhere more remote than that. I'd urge farmers to check outbuildings. Barns they haven't used in a while. There are plenty of empty factory units in and around the city.'

'So you're asking the current key holders to go open them up and check?' Kavanagh said.

That's exactly what Reece wanted.

Chapter 29

'Can you believe the stupidity of that man?' They were back upstairs in the incident room, Reece seething over the episode with the reporter. 'One sentence that nearly brings the whole appeal crashing down like a house of cards.' He clicked his fingers. 'Just like that.'

'Maggie got things back on track,' Jenkins said, plonking four mugs of hot coffee onto her desk. 'Shit. Ouch, ouch, ouch.'

Morgan took a couple of tissues from her bag and dabbed at the spills. 'Maggie has her uses when she tries.'

Reece reluctantly agreed, while Jenkins went to put her scalded fingers under the cold-water tap.

The reporter couldn't be altogether blamed for what he'd said, only for when and where he'd chosen to say it. Time was fast running out for finding Isla Kosh alive. Even if she wasn't already dead, with her father in custody, unwilling to divulge her whereabouts, it wouldn't be too long before she succumbed to thirst or the effects of the environment she was being held captive in.

The school had come up trumps, doing all it could to help with the search. Hundreds of laminated photographs were pinned to lampposts. Bag-tied to wrought-iron railings. Paper versions handed to passers-by in the streets. Images of Isla Kosh smiled from behind the glass of shop windows, flanked by freephone numbers to call if anyone got sight of her.

Her fellow students were busy trawling parks and other recreational areas, such as rugby and football fields. Some went to the hills. Others, the woods. Each party chaperoned by a member of the local constabulary, so as not to compromise evidence should they find any.

Council tips had been walked over. Builders' skips and restaurant bins rummaged through. They'd so far found nothing of any interest to them.

Not a bag, shoe, or anything else belonging to the missing girl.

There was one thing to be grateful for. They'd come across no teenage corpse either.

It was Jenkins who'd first suggested that, as a butcher, John Kosh would have been more than capable of turning his daughter into pies and sausages to sell to the local community. 'It's been done before,' she said, sending Morgan into raptures of loud heaving.

'He wouldn't have had enough time before the party,' was Reece's opinion. 'Besides, if you're going to get rid of the girl like that, then why not do the same with the wife's body?' Regardless of what he thought, Reece was a thorough detective, and had already had the butcher's shop forensically swept. 'Any CCTV?' he asked, helping himself to one of the coffees.

Ginge sifted through a few sheets of A4. 'Nothing yet, boss. They could do with an extra pair of hands going through that lot. It's taking an age, with there being so much of it.'

'Consider yourself volunteered.' Reece pointed to the door. 'Keep me posted.' He smirked as the detective constable left with an unashamed display of youthful enthusiasm. 'Have we found the wife's phone yet?'

The data analyst told him they hadn't.

'It's probably in the Taff by now.' Jenkins meant the main river flowing through the city and out into the bay and sea beyond.

No one in the room disagreed.

Chapter 30

Isla Kosh heard the helicopter approach overhead, the slap of its rotor blades making the ground beneath her vibrate. She couldn't see it. Couldn't see much of anything – held against her will in a room filled with darkness.

It was cold in there. Drafty, too. The place smelling of damp from what must have been several years of little use.

She kept her ears tuned to the sound. This helicopter wasn't passing by like the ones belonging to the air ambulance and electricity companies. Those were always going someplace fast. Point A to Point B. Responding to emergencies, or making surveys of storm damage on the network lines.

Was this a police helicopter? One of the yellow-and-black types she'd seen a hundred times or more, hovering high above the city and congested motorways at rush hour. It made complete sense that it might be. And if they were hovering and not moving on, that meant they were searching.

Searching for her.

Why else would they be there?

Isla was struck by a troubling thought. Could she still be in the city? Or next to a motorway? What if the helicopter wasn't searching? What if it *was* one of those she'd seen a hundred times or more? She refused to give the thought any further opportunity to drag her down. This helicopter was there for her and for no other reason.

She tried to scream; the tape holding her lips shut, preventing her from managing anything louder than a muted hum. 'I'm here,' sounded like *'umm, mmm.'* It was useless. Hopeless, even. She yanked her arms with all her strength, whimpering when the leather wrist-straps bit ever tighter into her skin. A length of chain attached to them slapped against the wall, grit and paint flakes raining down on her from its anchor point somewhere above her head.

The helicopter was moving away. Getting quieter. The sound of its rotor blades fading into the distance. They were off to search elsewhere. *'Ummm, mmmm!'* Even screaming it long and hard enough to make her head feel like it was about to split in two made no difference.

They weren't looking for her.

Did they even know she was missing? Mum and dad might think she was still over at Millie's place, staying longer than expected. But then, what about school? Her teachers would have done something in response to her being absent without explanation. Wouldn't they?

That got Isla thinking about time. How long had she been there? Wherever *there* was.

If she was made to guess, then she'd have said a day. Maybe a bit longer than that. Craning her neck high enough to look into the pee-bucket only an arm's-length to her right, she could just make out the fluid line. There was a different tone of grey marking its level.

How many pees, and what did that mean in terms of time? she wondered. After some frequency and volume guesstimates, she came to the conclusion it might have been her second day in captivity.

Mum would definitely have expected a call by now. She'd have contacted Millie, only to be told that Isla hadn't gone there after school.

Mum would have been frantic after that, sending Dad out to search the streets. The neighbours, on hearing of her disappearance, would have volunteered their services in a flash.

The helicopter *was* looking for her. Isla knew it was. '*Ummm, mmmm!*'

Cowering on the dirty floor, cold and afraid, she had so many unanswered questions. None of them pleasant. She willed herself to stop overthinking things, but couldn't help but do so.

Did her captor intend to rape her? She'd seen very little of him as yet. Except for when he came and went with the bucket.

Would he sell her overseas, perhaps? Into a life of drugs and prostitution. She'd read of such awful things and wished that she hadn't.

Not that. Not rape. Not the sex trade. Please God. She'd rather die.

Would he torture her first? Was he a sadist getting an extra kick from the hurt he was inflicting? The endless possibilities sent her into a new frenzy of flailing limbs and muted screams, the wrist bindings gripping her flesh like the jaws of an angry dog.

She used a series of deep breathing exercises to calm herself as best she could. Her captor had worn a woollen mask—she couldn't remember the name for it—only his eyes and a small area of cheek exposed. It wasn't entirely necessary, given the lack of light in the room.

If he was planning on killing her, then why keep his identity hidden the entire time? There was no reason for it. Not unless he intended to let her go.

That was it. He wasn't going to kill her. Sell her to the highest bidder, neither. She felt stronger for knowing that. She was going to survive this, after all. Was going to get home and hug Mum and Dad like she'd never hugged them before. They'd spend evenings in front of the TV together, with her telling them how much she loved them both. They'd respond in kind.

Isla was thinking happy thoughts when the rat returned.

It was big, black, and barely visible in the darkness. She could hear it scraping somewhere on the other side of the room.

The first time they'd met, she'd awoken from a shallow sleep to find the creature's furry pelt brushing against her nose. It had, no doubt, been getting ready to take a sizable chunk out of her face. Isla wasn't sure which of them had been the more surprised. Her, on opening her eyes to find it only inches away. Or the rat, when its intended meal sat up straight and went apeshit.

It was on the move now. Tentatively making its way towards her. Getting braver. Coming back for another sniff. Isla drew herself into the foetal position, cowering against the cold wall, waiting for the rodent to decide on its next course of action.

What if it had brought others with it? Hundreds of them come to overpower her. She stared into the darkness. Squinted. Into a pair of eyes that stared back. A single pair, as far as she could tell.

The rat had its nose to the ground, its direction of travel almost serpentine as it approached.

Isla swung a leg at it and missed.

The rat came again, unperturbed, its whiskered snout sampling the air.

She growled at it. Tried to scream. Managed a muted *'Ummm, mmmm!'*

It watched.

It came.

Isla Kosh was about to be eaten alive.

Chapter 31

Arvel Baines was cutting firewood on the far side of his rambling property when the police helicopter went over. No time wasted in beginning the search for the missing girl. Baines couldn't blame the authorities for acting with such haste, and would have criticised them heavily had they not.

In such cases, seventy-three percent of MISPERs were found alive. Half of them within two kilometres of where they were last known to be. Two-thirds within three kilometres.

Though Baines's smallholding was a little outside the perimeter of those distances, come searching the authorities had – if only by air, so far. He'd need to tread carefully if he was to stay one step ahead of them.

Baines's mother had died only two years previously. Succumbed to the poison running through her veins, was his initial thought on hearing of her sudden demise. In reality, her death had been from coronary artery disease. A massive heart attack next to the till in the local supermarket doing for her.

He'd not mourned the loss. Nor did he apply to the prison governor for permission to attend the funeral. Those sentimental things had been dealt with thirty years ago when the woman first turned her back on him. It came as an enormous surprise, therefore, when he'd inherited the family home in Bristol, and close on one hundred and fifty thousand pounds in post office savings.

He didn't delay putting the house on the market—too many bad memories to ever contemplate living there—an *on-price* offer accepted only two weeks later, by a conveyancer acting on his behalf.

He'd then used some of the money gained from the sale to purchase a rundown smallholding in a wooded area on the west side of the Cardiff boundary line. It was comprised of a slate-roofed cottage, a medium-sized barn, and one other stone-walled outbuilding. The property more than suited his needs. Was perfect for keeping a MISPER under lock and key.

Isla froze when the rat climbed onto her ankle. That's what they told you to do, wasn't it? Stay perfectly still. Like you would when encountering a venomous snake. Wait for it to realise you're neither prey nor predator, and go off again on its way.

But nobody had told the rat. Instead of moving off, it nibbled on Isla's shoe before turning its attention to the edge of a white ankle sock. She could feel its claws pricking her skin as it kept its balance.

What if she brought the shoe of the other foot crashing down on it, squashing the thing dead – or forcing its sharp teeth into her exposed shin if she got it wrong?

Then what?

Rabies, maybe? Frothing at the mouth while going mad. No thank you.

It started moving again. This time along her bare leg, stopping at the knee to clean itself. Isla was about to take a chance and swing the other foot when she heard a key turn in a lock. The rat must have heard it too—or via a sixth sense, realised it was imminently about to get its head caved in—and leapt away into the safety of the darkness.

Isla pressed herself against the damp wall, her body twisting counterclockwise to face away from the opening door. The helicopter was gone, its search over before it had properly begun. The room brightened—marginally—a weak patch of light *illuminating* a small section of wall on the far side of it. The light bobbed in sync with the sound of footfall descending the steps to her left.

He was coming. Her captor, rapist, or sex trade merchant.

Isla held her breath, the chain rattling like a charity bucket part-filled with coins. She pressed herself tighter to the wall, trying to push through to the other side.

The wall pushed back, rough, cold, and damp, allowing no such escape.

He was close by, but hadn't yet spoken a word. She could hear his breathing. Could smell a musky cologne. Not one she was familiar with. Not something Dad or the boys at school wore.

He, was as good a label as any, and several times less scary than the alternative terms flooding her mind with horrific imagery.

He came around to her other side, stopping to stare on the way. Isla used a knee to drag at the hem of her short school skirt. She couldn't exactly tell where he was looking, his lazy gaze hidden behind a halo of what must have been a runner's head torch.

She closed her eyes, the bright light causing an ice-pick pain across her forehead.

The chain rattled in time with her tremor.

He squatted to lay something on the floor next to her, his cheek coming so close to hers that she felt the woollen mask rub against her own soft skin. When she leaned away from him, he pushed into her, breathing hot air against her ear. He drew the tape slowly from her mouth and left it to hang from one side of her chin.

'Evening, Isla.' There was no warmth or sincerity in the whispered greeting.

Evening. That would make it Thursday. Two nights there so far. Or was it only Wednesday, still?

'Not talking?' His tone was mocking. 'After I'd gone to all the bother of making you an omelette.'

'My father's going to kick your arse when this shit's over.' The force of the retort surprised her. With the flash of bravado gone as quickly as it had come, she sank back against the wall, defeated, her head turned to the ground.

'Is that so?' He was upright again. 'Eat. There's milk as well.'

Isla swung a leg at the meal—it was good practice for walloping the rat—knocking the contents of the glass onto the plate.

'As you wish.' Strangely, he didn't sound angry, and used his foot to drag the spoiled food to the far corner of the room. 'Your new pet can have it. Him and the rest of the family.'

Isla shuddered. 'I need the toilet.'

'There's plenty of room left in the bucket.'

'I can't do it in that!'

'I beg to differ,' he said, bending to look inside.

'It's not a wee this time.' She started to cry. 'Why are you doing this?' She pressed her forearm to her nose and wiped a mix of tears and mucus in the sleeve of her school cardigan.

Grabbing her by the left arm, he took a small key to the lock on its wrist strap and opened it. 'You've got five minutes to do whatever you need to,' he said, shoving the bucket and toilet paper towards her.

Chapter 32

Arvel Baines tucked himself into a quiet corner next to the stone chimney breast in the lounge of the Druid's Inn. The very same position, if not chair, he'd sat on that fateful night some thirty years earlier.

The dartboard was gone. He noticed that almost immediately. He imagined it still being locked away somewhere in the bowels of a police records and evidence department.

Lost would be a more likely explanation if the local police had anything to do with it. Lost before more modern forensic techniques proved that a lazy Idris Roberts and his team had put away the wrong man.

If he wasn't so incensed, Baines would have laughed off the whole affair. He'd met so many others like himself in prison. Men—he didn't doubt there being women also—who'd been incarcerated on dodgy evidence that would later go missing from *secure* vaults.

The Druid Inn looked as though it had undergone at least one major refurbishment since his previous visit. That said, it still maintained much of the olde-worlde charm that had always made it such a popular watering hole for locals.

Baines recalled seeing brightly coloured Christmas trimmings hanging from the beamed ceiling. A decorated fir tree leaning slightly left of centre next to the bar. A collie dog warming itself on the fireside rug, its nose tuned to the smell of hot cawl wafting in through the open kitchen door.

The dog was long gone. No surprise there. Replaced by the hairiest cat he'd ever seen. It was practising feline yoga on a chair. Cleaning itself while watching the newcomer with one open eye. Baines stared back and wondered if the shaggy animal had sussed the true purpose of his return.

Should he take it outside and kill it? Skin the thing like the rabbits of old?

Probably not. Unlike its owner, it had done him no harm.

The pub's clientele was another change. There were tradespeople in work gear gathered at the bar, telling jokes and laughing loudly.

There were no vets or farmers. None that Baines could see.

And the air he breathed was another thing. It smelled of vinegar-doused chips and curry sauce. Even the simmering wood burner gave off no smoke.

The overweight landlord hadn't so much as looked up when Baines strolled in and took a seat on his own. Didn't tear his gaze away from the crossword puzzle he was engrossed in. The man was drinking red wine from a long-stemmed glass, his elbows supporting his hefty weight on the far end of the bar, his spectacles balanced perilously close to the end of his nose.

He hadn't recognised Baines's voice when the newcomer stepped up to order a cheese and pickle sandwich with a pint of Guinness. Not even when Baines flirted shamelessly with one of the bar staff.

And why would he, after all these years? Wasn't Elgan Collins—aka Badger—entitled to forget the existence of the man whose life he'd helped ruin?

The pub landlord looked more like an arctic fox now that the white streak of hair had fully invaded the front, back, and sides of his head.

With the sandwich long-since eaten, Baines kept to his corner, watching the clock, biding his time. Waiting for an opportunity to skulk upstairs and jog the fat man's memory.

Reece was showered, dressed, and sat alone in the darkness at his home in Llandaff, Cardiff. His heartbeat raced; an area of flesh at the side of his neck pounding an uncomfortable beat. So much so, it gave him a headache. He counted out a slower time signature, his fingernails gripping and releasing the soft fabric of the armchair like the paws of a house cat. He was breath-holding. When he realised, he took a few greedy lungfuls of air to compensate for the oxygen deficit.

His mobile phone had rung once already. Only a minute or two earlier. *Miranda Beven,* it read in white block capitals across the narrow screen. It was ringing again. One red, one green telephone icon offering a choice of response. The handset vibrated its way along the arm of the chair, Reece watching until it fell to the floor, unanswered.

But still the phone wouldn't shut up, the block of black plastic demanding a response from him.

He raised his shoe above it, poised to strike, hesitating when an awkward voicemail prompt to *'leave a message after the beep,'* kicked in only a moment later.

'Brân, it's Miranda . . .' She waited for him to pick up. When he didn't, she spoke again: 'Did I get the meeting place wrong? The time perhaps? I'm sure it's my fault.' Several seconds passed. Then a gentle hum on the line.

The phone rang a second time. Reece wasn't sure how much later, but hadn't moved from where he was.

'I guess you're not coming . . .' Another awkward pause. 'I'm going home. I'll try ringing again tomorrow.' The line went dead, the room silent save for his heavy breathing.

He flicked the switch of a small table lamp next to him, staring at the white envelope propped against it. He picked it up and read the handwritten message on the front of it: **Brân, How can I ever thank you enough?** It was signed, **Miranda**.

The writing was neat and reminded him so much of Anwen's. Inside the envelope were a pair of tickets for the TRIBUTE Concert, *Rumours of Fleetwood Mac.* The venue: Wales Millennium Centre in the bay.

Reece rose from the chair, soft lamp light guiding the way to the other side of the room. He took the Blueridge acoustic guitar from its corner and tuned it by ear. Finger picking a familiar song when done, his body swayed as Anwen's sweet voice sang the lyrics to 'Beautiful Child.'

He couldn't share that with anyone but his dead wife.

Chapter 33

It was just after closing time when Arvel Baines took his long-awaited opportunity to get even.

The young barmaid was almost finished clearing glasses and collecting plates. Someone else was scraping and loading them into a dishwasher with scant care for the items' wellbeing.

Glasses rattled. Plates clinked and clunked. Cutlery tossed into wash-trays with the sound of clashing cymbals.

Someone else was off to the toilets, armed with rubber gloves, a mop, and a bucket of frothing lemon detergent mixed with hot water.

They couldn't wait to lock up and go home for the night.

None of them had any clue that Baines was wedged between the wall and a bulky Chesterfield sofa on the far side of the room. Lying lengthways against the dusty skirting, he'd have been able to reach out and catch hold of the barmaid's tattooed ankle had he so wished.

With the tables cleared of clutter, he waited for her to finish vacuuming. The machine roared like a big cat as it came towards him. He lay very still while she moved chairs and cleared the carpet of crumbs. Separating some of the smaller tables, she repositioned them elsewhere. Others, she pushed together with the knock of wood on wood.

There were voices. Conversations about how *Fatso* upstairs always pissed off and left them to it when it was time to clear up. How he had a habit of falling asleep in the bathtub with a bellyful of Beaujolais wine and soft cheese.

'He'll drown in there one day,' the girl said, forcing an arm into her coat sleeve.

'Hopefully not before he's paid us for the week,' said the man with the mop and bucket. He shut them away in a cupboard near the bar and took three attempts to close the door; the mop's handle wedging in the jamb each time.

Baines congratulated himself on his choice of hiding place. He had, for a short while only, considered that very cupboard. The heavy sofa was perfect for his needs. No one would shift it to clean behind. The amount of fluff and bits of foodstuff sharing the tight space with him was testament to the fact staff hadn't done that in a long, long while.

One of the trio opened a door at the foot of the stairs leading to the upper level of the inn. Its hinges squealed. 'We're finished,' the man shouted into the gloom. 'He's sleeping. I can hear him snoring from here,' he said in a quieter voice.

The girl's feet were visible from Baines's letterbox view on the floor, moving from one end of the room to the other as she spoke. 'Do you think one of you should go up and make sure he's all right?'

'Sod that,' said a voice Baines recognised as belonging to the mop man.

'I'd never be able to erase the sight once seen,' said the other.

The two men laughed, while the girl put a foot on the bottom stair. She withdrew it. 'I need those wages tomorrow. I'm skint.'

'He'll be all right.' Mop man again. 'He sleeps in there all the time. It's never been an issue before.'

They were headed towards the exit at the front of the room, one of them jangling a set of keys. 'Besides, there's not enough space in that tub for him to go under and drown.'

A door opened and shut. Lights turned off one by one. 'Are you sure?' The girl's voice was more distant than it had been and was now accompanied by a chilly draft. '*Cat!*' The girl was back, or at least her feet were. 'Did either of you put it out?'

'I didn't.'

'Me neither,' mop man said.

'Ah, Christ. Where do you think it's hiding tonight?' she asked.

'Same place as always.'

Baines kept still. Mop man's Timberland boots crossed the room towards him. He had no stomach for killing innocents, but if it came to it . . . He tapped the knife in his pocket, making sure it was still there.

'There it is,' the girl said. 'Behind the bar. Look. There.'

The Timberlands about-turned and marched away from the Chesterfield.

'Grab it,' said the girl.

'I'm trying!' Tempers were fraying.

Baines saw the cat scarper from one side of the room to the other. A ginger flash. He closed a hand over the bulge of the knife's handle when the annoying moggie turned and headed in his direction. *Don't even think it. You wouldn't look the same, naked.*

The animal must have read his mind and stopped in its tracks.

'*Now!*' the girl shouted. 'While it's stood still.'

'Aw, fuck.' The cat was gone again, the Timberlands zig-zagging after it. 'That's it. No more.'

'We can't leave it in overnight,' the girl said.

'We can't catch it, either.'

'It'll shit on the carpet like last time.'

'Tough. I'm going home.'

'Me too,' said the other man.

'And leave me here on my own?' The girl sounded rightfully narked.

'Your choice.'

She took a moment to think it over. 'You're right. Come on, let's go.'

Baines lost touch with the conversation when the main door closed with a solid bang, footfall passing the window above him only seconds later.

He was alone with Badger. The cat now nowhere to be seen.

Chapter 34

When Baines switched the table lamp on not ten minutes later, he agreed totally with the opinions of the bar staff. Elgan Collins was wedged into a bathtub that was clearly not intended to accommodate a man of his hefty girth.

Placing the lamp at the head-end of the tub—its electrical flex at full stretch to the socket on the landing—he shook the sleeping man's shoulder. 'Wake up.'

Elgan Collins opened his eyes, squinted, and looked away from the bright light. His shoulder bumped against the bowl of the lamp, making it wobble.

Baines steadied it with a gloved hand. 'Careful. You could do yourself some real damage with that.'

'Who are you?' Collins asked, dragging the wet, folded newspaper across his exposed groin. He wasn't yet properly free of his wine-induced stupor. 'What time is it? Who let you up here?' He called someone's name. It might have been the barmaid's. It mattered little, there being nobody left downstairs to answer him.

'They've all gone home. It's just you and me now.' Baines took a set of darts from his pocket. 'Shame about the lack of a board. I was going to offer you a rematch.'

Collins's eyes narrowed. A look of suspicion replaced by one of fear.

'You're the second person to play dumb with me this week.' Baines gave the other man's head a rap with his knuckles. 'It's in there somewhere. It's just a case of teasing it out.'

Collins looked like he might say something. Either that, or succumb to a massive heart attack at any moment.

'Don't.' Baines wagged a finger. 'Don't you fucking dare claim it was nothing to do with you.' He gripped the lamp. Caught it too close to the hot bulb and complained when it burned him. The gloves were made of thin rubber, not a more substantial material, a small hole and blister appearing over his first knuckle. 'Thick as thieves,' he said, licking the reddening skin. 'And I was the victim.'

'If I'd only known they'd send you down.' Collins didn't look at him. 'I honestly thought they'd acquit you at trial. Before it got that far, even. Especially with that young detective pointing a finger at Dai.'

Baines stood and offered the lamp like a sommelier might present a carafe. 'Are you ready for *your* trial?' He allowed himself only the briefest escape of laughter. 'It's gonna be a short one, this. Let's see what verdict the jury return in the case of the *Crown versus the Fat Lying Fuck.*'

Chapter 35

When Arvel Baines strolled into the drab Probation Services building on an equally drab Friday morning, he resembled any other pasty-faced release prisoner out on licence. A little more than a week's freedom being nowhere near enough time to counter the effects of thirty years spent predominantly indoors. Wearing navy jeans with matching jumper and no-brand trainers, he blended in quite nicely and didn't look at all like someone just getting started on a vengeful murder spree.

He preferred the term *spree killer* over *serial killer*. It better fitted his intention of getting things done quickly. Serial killers were often indulgent people who murdered more than three victims over a time period exceeding thirty days. He'd read that factoid while surrounded by murderers.

Baines was there to meet his supervising officer: an unfortunate-looking woman—and that was being kind—named Olga. He finger-combed a side-parting in a reflection kindly provided by a brief burst of sunlight on the glass of an automatic door. He'd lost a little coverage on the crown of his head, but not much. The sides carried some grey. Not that it bothered him. Not since someone *in the know* had said women aged, whereas men grew to look distinguished.

That was another factoid he'd picked up while inside. Prison had its plus points. Gave you plenty of opportunity to read and educate yourself.

He'd aged way better than Elgan Collins had, that was for sure. He smelled a lot better, too. Fatso had given off the stink of burning bacon when the lamp fell through his flailing hands and contacted the swishing water. He'd bitten off his own tongue, Baines watching with interest as the stub of severed muscle first contracted to half its normal size on the man's pot belly, before rolling off to float on the surface of the bathwater.

Collins's mouth had bled little after the agonising injury; two-hundred-and-forty volts quickly cooking up a nice bit of black pudding.

Parts of him smoked. Crackled, and split open in several places, a deep guttural moan rising in pitch before the man fell abruptly silent.

And the beauty of it was, there had been nothing to clean up afterwards. The abandoned scene told the unfortunate story of a foolish, yet tragic, accident. Collins's death would be documented as another statistic involving the terminally stupid.

Darwinism at its finest.

Perfect, any day of the week.

Olga sat opposite, looking like a bog-eyed fish. Baines had no idea what one of those was, but it painted the right picture in his mind. Peering through milk-bottle-thick glasses, she reminded him of the terms of his licence with abject disinterest, the features of her face not altering one bit as she spoke.

Yeah, *bog-eyed fish* described the woman just perfectly.

In prison, Baines had read of the ludicrous modern-day fad of injecting parts of the human body with fillers. Fat arses and Daffy Duck lips being all the rage, apparently. Women willing to part with small fortunes in exchange for that *punched in the mouth* appearance.

He hadn't believed such a thing until witnessing it for himself.

Each to their own, he supposed.

Definitely not a distinguished look. More of a joke shop fad.

Olga babbled on—her stiff mouth opening and closing as she drew air through invisible gills—telling him where he could live. Where he could not. What he could do, and what he wasn't allowed to do. There were places he was prohibited from visiting. People he shouldn't be seen around. Then a list of jobs he was never to apply for.

It was endless. Rules, rules, rules. Blah, blah, blah. Like being in prison all over again.

But he played the game.

Gave the right answers and made no fuss.

Signed the required forms and was out of there in no time at all.

As he exited the building through the same glass door he'd used on the way in, Arvel Baines had a skip in his step.

Chapter 36

Isla Kosh looked like she didn't have a care in the world.

Baines stopped to smile at her. It would have been rude not to. He read the numbers alongside her photograph in the corner-shop window, making no attempt to commit them to memory. The property next door displayed the very same picture. As did those across the road.

With no time to dawdle, he was on his way again, walking along the pavement with the confident swagger of a man who was moving up in the world. He'd already ruined the life of John Kosh: the toss-pot son of the farmer responsible for fitting him up for murder. '*Freedom!*' Baines shouted with a fake Scottish accent. He punched the air, drawing looks of bemusement from all those around him.

He didn't give a shit what they thought. Never had. He knew exactly what he wanted and was well on his way to getting it. He was still chuckling to himself when the world around him went dark. His neck was violently yanked backwards, the muscles stretching until they threatened to snap. His right arm was drawn up behind him and pressed close to his shoulder blades.

Whoever it was, had him running along the pavement at a fair pace.

Police. It had to be. Yesterday's helicopter crew must have reported to a ground patrol, who'd then waited for better light before coming back to check out the smallholding. They must have found the girl and used Land Registry records to ascertain ownership details.

A car door opened. There was a solid click of the mechanism and squeak of its hinge. The engine sounded powerful; the driver revving as though preparing to pull away from the kerbside at speed. A hand pressed heavily on the top of his head, making him bend. It wasn't enough to stop his forehead striking against the vehicle's metalwork as he was shoved inside. When he objected, someone told him to 'Shut the fuck up.' It might have been the driver. He couldn't be sure and landed in the narrow gap between the front and rear seats.

The assailant refused to remove the hood, leaving him totally reliant on non-visual cues for information gathering.

Frustratingly, there were few of those to be had.

It wasn't a bit like his own snatching of Isla Kosh. *That* had gone incredibly well, with almost nothing in the way of violence required. He'd simply pulled up alongside the wide expanse of playing field to ask the schoolgirl directions to Kosh's Butcher's. 'I've got a delivery for someone called John,' he'd said, pointing into the back of the van.

'That's my dad,' the girl had replied. 'Small world.'

Not really. It was perfectly planned and had nothing to do with chance.

'It is indeed. Can I give you a lift round there?' Baines had asked. 'I'm running late and it would help me a lot.'

'I don't know.' The girl began to reverse away, her head jerking left and right. There was no one else there; a new shower of rain keeping most people indoors. 'Oh, what the hell,' she said, reaching for the handle of the van door. 'I'll get soaked to the skin out here.'

When Isla first realised she'd made what might be a fatal mistake, they were already travelling at speed along the dual carriageway. Her screaming was lost to the noise of traffic, the van's blacked-out windows obscuring her contorted face pressed against the glass.

Baines drew his thoughts back to the present. He had his own problem to deal with.

The vehicle moved off before the door slammed shut, a menacing voice telling him to lie still, or else. How could he refuse? What with the dirty boot pressed firmly against the side of his head. He chose not to object. Thought it best, given he still had no idea who or what he was up against.

The journey was a short one. Little more than twenty minutes, if he'd had to guess. At first there was the monotonous stop-start of busy roads as they negotiated city traffic, other motorists oblivious to the fact they were witness to a real-world kidnapping.

Then came the uncomfortable body-roll of several roundabouts.

A series of winding roads after that.

And only seconds earlier, they'd turned onto a bumpier surface that gave the car's suspension a proper spanking.

When they swung in a wide arc on what sounded like a patch of coarse gravel, Baines was wedged more tightly against the seat, the raised axle channel running along the centre line of the vehicle digging uncomfortably into his left flank.

The engine went silent after a final growl, the boot of his captor catching his head on the exact same spot the roof of the vehicle had on his way in. The man had done it on purpose, showing him who was boss.

Baines was dragged out by a hand clamped to the back of his neck. It pinched and pushed in simultaneous movements. He had no idea where he was. Or for that matter, who had taken him there.

Definitely not the police. He'd discounted that possibility early on.

Even with his head stuck inside the disorientating hood, he could tell they'd moved from an area of natural lighting to one that was several shades darker. His footsteps echoed. They were somewhere enclosed. A warehouse or barn of sorts, by the smell of things.

'This him, is it?'

Baines didn't recognise the voice. It was local. Proper Cardiff, as they say. Not someone he'd done bird with. Not as far as he could tell from the few spoken words.

The hood came off with the yank of a rough hand. Baines's head jerked back then forward as though attached to a spring coil. Even though it was gloomy inside the building, he still had to squint to compensate for the sudden change in lighting. A door slammed shut behind him. Heavy and metallic sounding. Like the ones that had, until recently, held him prisoner.

Ahead, and illuminated in a prism of light thrown by a window in the corrugated roofing, was a bald man with a tattooed head, face, and neck. Motes of dust danced all around him. He looked like he'd been beamed to Earth by a higher entity; standing there in a long leather coat, leaning on a polished cane. The tip and handle of the cane were embellished with a highly reflective metal. Silver was Baines's best guess.

'Arvel, we meet at last.' The greeting was as polite as it was succinct, yet oozed menace.

'Who are you?' This was how he'd done it in prison. Held his ground and shown no weakness. He turned his head and saw a monster of a man with what couldn't possibly have been a real jawbone. Next to him was more hired muscle, this one with a badly pockmarked face.

Baines was outnumbered three to one. *Fucked,* was his initial assessment.

'I'm Billy Creed. I'd be disappointed to know you haven't heard of me.' The gangster let out a brief chuckle. 'Don't mind the boys,' he said, helping himself to a cigar taken from a leather pouch. 'They've been fed.' He drew the full length of the cigar under his nose. 'They can be a tad dramatic at times. I blames it on too much TV, myself.'

Yes, the accent and dialect were *proper Cardiff*.

Baines waited patiently for a punchline that was likely coming anytime soon.

'Not that you're any stranger to violence, hey Arvel. I'm told you've got plans.'

How much did the gangster know? Baines shouldn't have been surprised, there being no such thing as a secret in prison. 'You've lost me?'

The cane tapped the ground twice; the air charged with danger. 'You wouldn't be taking the piss, would you?'

'What I'm up to is none of your concern,' Baines said, maintaining the show of bravado. It was a dangerous game he was playing. Walking a fine line. 'This is between me and them. Not you.'

Creed waved the cigar as though handling a sword. 'Not when you're working on my patch, it ain't.'

'It won't come back to bite you.'

Another throaty chuckle. 'You hear that, boys?'

There was a blast of short-lived laughter behind Baines. He swivelled to look at Pockmark and the man with the huge jaw. Both stopped laughing and scowled instead.

'Don't look so nervous, Arvel.' Creed pointed the silver-tipped cane at him from the confines of the prism of blueish-white light. 'You and me are on the same side. We want the same thing.'

Baines had no idea what that meant. 'Go on.'

'There's a detective I know you're interested in. A thorn in my side for more years than I'd care to admit.' Creed shifted position; the movement awkward. Grimacing, he leaned his weight on the cane for added support. 'You need my permission for what you're doing. Dead folk have a habit of bringing the police to my door.' Creed nodded slowly. 'One officer in particular.'

Baines's eyes narrowed. 'Where are you going with this?'

'Don't play dumb, Arvel. You're going to kill him.'

Baines shook his head. 'I'd never be a free man if I did. Besides, I now know he wasn't involved like the others.'

'Copper is on your list. I put him there.' Pockmark and Jaw lifted Baines off the ground by his armpits, the skin pinching as he hung in silence. 'This ain't up for negotiation,' Creed said. 'It's you or Copper. Take your pick.'

Chapter 37

The razor-sharp blade of Arvel Baines's axe split the log as easily as it might the flesh of an overripe melon. Or a tattooed head. Resting a boot on the heavy chunk of wood, he freed the axe with a hefty tug. He hit the log a second time; polished steel arcing through the air in what was almost a full circle. Then he swung it twice more in quick succession, stopping only to catch his breath and wipe sweat from his eyes.

When he started up again, he lost his grip; the axe's handle rotating in his wet hands. Its head, not blade, hitting the chopping block, causing it to rebound back at him. A slower man might have done himself a serious injury. Not so Arvel Baines. His trained reaction time meant the axe flew over his left shoulder, landing on a patch of grass behind him.

'For fuck's sake!' He sat down on the gouged tree stump with his head in his hands, grappling with his latest predicament. The light breeze cooled the bare skin of his arms, leaving goose pimples in place of shiny perspiration. This wasn't supposed to be happening. Not with the time he'd invested in the planning of his violent vendetta.

John Kosh had already been dealt with. His wife playing a tragic, yet vital, role in the man's fall from grace. Baines wasn't exactly proud of himself for murdering the woman while Kosh slept off the effects of the herbal offering deposited in his party drink.

There'd been no need for an improvised shank on that occasion. Not when there was such a fine set of expensive carving knives to be had.

It was Isla who'd let slip about the house party. Blurted it out like some gibbering wreck while Baines chained her to the basement wall. Knowing the hosts were new to the village and invitation was mostly on an *open-door* basis, he'd altered his plans, and would have been a fool to turn his back on such an opportunity.

He'd simply wandered into the house, bottle in hand. 'Hi, I'm Dan,' he told the homeowners. 'I live towards the end of the street.' He'd pointed in the general direction of where he meant and used the other hand to relieve himself of the supermarket Merlot. 'Sara invited me. I hope that's all right?' He had no idea who Sara might be, or if she was there. But then again, neither did the hosts.

With a welcoming smile, he was escorted through to a kitchen that needed some modernisation and invited to help himself to any number of curried dishes presented in plastic Tupperware containers.

Locating his targets among the dancing partygoers had been a simple enough thing to do. He'd previously watched John Kosh through the window of the butcher's shop. Had stood staring at boy-turned-man. Then he'd followed Kosh home and observed the comings and goings of the household. It had been as easy as that.

The sedative was easily deposited in Kosh's drink while he used the bathroom. His wife, Helen, had been in conversation with someone and showed Baines no interest. It was then a case of waiting in the garden until husband and wife came staggering down the path. 'Let me help you with him,' Baines said, offering his services. 'You go ahead and open the front door.'

Helen Kosh hadn't refused and looked relieved at no longer having the weight of her husband draped around her neck and shoulders.

Baines was in and couldn't believe his good fortune.

He'd stabbed Helen Kosh only moments after she poured him a drink in gratitude for his help. When she turned, wineglass in hand, he'd plunged a heavy carving knife deep into the front of her neck. The woman tried to scream, but comically, managed little more than to blow red bubbles of saliva instead. That's when Baines hit her a few more times. He wasn't sure how many. Chest, abdomen, and once round the side, where he imagined her kidney to be. Withdrawing the blade at speed between strikes is what had showered the otherwise pristine ceiling with red blood spots.

Helen's knees had buckled, sending her to the floor with an arm pointing towards the ceiling.

'I've already taken her,' Baines said. Unkind. But true.

The woman had died only seconds later. Blowing more bubbles and hissing gas from the open chest wound. It took John Kosh another forty-five minutes to wake up, knife in hand, but way too late to save his wife. That had given Baines ample time to change out of his blood-stained party clothes and bag them for incineration.

The entire event couldn't have gone any more smoothly.

Good old Isla.

Thoughts of the girl made him wonder what to do with her now her parents had been dealt with. Killing her was an option he hadn't fully ruled out.

But there were more pressing issues to deal with first. Billy Creed had introduced the mother of all complications. Killing Brân Reece would, without a doubt, bring a whole heap of shit his way. The authorities wouldn't stop hunting until they'd found and locked him up again. He'd forever be a fugitive. And that was worse than being in jail.

Chapter 38

'Hello,' was what Isla tried to shout. It came as more of a muffled bi-phonic hum. She pressed her tongue against the duct tape and tried in vain to push it away. Forcing her jaw open only threatened to tear the tender flesh from her lips.

Her shoulders ached. Despite her arms being suspended on the end of a chain, the awkward positioning took it out of them. Her fingers were numb. The cold environment and overly tight wristbands to blame.

Adding to her expanding list of woes was a mounting sensation of hunger that gnawed at the pit of her stomach. She'd eaten very little since her abduction. Scant morsels of food shared with a rat that visited with monotonous repetition. It was as though the thing, wherever it was, could hear the ringing of a dinner bell. No sooner was the door to the basement closed, and Isla thrown into darkness, than the rat was there, trying to get at the plate of food before she could.

Eating also made her want to use the loo. Peeing in a bucket for somebody else to empty was one thing, but doing a . . . She held the thought and squeezed her eyes shut with embarrassment. She was cycling through a whole raft of emotions. None of them helpful.

There was *anger* at being so stupid for getting into the stranger's van in the first place. Its driver had leaned across the passenger seat to ask directions, careful to keep his head down, the peak of a red cap obscuring the upper two-thirds of his face. His wicked intentions had seemed nowhere near as obvious as they did now.

Hatred for what he was doing to her. Or would do. That thought brought with it an intolerable level of fear.

Sadness didn't adequately describe the feeling of being away from her parents. It was like that hideous *pit of the stomach* response, when, as a young child, she'd wandered off at a busy beach or shopping centre and suddenly realised she was all alone in the world. That terror-filled few seconds before Mum and Dad's faces pushed through the crowds to rescue her.

But there was no familiar face in the crowd today.

No rescue as yet.

That sick-to-the-stomach feeling was showing no signs of easing up anytime soon.

It was dark outside, with something of a nip in the air. Summer hadn't yet arrived and spring was busy reminding everyone that it would leave only when it was good and ready.

With more than enough logs cut to keep the wood burner supplying heat and hot water, Baines decided it was time to get working on the van.

The police would have already reviewed all CCTV images available to them. There would be plenty of those in a city like Cardiff. The place was crawling with cameras. Most secured to lampposts and buildings. Some strung across the road on lengths of wire.

He knew there was a chance that someone had seen him drive away with the schoolgirl. Or the possibility that Isla's frantic slapping of the van's side window had caught the attention of another motorist. Neither of those things could be ruled out completely.

He pulled on a short length of rope, like the anchorman in a tug-of-war contest, the barn door coming unstuck with a shudder and squeal. He'd used a full can of WD40 on all moving parts—would have used grease if he'd earlier thought to buy any—and it seemed to do the trick once he got the door moving.

When the floor-to-roof door slammed shut, the sound passed through the outbuilding like a gunshot. The inside was illuminated by three overhead strip lights screwed to its dusty rafters. There was a tower of browning hay bales piled against the far wall. A few individual bales dotted about like sofas in a sixth-form common room. There was a barrel of engine oil. A workbench playing host to an array of old tools. And at the centre of it all, beneath the glare of the lights, was a Ford Transit Connect van. Next to that were a few cans of blue paint and a spray gun.

Baines spent a good forty minutes spreading newspaper and tape over the wheels, windows, and anything else he didn't want changing out for new.

The licence plates used for abducting Isla were discarded at the bottom of an aluminium garden bin, waiting for the waste paper and used rags to join them for a good burning. If any sightings caught on CCTV resulted in the police running ownership checks with the DVLA in Swansea, they'd find the vehicle registered to a window cleaner in Pontypridd.

Isla remained silent when the door to the basement opened and banged against the shoddy plasterwork. She turned her head the other way and felt a cold draft reach for her bare legs.

She crossed them. Pulled them under her as best she could. For a few seconds only, shadows moved on the far wall, disappearing again when the door creaked its way shut. Something landed on her lap. Not the rat. This was larger. Heavier. It made her jump all the same.

'I've brought you a change of clothes.'

It had been more than two days. Possibly three since she'd got dressed for school. Isla mumbled beneath the tape, wincing as it was peeled away. She licked her lips and tasted blood. 'I need a shower.'

'No can do.' The reply teased with a sing-song lilt to it.

Isla shifted position. Most of her bodyweight was supported by her right hip, the grit floor digging into her skin like a box of spilt tacks. 'Please. It's been days since I washed.'

He walked towards the door and hadn't yet reapplied the tape. 'If you behave yourself, I'll think about it in the morning.'

Chapter 39

Events were taking place at an alarming speed. Mostly because of John Kosh's extraordinary compliance with proceedings.

He'd not fled the scene.

Was found in possession of the bloodied murder weapon.

Had readily confessed to killing his wife, though oddly, could not be engaged in any discussion regarding his daughter's whereabouts.

Given the severity of the crime in question, his case had been referred to Crown Court by a panel of three magistrates.

Mr Justice Laing stared from his lofty seat on the bench, a pair of half-rim spectacles held in place with the help of a strawberry-like wart at the end of his blue nose. 'Take him down.'

The order made Kosh fold at the waist. Though he'd later return to court for sentencing, Laing's words sounded terrifyingly final. Turning his head in all directions, Kosh searched for a sympathetic face with which to share the awful news. He saw none other than the lowered head of the police detective.

A guard who'd previously been sitting next to him got to his feet and pointed to a doorway in the wall of the courtroom. When at first Kosh didn't move, the same guard took him by the elbow and steered him towards it.

They descended the stairs together. Waiting at the bottom was a court official dressed in a sombre black suit. 'Name?' he asked.

'John Kosh.'

'Age?'

'Forty-one.'

'Weight?'

'Twelve and a half stones.' Kosh hesitated. 'I don't know what that is in kilos.' As a butcher, he knew there were two-point-two pounds in a kilogramme. And he thought there were fourteen pounds in a stone. But given his current predicament, he couldn't manage the conversion.

The official did the maths and scribbled a rounded-up number of eighty kilogrammes on the form. 'Sign here,' he said, offering the clipboard. Kosh was then led away by the guard. Taken along a narrow corridor and made to wait while a steel door opened at the other end. 'In you go,' the guard said with what might have been his first words of the day.

The cream-walled room beyond wasn't much larger than a snooker table. At the far end—not *that* far away—was a wooden bench that might have been better placed on display as a museum exhibit of Victorian classroom furniture. The door slammed shut, a cushion of air pressing Kosh against brickwork scratched with countless threats to individual members of the police and judiciary.

What would happen next?

He'd done exactly as the stranger had asked of him. Pleaded guilty and taken his punishment. He was busy rearranging things in his overwhelmed mind when the door to his cell opened.

'You've got a visitor,' the guard told him.

Kosh flew off the bench; the guard adopting a defensive stance in response. 'Is it Isla?' Kosh asked.

'Looks nothing like an Isla to me.' The guard visibly relaxed and ushered his charge back down the corridor and into a room barely larger than the one they'd just vacated.

Reece looked up when the door opened. 'Sit down, John.'

'*Isla. Is that you?*' Kosh turned to the guard when he saw it wasn't. 'I don't get it. What's going on?'

Reece repeated his instruction. 'We don't have long. I'm calling in a few favours just being here.'

Kosh shrugged and didn't sit. 'Why?'

Reece stood and leaned against the wall with his hands held deep in his pockets. 'Who put you up to this?'

Kosh looked away. There wouldn't have been much to see. 'I don't know what you're talking about.'

'Just then, as you came through the door – you genuinely thought Isla might be in here.'

Kosh grabbed at his ears, grimacing as he pulled down on them. 'Leave me be.' To the guard, he said: 'Get me out of here.'

Reece blocked their way. 'Give me one more minute.' He put the flat of his shoe against the metal door and rested both hands on his raised thigh. 'You were drugged, John. That's what the tox screen says.'

'What I told the judge and jury was true. I bought and took those drugs myself.'

'Like hell you did. That stuff doesn't come up for sale.'

Kosh stared at the floor. 'No comment.'

'If Isla's alive, I can get her back to you.' Reece took his foot off the door. 'Do you hear me, John? I can save your daughter's life. But only if you're willing to help me.'

John Kosh stood in the signing-out room. Yet more forms to complete. He removed his watch, handed over a rollerball pen, and waited for the court officer to place them in a clear plastic bag.

'Where do you want these sent?' the officer asked in a tone that suggested he didn't really care.

Kosh could think of no one and kept quiet.

'They have to go somewhere,' the guard insisted, his manner bordering on irritated.

'Send them to my home address. For the attention of Isla Kosh.'

The guard raised his head. 'Your daughter?' He sniffed. 'Okay, your daughter it is.' With that done, the handcuffs were reapplied, just as tightly as before. Kosh was then escorted out of the building to the waiting prison van.

The area outside was crawling with journalists. The case was big news, attracting the likes of the BBC and Sky TV. Camera shutters clicked like sticks dragged along iron railings. Flashes of light almost blinded him. An egg hit him square in the face. Rotten. Pungent. He couldn't wipe it off with hands pinned to his waistline. No one came to his aid.

'Murdering bastard!' one of the angry crowd shouted. More of them started up. They wanted his blood. Several of them delighting in telling him he wouldn't survive five minutes of prison life.

Kosh had never thought he'd one day be grateful to have himself shoved into a cage. It slammed shut behind him, bolts drawn, keys turning in the locks.

It went dark momentarily as the back door closed. Quieter, too. A light flickered into life above him, illuminating the small space. There were windows high up. Some of them blacked out. Others with red-tinted glass.

The vehicle's engine started, the cage rattling in tune with it. There was banging on the sides of the van as it moved off, its windows lighting up as cameras sought him out.

Their route was through the centre of the city. A brief journey from one side to the other. John Kosh had lost count of the number of times he'd driven the first part of it.

With Helen.

Isla.

Both.

To concerts at St David's Hall.

Shopping on Queen Street.

Coffee and a pastry before returning home.

But never once had he witnessed the spectacle from the rear seat of a GEOAmey van headed for **HM PRISON CARDIFF.**

Chapter 40

IN THE PRISON'S RECEPTION area was a large *glass* cell holding another four inmates. Presumably the same arseholes who'd goaded and threatened Kosh throughout the journey from Crown Courts.

One of them came closer: a man in his mid-twenties, dressed like he'd never before worn a suit. The jacket and trousers were creased. Shirt hanging free of his belt. Tie knotted to leave it hanging at half the length it should have been.

Kosh slid along the bench a few inches, increasing the distance between them. He didn't dare look up and make eye contact.

Another of them came and sat on his other side, preventing him from moving any further away. 'Wassup, Kiddy-Killer?'

Kosh pushed to his feet and stumbled to the floor when the second man ankle-tapped him.

A screw knocked on the glass. 'Cut it out!'

The prisoner grinned, exposing a half-dozen black teeth that were worn to little more than short stumps. 'I'll be comin' for yer,' he said, putting a hand over his lower face. 'I hates nonces.'

Kosh considered driving his forehead smack into the idiot's face. Squashing his nose and then some. He didn't. The detective had warned him, during their brief encounter at the Cardiff courthouse, to never react with hostility once inside. 'It'll get you killed faster than anything.' Kosh wished he could have confided in the detective and told him everything he knew. But the risk to Isla was too great and so he'd keep to doing as told. For now, at least.

'John Kosh.' For how long had the screw been calling his name? '*Kosh!*'

'Yes.' More forms. The same questions. His answers no different to those previously given at the courthouse. Once done, two screws he hadn't previously laid eyes on took him to a private room.

'Stand under the light and strip naked,' said one of them. Kosh wondered if he'd heard correctly. 'Don't be shy. You'll be shitting in front of an audience soon enough.'

Off came the jacket, shirt, and tie. Shoes and socks. Trousers, then underpants. Kosh stood naked in the light, his hands cupped over his groin.

'Hands above your head. Turn in a full circle.' There was a video camera on the wall, its red eye blinking. 'Bend at the waist.'

'You what?'

'Bend.'

There were two bags on a table. One intended for things to be sent home. The other, for possessions allowed on the inside. One of the screws handed Kosh his prison clothing: a white T-shirt, grey sweatshirt, and black trousers. He got dressed, doubting he'd live long enough to give them their first wash and iron.

Once returned to the holding cell, Kosh stood with his back pressed against the *glass*. His head was close to exploding.

Meth Mouth stopped walking circuits. 'I've seen pictures of your daughter on the telly. Smart piece of skirt, I'll give her that.' He came closer and put his face next to Kosh's, his stinking breath fouling the air between them. 'I bet you gave her a right good—' He got no further before his nose erupted with a fine red spray.

An alarm went off.

A five-man fight broke out. Four against one. Not great odds in anyone's book.

There was shouting.

The clatter of boots on metal.

The sound of heavy keys in heavier locks.

More shouting. Screaming even.

Utter mayhem.

Kosh raised his arms in defence against the fists raining down on him. At least one of his attackers was kicking at anything he could target.

Meth Mouth lurched towards him with bloodied hands and face. 'I'll fucking kill you for that!'

Kosh punched the man at least twice before a heavy blow from behind took his legs from under him. He buckled, surrendering to the weight of the screws pinning him to the floor.

So much for the detective's words of warning: "*Heroes get carried out of prisons in boxes.*"

'You're a dead man! A *fucking* dead man!'

That sounded like an option he might be willing to take. A knee pressed on his neck, pinning his face to the floor. 'I can't breathe.' He only just got it out. 'I said I can't breathe.'

They'd whisked him off to see the prison nurse. A quick health check after his heavy mauling. He felt like he'd been run over, and in many ways, he had.

'You're going to get yourself killed, young man.' The nurse spoke with a broad West Indian accent and wore a uniform that was struggling to keep all parts of her tucked safely inside. 'First day here and already you're making enemies.' She wagged a finger in his face. 'You must have shit for brains, boy.'

'*He* started it,' Kosh said, just as he had that day with the snowman.

'And it ain't over yet,' the nurse told him. '*Oh*, sweet Jesus, no.'

For a moment he expected the doors to fly open and a gospel choir to appear—with feathered wings on their backs—singing him all the way to the Pearly Gates. When they didn't, he went back to whinging every time the nurse dabbed his face with cotton wool balls and a stingy solution.

'You and me will be seeing a lot of one another,' she said. 'You mark my words.'

'I didn't kill my wife.' There was no harm in telling the nurse. 'And I've no idea where my daughter is.'

'I'm just here to patch you up.' She was done and took her tray of equipment over to a counter running along the far wall. 'They'll be putting you on the medical wing overnight, to keep an eye on you.'

Maybe that wasn't such a bad idea. Whether he liked it or not, Kosh desperately needed to sleep.

Up two flights of iron steps and through several locked gates was the route to his room for the night. Was it his imagination, or did everyone else there look heavily medicated?

Some were mumbling to themselves. Others argued with invisible demons. One man of about seventy years of age walked in circles holding a handful of watery faeces.

Kosh kept out of the old man's way. 'I've changed my mind,' he told his escort. 'I don't need the hospital wing.'

'Take it up with the governor in the morning,' she said, pushing on the cell door. 'But if I were you, I'd pray he kept me here for the rest of my sentence.' She ushered him inside. 'Your back is covered with a great big *X marks the spot*.'

Chapter 41

It had been more than a couple of weeks since Reece last made it out to his cottage in Brecon. Since he, personally, had got anything resembling a decent day's work done on the place. His best mate, Yanto, had finished the slate roof in his absence.

The place was at last watertight – if leaks around the rotten window frames didn't count. That's what he intended to see to next. After that, he'd re-point, then repaint the stonework.

Police work had well and truly got in the way lately, one case after another demanding much of his attention. The current murder and MISPER were no exception and had him spending extraordinary lengths of time at the station back in Cardiff. He hadn't yet given up all hope of finding Isla Kosh alive, but in quieter moments like these, had acknowledged, to himself at least, that his team was very much operating on borrowed time where Isla's wellbeing was concerned.

The teenager had last been seen four days earlier. In school, and not once since. The same evening her mother was brutally murdered by a husband who'd wasted no time in confessing his guilt.

That still didn't sit right with Reece. No matter how he tried to square it.

He'd stopped off at the Penderyn distillery on the way to the cottage, purchasing a couple of bottles of his favourite Sherrywood whisky. There was a crate of beer in the boot for Yanto. The heathen didn't touch whisky. Would *"rather drink petrol."* The beer was called Cwtch—the Welsh word for hug—brewed at the *Tiny Rebel Brewery* in Newport. *"And none of that fizzy piss for me either,"* Yanto had so eloquently warned him, referring to lager.

The memory made Reece smile. They were boyhood friends who'd do just about anything for one another. Though Yanto would have it that Reece wasn't pulling his weight where the cottage renovation was concerned.

"It all comes down to priorities," the farmer-cum-builders' merchant had told the detective on more than one occasion. *"And you've got yours all wrong."*

With the distillery well behind him, Reece accelerated towards the mountains, the clear sky rewarding him with spectacular views of the rugged landscape. There were undulating fields peppered with outcrops of rocks, ferns and bracken. Steep green slopes pitted with gorges and fast-flowing streams. And not much further ahead, the *twins* basking in the spring sunshine – Pen y Fan standing on tiptoes over her slightly shorter sister, Corn Du.

There was moisture in Reece's eyes. A blurriness to his vision. Not only did he consider himself blessed to be witness to such natural beauty, but the summit of Pen y Fan was where he'd scattered the ashes of his wife and father-in-law.

Chapter 42

Free of the duct tape, Isla could shout and scream. 'Hello. Is there anybody there?' She slapped the chain against the wall. The sound it made might be more successful in attracting *his* attention.

Voice alone was getting her nowhere, and the act of hitting something hard went some way in controlling her mounting anger. Again and again, she called and slapped. 'I need the toilet.' She couldn't soil herself. Anything but that. Her head was pounding. Several nights of cat-napping taking its inevitable toll. 'I said I need the toilet!'

She let her head flop forward in resignation of her fate. He'd gone. Left her to starve. Left her to be eaten by the rodent. Even that hadn't shown its ugly face in more hours than she was able to keep track of.

There was the sound of a key in the door.

The key.

The door.

At first, she thought she was imagining it. But no, it was opening, albeit slowly. There was light, of the natural kind, but not much to go around. That meant it was day. Another day. The fourth? Fifth? Was that really how long she'd been held captive? Was no one searching for her? Had they all given in, even though she'd refused to do any such thing herself? The thought made her angry. Then more afraid. 'I need the toilet. I can't use the bucket again.' He said nothing in reply. Just stood there staring. 'And a shower. Please. You promised you'd think about it,' Isla said, not wanting to sound too desperate.

But desperate she was. Not having felt this dirty, ever. She watched him reach into a pocket, and recoiled against the wall. It was far too gloomy to tell what was in his hand. It looked smaller than a knife.

He moved off to one side of the room to put a light on. Its orange glow might have looked homely under different circumstances. But not so in a rat-infested hellhole in the back of beyond.

When he returned, his head only just passed under the swaying bulb, leaving Isla thinking he must have been well above average height. He wore the balaclava still—she'd remembered the name—and straightened it with hands specked with blue paint.

Isla noticed that—the blue paint—but had no clue of its relevance to her situation. She was trying to be observant. It might help at a later date. When she was rescued and interviewed by the police, perhaps.

He reached across her and turned the key in the lock that secured the chain to the wall. 'You make any attempt to escape and I'll punish you.' He pulled her to her feet with no attempt made to be gentle. She stumbled under the burden of her own weight and grabbed a handful of his navy overall for support. A few of the top buttons popped open, offering a glimpse of what might have been a butterfly tattoo.

Isla filed the image away in her memory bank.

He rebuttoned the garment. 'I said no funny business.'

'It wasn't my fault. You shouldn't have pulled me like that.' She took small steps towards the door, following on the sagging chain like a downtrodden bear at an illegal circus.

He wasn't as tall as he'd looked from her position on the floor. Isla ducked to clear under the bulb, but needn't have.

There were three stone steps leading up to a door offering the only exit from the room. When she put her foot on the first, her other leg wobbled. She reached for the wall. He yanked the chain, causing her to stumble and hit her left shoulder. She cried out in pain.

'I'm warning you.' He stood on the top step, looking down on her, stooped and menacing. 'Last chance before I take you back.'

Isla pushed up off the floor. She'd had enough of his shit. 'I fell okay. If you've got a problem with that, stop pulling my chain.'

He stared as though considering his next move. Without speaking, he turned his back and passed through the doorway.

They entered what looked to be an old boot room, the once white floor tiles cracked and dirty. There were a few dried leaves resting against a skirting board ravaged by wet rot. In the corner of the room was an enamel sink; water drip-dripping from a short length of rubber hose fastened to a solitary tap. A stained towel hung limply next to it.

'I must remember to leave a TripAdvisor review,' Isla said, looking around. She had no idea why she'd started goading him, except that it made her feel heaps better than playing the victim.

'Shut it.'

'No, really. A nice set of curtains and—' She stopped when he put the blade of a utility knife to her face.

'I can turn you into a freak,' he said, resting it on the bridge of her nose. 'What will the boys think of that?'

'Don't.' Her voice quivered. All signs of bravado quickly gone. 'Please.'

'I mean it.'

Isla followed in silence. She was tearful, but trying not to show it.

'In there.'

The wet room smelled of damp and was barely larger than a double wardrobe. 'Is there a light?'

'I'll leave the door open.'

Isla hesitated. Being naked with him so close terrified her. She checked for spiders on her way in.

There was a chair outside. One of those cheap white ones found in gardens. He wasn't going to sit there and watch the whole time, was he? Then walk in and take advantage of her once she was good and clean? She willed herself to be strong.

He stepped into the cubicle with his body pressed against hers. 'Arms out in front.'

She twisted away from him. 'I can't undress like that. Not fastened to a pipe.'

He let his end of the chain drop to the floor. 'You've got one minute before the water comes on, clothes and all.'

She waited for him to leave, checking over her shoulder two or three times before getting undressed. She started with her shoes and socks. When the sleeves of her cardigan caught on the wrist-straps, she used a bare foot to trample the heavily creased garment along the length of chain to the dirty floor. Squatting to pick it up, she tied it around her waist before removing the rest of her clothing.

Without warning, there was a clicking and banging sound from the pipes high above, a torrent of water gushing forth from the broken shower head. Isla shrieked and jumped out of its range, slipping on the floor tiles, stubbing her little toe. She pulled at the sleeves of her cardigan, tightening them to make sure it covered as much of her modesty as was possible. 'It's cold! The water's freezing cold.'

'What did you expect?' He laughed at her expense. 'Like you already said: this ain't no five-star hotel, darling.'

That pissed her off more than the frigid water had. She wasn't his darling, and he'd better watch his mouth.

'You had enough yet?' Thankfully, he wasn't in sight. Wasn't ogling her young body like she'd expected him to.

She reached a hand under the water and dabbed some on her face. 'I haven't started yet.' She heard him lower himself onto the plastic chair.

'Two minutes,' he said. 'The clock's already running.'

Chapter 43

Reece got out of the car and slammed its door shut. The corresponding window dropped a few inches and came to rest at a tilt. He left it where it was and grinned. 'All right?'

Yanto squinted. 'Look who the cat's dragged home.' He scratched his head and clicked his fingers. 'I'll remember the name if you give me a minute.'

Reece went round to the boot of the Peugeot, still chuckling to himself. 'I've got your beer,' he said, taking the box under his arm.

Yanto didn't look any more impressed. 'Slave labour this, you know.' He pointed at a dozen primed window frames leaning against the wall of the cottage.

'I offered to pay you.'

'I don't want paying.'

'How can it be slave labour, then?'

'I dunno. It just is.'

'How?'

'I said I dunno!'

Reece reached into the box and removed a couple of bottles. 'Not too early for a cheeky one?'

'Oi. Those are mine.'

'Technically, they're still mine,' Reece said, using a bottle opener on his keyring. 'I haven't given them to you yet.'

Yanto snatched one, the sudden movement causing the bottle to froth over and spit.

'You're wasting it,' Reece said, twisting out of the line of fire.

Yanto grabbed for Reece's bottle. 'Give me the other one.'

'Sod off.' Reece pulled away from him, the remaining bottles of beer rattling in the box.

And so it continued for a few minutes longer. Banter between the best of friends.

Reece sat on an upturned bucket. Yanto on a flat bit of ground next to a waist-high section of drystone wall. There were sausages sizzling in a pan on top of an outdoor grill. Reece turned them, licking hot fat from the back of his hand. He slid a few eggs in alongside.

'How many you doing?' Yanto asked, craning his neck to see.

'Sausage or eggs?'

'Sausage.'

'Eight.'

'Where's yours?' Yanto asked. They both laughed easily.

Reece lobbed a loaf of bread. Then a knife. 'Make yourself useful and cut a few slices of that.'

Yanto pulled the knife out of the ground and wiped dirt on the knee of his jeans. 'Did you hear about Badger?'

Reece couldn't place the name. 'Never heard of him.'

Yanto paused, a slice of partly buttered bread resting on his palm. 'Yes, you do. Elgan Collins was his proper name. Landlord of that pub in Radyr we used to go to. Years back, it was.'

'You mean the Druid's?'

'That's the one.' Yanto got to his feet, wagging a few slices of bread like limp flags. 'Where do you want these?'

Reece took them. 'So, what happened to this Badger fella?'

'Killed himself, didn't he. Stupid bastard took a lamp for a bath.'

Reece angled the pan to get hot oil under the eggs. 'In the water with him?'

'Aye. I don't suppose he did it on purpose, though. The news said he knocked it over and electrocuted himself.'

'Ouch.'

Yanto pulled a face. 'Bet he said a damn sight more than that.' He paused. 'Come to think of it, I don't suppose he said much at all. Well, you can't, can you? Not when there's two hundred and forty volts frying your insides.'

'Give it a go after we've eaten,' Reece said, plating the food. 'See if it's possible.'

'And who's gonna finish these windows if I'm dead?' Yanto nodded deeply. 'Didn't think of that one, did you?'

'Stop going on about the windows.'

'You started it.'

Reece forked a sausage and waited for it to cool in the mountain breeze. 'You coming with me tomorrow? I've got daffodils for Anwen.'

Yanto held half a sausage to his mouth and swallowed. 'Yeah, okay.' He wiped greasy fingers on the front of his rugby shirt.

Reece used a chunk of bread to blot the yolk of a broken egg from his plate. 'Cheers. I appreciate it.'

Yanto lay back on the grass and burped loudly. 'She was a good-un, was Anwen.'

Chapter 44

Arvel Baines stopped at the main entrance to the Midnight Club. Or rather, *was* stopped – by a thick-necked man wearing a black bomber jacket and trousers. The doorman was busy letting some people in and turning others away. He stooped to get a peck on the cheek from a woman wearing a dress so short it rode an inch above her stocking tops when she leaned to meet him somewhere in the middle. When he slapped her backside, she squealed and wriggled in his hands.

'See you later,' she said, straightening the doorman's snap-on tie. 'I'll keep it warm.'

He waved her off and went back to scowling and smiling, whichever way the whim took him.

The doorman's clone stood a little further inside the entrance hall. His function: to pummel anyone who got through the first line of defence without invitation. He was busy holding apart two screaming women. They were arguing over possession of a coat and were threatening each other with all manner of violent acts. One of them spat, setting the whole thing off again.

A third woman appeared. She was carrying a coat and a look of irritation. 'I found it in the bogs,' she said, dragging her friend towards the door before she could get beaten up. 'You must have left it in there when you went for a piss, you silly bitch.'

Baines did his best to ignore the ensuing mayhem and read the sign above the door while he waited. He considered it a poor choice of name for such an establishment. *Midnight Club*—to him at least—suggested the place shouldn't open for another couple of hours.

With the coat-fracas over, the doorman gave him his full attention. 'You on your own?'

Baines's toecaps scuffed against the stone doorstep. For a fleeting moment, he thought about saying something clever in reply. Knowing he'd get hurt if he did, put him off. 'Yes.'

'No single men,' the doorman told him.

Baines had seen several women go in alone. One or two of them not stopped to pay the entry fee. So much for equality.

There was no way to pass the gorilla. Not without a significant amount of firepower to hand. 'I'm here to see Billy Creed,' Baines said. 'He's expecting me.' *Summoned* would have been nearer the truth – from the other end of a burner phone given to him only twenty-four hours earlier. He couldn't help but think this new meeting had something to do with the detective.

'What's your name?' Once the doorman had his answer, he turned side-on to speak into a mic clipped to his jacket. A bruised finger held an earpiece in place. The flesh on the back of the man's neck formed deep rolls as it pressed against a white shirt collar. The skin on his wide forehead likewise as he spoke. There were nods and shakes of the head. Once or twice, he looked Baines up and down before speaking into the mic again.

Someone was checking him out. Making sure he was who he claimed to be. That meant Creed was taking more care with visitors since the shooting. Baines couldn't blame him. There'd be plenty of wannabees thinking the gangster had been weakened by his ruined knee. Foolishly believing it had somehow made him less dangerous.

What was it they said about wounded animals?

Baines shoved his hands in his pockets and stared along the street. The night had brought heavy showers of rain that came and went like the traffic. Roadside street lamps and neon signs from local businesses painted abstract collages of colour on the wet tarmac. He shifted closer to the building, using the overhang from its roof as shelter, all the while waiting for a *yea* or *nay* from the man with the thick neck.

A black Mercedes skulked by, the surrounding air pulsing to the beat of a bass machine. The driver's window came down slowly, the man behind the wheel cocking his fingers like a pistol. He blew on them and smiled, exposing a tooth that glinted reflected light.

Everyone wanted to be a gangster these days.

All Baines wanted was to get even.

The doorman hadn't noticed the threat. Was it a threat, or just some kid come to act tough? The doorman kept talking into his mic. Clone was leaning against a glass kiosk in the same hallway, a muscular forearm holding some poor unfortunate drunk in a tight choke lock.

No one seemed to care.

It was Saturday night in the windy city.

All things to all comers.

Welcome to Cardiff.

The doorman was finished with his conversation. 'Sorry about that, Mr Baines. You can go straight up to the office.'

Mr Baines, eh? Arvel felt no less nervous.

Chapter 45

The air in the room smelled of cigar smoke and patchouli oil. Plus, a heady mix of feminine perfumes. Baines cast an appraising eye over the mezzanine-level office and its material contents. He could have fitted several prison cells in there. It was the size of an exercise yard, almost.

The wall-hung television set was only slightly smaller than his prison bed had been. And in this place, the scantily clad women were for real and not of the paper variety – even the ponytailed blonde who was now making her way over to him. Her smile was as wide and white as any he'd seen. Her chest fresh out of a catalogue of shapes and sizes.

There were a couple of black leather sofas turned to face one another, a Union Jack floor rug and a glass table holding court in the space between them. On the table was a ship's decanter, a good measure of something already poured and waiting in a pair of expensive looking cut-crystal snifters. 'I've taken the liberty,' Billy Creed said, opening a hand over one glass. Next to it was a line of white powder.

'Not for me.'

Creed looked from Baines to the blonde who promptly draped an arm around the newcomer's shoulder, her tongue flicking at his earlobe.

Baines pulled away. 'I don't know what you had in mind, Billy, but I've got things to do.' He knew Isla couldn't escape from the basement, but what if someone came snooping around? Someone who'd recognise her from the photographs displayed in countless shop windows.

Creed laughed. 'Did you hear that?' he asked no one in particular. Several of the women laughed with him. Forced and nervous. 'Our Arvel's too busy to party with us.' The gangster rubbed together a pair of tattooed hands. 'Our parties are legendary, Arvel. Believe me, you don't want to miss one of these.'

The blonde put the flat of a hand to Baines's chest and let it snake its way lower.

He caught her wrist when she tried to unfasten the buckle of his belt. 'It's not that I'm ungrateful or anything, but—'

'Shut the fuck up!'

'Billy, I—'

'Are you deaf?' The air was suddenly charged. Several of the women lowered their heads, all signs of laughter long gone. '*I'm talking now.*' A half-smoked cigar dropped ash down the front of the gangster's silk shirt. 'Your place is to listen.'

Baines had experienced similar moments in prison. The trick to surviving them was to keep quiet and agree to just about anything asked of you. He watched the girls file out of the room on Creed's order. There were seven in total. None of them older than twenty, he guessed.

Creed blew smoke across the glass table and waited for it to clear. 'You and me needs a proper talk,' he said when at last it had. 'I wanna know what you did with the Kosh girl.'

Baines couldn't risk Creed bringing Isla to the club for his own perverted use. That might ruin everything if she was seen. 'Impossible. She's dead.' He was playing a dangerous game and had better not get caught.

Creed reclined on a leather sofa and took another deep drag on his cigar. 'Shame that,' he said, spewing smoke like an old bus. 'She could have had a cage downstairs all to herself.'

Baines feigned disappointment. 'I'll know next time.'

Creed stared at him. 'Ain't you gonna ask why I sent for you?'

There was no need to ask. Baines already knew. 'If this is about killing the detective, then—'

The gangster raised a finger. It *spoke* a clear message.

Baines tried again. 'I'm getting even. Then I'm going abroad.'

'Arvel—'

'Look, Billy—'

'Sit the fuck down!'

Baines lowered himself onto one end of the leather sofa. 'Reece wasn't like the others. I didn't go to prison because of him.'

'You killed two innocent women,' Creed said. 'We both know you've got it in you when it suits.'

Baines was in a corner he couldn't get out of. His head flopped onto his shoulder. 'I don't know, Billy. I'd be on the run forever more. They don't let up when they're hunting cop killers.'

Creed grinned. 'The trick is to never let them find the body. Pig food. Fish food. Whatever it takes.'

John Kosh couldn't imagine who he'd pissed off enough to cause such a level of hatred.

Who?

When?

Where?

There were no answers to any of his questions.

Unseen doors opened and closed all around him. Heavy pounding sounds echoing through the medical wing like gunshots. Every one of them made him jump.

The jangling of the screws' keys was already starting to grate on him. But not nearly as much as the shouting and screaming of the other inmates. There was no let up to any of it.

He paced and counted his steps. 'Five, across the length of the cell. Three, across its width.' He repeated the measurement in case he'd made a mistake. He hadn't. Five by three, true enough. It was a stark, in-your-face reality of a life to come.

He lowered himself onto a mattress as thin as a wafer biscuit, finding it difficult to believe that anyone, including the government, would have knowingly parted with good money for such rubbish. Maybe someone was on the take? Creaming off a cut for themselves. Importing cheap imitations from overseas.

He swung a foot at the tiny bed. Bent over and pummelled the mattress until his knuckles were red-raw and bleeding in places. Breathless from the exertion, he leaned against the table on the other side of the room. An easy enough thing to do with it being only a little more than an arm's length away.

To one side of where he stood was a steel washbasin and open lavatory, both bolted to the thick wall. Searching for the flush—button or lever—he found none. It had no lid and smelled rotten.

Behind him was a window, if several thick layers of laminated Perspex set behind stout iron bars qualified as such a thing. A thought caught Kosh unawares. He got to the door in four wide strides and banged hard on it.

'What?' The voice on the other side was less than welcoming.

'My wife's funeral. What happens with that?' The flap slammed shut with no response from whoever was out there. 'I *have* to go.' Doors slammed. Keys jangled. The screaming went on and on. 'Will you tell me if they find Isla?' John Kosh's fingernails dug against the door's paintwork, scraping their way downward as he slumped to his knees.

Chapter 46

Reece pulled twice on the cottage door before the lock properly engaged. The winter rains had made the wood warp and swell, multiple layers of flaking paint not helping the cause. It was nothing a heavy sanding session wouldn't put right once he had time. *If* he found the time. The door had character. He'd already decided to keep it. Not so the windows. Most of those were beyond repair, hence the stack of new ones stored beneath a tarpaulin against the side of the building.

The morning was still dark. 'All set?' Reece asked, his breath condensing on the cold air.

Yanto nodded. 'You've got Anwen's daffs, haven't you?'

Reece tapped his rucksack. 'I put them safe in a cardboard box.'

'I didn't want us getting all the way up to the top, only to realise you'd forgotten them.'

Reece patted his friend's shoulder as he went past. 'I've got the flowers. Stop worrying.'

Yanto followed across the gravel forecourt, breaking into a brief trot to catch up. 'I wasn't worrying.'

They got going not long afterwards, sticking to a few miles of meandering dirt track, marching quick-step along it like countless regiments of the British Army before them. Grit and gravel crunched underfoot with a rhythm that was not unlike the sound of a steam-powered train.

Once they were off the track, the rugged moorland sucked and soaked their boots, making things heavy going. They were exposed out there. Shoved by a bully of a wind that was unusually dry.

In the distance, the day's first fingers of sunlight gripped the mountaintops. A yellow crescent rose above them only a few minutes later.

The sky, in places, looked like it had been beaten with a leather strap; several long welts of purple running in straight lines along it.

Reece loved it out there. Being one on one with nature in its rawest form.

'Are we skirting round the edge of it?' Yanto asked when the wide expanse of the Taf Fechan forest loomed ahead. 'It's a bit dark, still.'

'We'll cut through over there,' Reece said, leading the way into it. He ducked and held to one side a branch belonging to a tall pine. 'Watch your head.'

Yanto kept unusually quiet, the branch springing back to its starting position once they were clear of it. The manoeuvre was repeated several times over before they were able to pass without obstruction.

The air inside the cavernous forest carried a heavy fusion of pine sap and rotting foliage. Cold. Damp. Yet deeply alluring. They walked on a soft bed of browning pine needles and small sticks that snapped underfoot.

An owl announced its displeasure at them trampling through its feeding grounds. Something moved up ahead, the noise it made suggesting it wasn't small.

'You know this place is haunted?' Reece teased.

Yanto's eyes narrowed. 'Don't start.'

The rustling sound came again. This time from somewhere off to their left. An animal stalking them, perhaps?

Reece made the childlike *'Wooo'* of a ghost. He couldn't keep it up and burst into raptures of laughter. Just as he had issues with heights—*issues* didn't come anywhere close to describing the phobia accurately—so did Yanto with thoughts of the afterlife.

It had something to do with a years-ago early morning sighting of a woman in one of the farm outbuildings. A woman who was known to have hanged herself there on hearing of her young husband's death during the Great War. Yanto had refused to set foot in that particular barn ever since.

'Wooo.'

Yanto raised a clenched fist. 'I'm warning you, Brân. Friend or no friend, I'll lamp you one, all the same.'

Reece thought it unlikely, but knew when to give it a rest where Yanto's fiery temper was concerned.

They broke free of the forest—ghost talk and trees left behind—out onto a stone track put there by the Romans. Then up to the Windy Gap junction at the foot of the south facing slope.

Yanto checked the skyline with a farmer's eye. It was fully light. 'It's gonna be a good un today.'

'It's always a good un out here,' Reece said, taking in the view. 'We going straight up?'

Yanto stepped to one side of the path. 'You lead the way.'

Chapter 47

Baines had no idea how he'd got himself involved in what was about to go down. He hadn't agreed to it exactly. But then again, he hadn't refused either.

'Fucking place is full of inbreeds,' Creed said as the BMW hammered along the winding road. 'Sheep-shaggers, the lot of them.'

Jimmy Chin played out a competent verbal rendition of 'Duelling Banjos'.

Baines added nothing to the conversation from his seat in the back.

'What's wrong with you?' Creed used the rear-view mirror to catch sight of him. 'Roast pig not your thing?'

Roast pig and dead detective were two *completely* different things, in Baines's opinion. The former, you ate with an apple sauce some Sundays. Whereas the latter got you jailed for the rest of your miserable life. That didn't appeal to him. Not one bit.

And all the while, Isla was alone and at risk of getting herself found. He knew he couldn't come clean and tell the truth about her. Not yet anyway. 'How do you even know Reece is out here?' he asked.

Creed tapped his nose. 'A little bird told me.'

'Someone at the police station?'

It wasn't denied. The BMW pulled to a stop on a dirt track leading to what was little more than a white speck in the distance. 'Here's your time to shine, Arvel.'

Baines stared through the window. 'I'm walking the rest of the way?'

Creed's eyes bulged. 'Well, I ain't calling you a fucking taxi!'

'I meant it's a long way to be carrying a couple of full jerrycans.'

The gangster tuned side-on in his seat. 'Will you listen to him, Jimmy. Always moaning, this one.'

Baines got out before the situation escalated. It wasn't that he couldn't do what was being asked of him. He'd already stabbed a woman, as well as fried a man in his bathtub. But Reece wasn't his problem. He had no beef with that particular detective.

Jimmy Chin went round to the boot of the vehicle and lifted a pair of jerrycans onto the ground. 'That should be more than enough,' he said, tapping one of them with his foot.

Creed took a pair of binoculars from his jacket pocket. 'I'll be watching you, Arvel,' he said, focussing the lenses on Reece's cottage. 'Any fuck-up's and you'll be the early Guy Fawkes, not him. You got me?'

Baines nodded as he went past with a sloshing jerrycan held at the end of each arm.

The view from the summit of Pen y Fan was breathtaking. The Brecon Beacons National Park spread out before them like a colourful patchwork quilt.

When they'd first arrived, Reece wasted no time in going to *see* Anwen and Idris. There was plenty to say. Much to catch up on. Work was progressing on the cottage. So much so, the new windows were going in later that week. The boiler and roof were done. Anwen knew that already. He'd told her on his previous visit.

'Jenkins thinks I'm nuts selling the place in Llandaff and moving out here full time. She reckons it's too far for me to travel each day. I think ninety minutes is doable. What about you?' Anwen didn't disagree and listened to him babble on without interrupting.

The daffodils made it to the summit mostly intact. One or two of them in need of a tweak before he was willing to hand them over. He'd tied the stems using a hairband once belonging to his deceased wife – holding it to his nose beforehand, inhaling memories of happier times.

Yanto paid his respects. Spoke in his own clumsy way and without any swearing, proving he could manage it when he tried.

The two of them had then stood in silence, their heads bowed to the ground, each with a hand on the other's shoulder.

Creed was hanging onto the passenger-side door of the BMW when Baines got back from the cottage. 'I don't see no smoke, Arvel.' The gangster came away from the car using a cane to maintain his balance on the uneven road. 'What part of torch the fucking thing did you not understand?'

Baines lowered the two full jerrycans and rolled his aching shoulders. He was soaked in sweat and breathing heavily. 'Reece wasn't there. No point in us giving the game away.' To say he'd been relieved to find the cottage unoccupied would be an understatement. 'The doors were locked. Curtains open. The place was definitely empty.'

'I've seen Copper's car.' Creed waved the binoculars with his free hand. 'With *these*.'

'You can say what you like, Billy. There's no one at home.' He took the jerrycans round to the back of the BMW, leaving them there for Jimmy Chin to lift into the boot. 'We should have been here hours ago. Looks like your inside man's given you duff information.'

Creed's eyes narrowed. 'Who said anything about it being a man?'

Baines wiped his hands on an old rag while he took in the scenery. 'Whoever it was, they forgot to remind you that Reece is a runner? I bet he's out there now, watching us.'

Creed's eyes scoured the same terrain. He looked edgy and exposed. 'This ain't finished,' he said, struggling to get into his seat. 'And next time, you won't be giving me any of your bullshit.'

Chapter 48

It being Sunday morning—the day after his admission to the prison's hospital wing—John Kosh was on the move again. This time, headed out into the general population.

The *jungle*.

He imagined it being many times worse than that. Even the thought of it had his guts in a turmoil. The comments about him having drawn an *X marks the spot* on his back, did little to calm him. Why had the woman even mentioned it? It was always going to play on his mind.

He'd already taken a shower, and that meant he'd need one less where he was going. That might keep him out of Meth Mouth's way a little while longer before the man could exact his violent revenge. Because exact it, Meth Mouth would.

That's what went on in places like this. If you pissed off the locals, then you paid your dues to the ferryman – meaning you were as good as dead.

At first, Kosh couldn't recall the name of those knife-type weapons prisoners made from everyday items. He'd seen several Ross Kemp documentaries on TV and YouTube, yet the exact term still escaped him.

Shank. The word came at last. He wished it hadn't. It was graphically ugly and suited its purpose almost perfectly.

'So it begins.' Wasn't that what King Theoden had said before the battle of Helms Deep? Kosh had intended it to be for his ears only.

The screw held a gate open and stood to one side. 'What?' He let it clunk shut behind them.

Kosh recoiled from the sound. 'You're not a fan of Tolkien?' He couldn't tell if the man's vacant expression was one of abject boredom, or mere ignorance. Either way, he offered no response.

Kosh had been categorised 'A'. That meant he was considered one of the most dangerous prisoners there. A ruling he believed he neither deserved nor was likely to live up to.

Arvel Baines reached for the scoreboard and added fifteen points to his by drawing a plastic slider across the marker. He then retreated into the darkness and took a swig of water from a plastic bottle while balancing the butt-end of an ash snooker cue on the upper surface of his shoe. Deciding it might be some time before he got back to the green baize, he sat and put the bottle down on a small, circular table.

He knew he shouldn't be there. Isla needed him. Didn't want him, granted. But *needed* him, nonetheless. What was he going to do with her now her father had done as told? John Kosh was awaiting sentencing and could still change his plea and tell all. No one would believe him, obviously. But the girl being dead would surely scupper any remaining leverage Baines had over him. Isla would be kept alive for a little while longer. After that – he was wasn't so sure.

Billy Creed chalked his cue tip in silence. He put the small green cube near the centre pocket when he was done and bent at the waist to line up his next shot.

The red ball went down with a satisfying pop, the white coming off two cushions to leave him on the wrong side of a blue into the same centre pocket. 'Bollocks.' He leaned on the heels of his hands and whistled like an old kettle coming to the boil. 'Gonna have to force the fucker in,' he said, going down again. He held his elbow perpendicular to the floor, the lower part of his arm swinging from its anchor point like a well-oiled pendulum.

As he struck the ball, his head came up early, the cue digging into the white in a downward motion, making it bounce and fly off the table into the darkness beyond. He launched the cue up the table, its tip leaving a nine-inch skid mark in the baize.

Baines looked away. The gangster wasn't having the best of days. For a moment, he considered telling him he'd had enough and was going home. When it came to it, he kept his mouth shut.

Creed turned to the scoreboard and did some basic arithmetic. 'Looks like *I* won that one.' He grabbed for the walking cane propped against the neighbouring table and headed towards the office with a pronounced limp. 'Time for you and me to have a proper talk, Arvel.' He tapped his back pocket like he was summoning a pet dog. 'Get your arse over here.'

Kosh carried his bedding and a couple of clean towels into the prison's general wing. He was beyond scared and wanted to vomit.

There was nothing resembling a welcome. No guided tour. Plenty of the inmates stared. Sized him up. He was a convicted wife killer and suspected child abductor. That put him one shade of shit above the status of *nonce*—Not of Normal Criminal Element—someone to be despised and got at.

One of the inmates clapped slowly. Others soon joined in. Some stamped their feet as things got going. More still knocked metal mugs against the railings.

Kosh fought the urge to look up, but lost that battle. He already had a pretty good idea of who'd started things off without having to search for a face in the crowd.

Meth Mouth grinned from his position on one of the upper landings. Clearing his throat with a great deal of noisy effort, he spat, the green ball arcing through the air to land on what had been clean bedding.

Kosh didn't retaliate and continued on his way with the minimum of fuss.

The screw led him up the steps towards them.

Towards Meth Mouth.

Kosh wondered what good a single prison officer might be against a group of thugs strung out along the landing. Pretty much useless, was his best guess.

'Watch yourselves,' the screw said once among them.

Kosh kept his terrified gaze to the floor. It was like running the gauntlet. Not that he was running anywhere. He willed the screw to speed up and get this over with.

When he did take a peek, they were glaring at him. A couple of them even dragged a finger across the front of their necks, their tongues lolling to one side of their open mouths.

Meth Mouth trailed a lazy foot. Kosh caught it with the toe of his shoe. Stumbling, he fell onto his elbows, skinning them on the metal floor. There was loud cheering, laughter, and a lot more clapping.

'That's enough!' Apart from the gruff order, the screw did nothing to help and stood there waiting for Kosh to get back on his feet.

He might have imagined it, but could have sworn the officer smirked as he looked in Meth Mouth's direction. When he retrieved his scattered bedding and towels, there were dirty footprints and more spit on them. He challenged no one, picked up his things, and followed the screw to his cell.

Chapter 49

THE CELL IN QUESTION was only slightly bigger than the one on the medical wing. The screw pointed him inside, to where a sea of dark green paint awaited him. It was drab. Depressing. And quite possibly his home for the next twenty to thirty years.

The lavatory, unlike the one on the medical wing, had a flush. He thanked God, his *lucky stars,* and whoever else might have been responsible. There was a washbasin alongside it. Made of a metal that might once have had a shine.

'Make your bed before you get settled,' the screw told him.

The bottom bunk was free. Its bare mattress stained. When Kosh checked, it was also soaking wet. He put his fingers to his nose. Piss. He turned the thing over to find it damp and not saturated like the other side. He dragged a sheet over it, careful to match up the deposits of urine and spit. If he was careful where he lay, he might just avoid them both.

The top bunk was empty, its owner presumably out on the landing somewhere.

Kosh had been sitting on a dry bit of mattress for only a matter of minutes, when he realised there was someone watching from the doorway. He raised his head slowly, expecting to see Meth Mouth. When he saw it wasn't, he let out an audible sigh of relief.

The man was tall and skinny and stood on one leg. 'You must be John Kosh,' he said, and introduced himself as 'Sykes.'

The office at the snooker hall was tiny compared with the one at the Midnight Club. Functional rather than comfortable was how Arvel Baines would have described it.

There were a couple of plastic chairs. An electric kettle and a few odds and sods belonging to Big Babs, the manager-cum cleaner-cum cook of greasy chip butties. The woman herself was busy in the kitchen out back, frying up a few for a league match between two local teams.

Creed lowered himself onto one of the plastic chairs, gritting his teeth and mouthing obscenities as he went down. The chair wobbled, and for a moment, looked like it might give up and collapse beneath him. He used both hands to grip his leg behind the knee and set it down where he wanted it. 'I'm having doubts about you, Arvel.'

The comment took Baines unawares. 'I don't get you, Billy?'

'Fucking leg!' Creed repositioned it before pointing an accusing finger. 'I'm beginning to think you're playing me.'

Baines swallowed. There was no way Creed could have seen him letting the detective's tyres down. Not even with the aid of binoculars. The Peugeot had been parked around the side of the cottage, out of sight of the upper road.

'Where's the girl?' Creed asked. It was a simple enough question.

'Girl?'

Creed slammed a fist against the table top. 'The butcher's *daughter!*' That got the attention of a few at the club. 'Get rid of them,' Creed told Jimmy Chin. 'All of them.'

Chin bounded out of the office, clapping his hands while shooing the regulars away.

'I wants to see her,' he said, putting a great deal of effort into getting up again.

Baines was in danger of going into panic mode. 'You can't.'

The veins in Creed's neck engorged with blood, his eyeballs straining in their sockets. 'What did you say?'

Baines pressed himself against the upright of his plastic chair. 'What I mean is, there's nothing left of her. Nothing for you or anyone else to see.'

Creed's fists gripped the table for added support. 'Tell me more.'

'I had her incinerated at the hospital.'

'I warned you about bullshitting me.'

'I'm not. I left her scattered about the place in orange bags. They burned her with the rest of the clinical waste coming in overnight.' It sounded implausible, even to Baines. 'Those people are used to dealing with amputated limbs and all sorts of blood-soaked materials. They wouldn't have bothered checking what was in there.'

'Incinerated, eh?'

Baines nodded. He might have got away with it. 'She's just a pile of ash, Billy. They'll have swept her up and thrown her out by now.' Creed called Jimmy Chin back to the office. Baines couldn't help but wonder if this was the end of the line. The finale. But how would they kill him? A single gunshot to the back of the head, perhaps? Strangulation? Slit his throat? The choices were almost endless. He knew he deserved it for what he'd done to poor Helen and Isla Kosh. Badger had it coming. But not the mother and daughter.

Chin appeared in the doorway and awaited his instructions.

Creed spoke over the top of Baines. 'Get the motor brought round the front. We're taking Arvel home.' He leaned across the table and held his face close to Baines's. 'If what you say is true, then I'm expecting to find one hell of a messy bathtub.'

Chapter 50

ARVEL BAINES HIT THE pavement running, his arms chopping through the air at his sides. He'd played his cards and showed his hand when all he'd been holding was a fistful of jokers.

He was now in survival mode.

Billy Creed righted himself on the doorstep of the snooker hall. He'd been knocked sideways during the brief scuffle, and was screaming all manner of threats at the fleeing Baines. He issued gruff commands to his men. Orders as to who should get in the car and who should go back inside to fetch the shotgun.

Baines didn't stick around long enough to hear any more than that. He raced up the high street, thankful for the extra puff gained through many years of squats, burpees, and mountain climbers.

A car engine started. The angry grunt of the BMW unmistakable even when heard from a distance. Doors slammed shut. Then a high-pitched screeching noise of tyres as the vehicle spun off the concrete hardstand at the side of the building and out onto the road. Other drivers braked. Several banging on their horns in what became a symphony of objection. Regardless, the BMW refused to stop for anyone and accelerated along the wet tarmac.

But that wasn't Baines's only problem.

Someone was chasing him on foot.

'I need to pee!' Isla had shouted the same thing a hundred times already. And a thousand more before she'd earlier soaked the clean clothes she'd been given only the day before.

Where was he? She'd give him a piece of her mind just as soon as he turned up.

If he ever again turned up.

That was a sobering thought. She was doing it again. Thinking the worst and dwelling on the negatives. That's not how people survived such situations. Not by thinking negative thoughts.

'Where are you, you bastard?' Isla didn't swear at home like some of her peers did. Mum disapproved. But even she would have excused it on this occasion.

Thoughts of Mum caught in Isla's throat. It was painfully dry, unlike the bottom half of her clothing. '*Bastard! Bastard! Bastard!*' She yanked the chain in sync with her protests. Then slumped, exhausted with the effort. She hadn't had a drop to drink for what must have been . . . She paused to work it out, but couldn't.

Hours.

Maybe an entire day.

For how long could a person expect to survive in such awful conditions? Dad had once told her—and she hadn't really been listening at the time, so could be wrong—that there was a rough rule of threes when it came to such things.

Up three minutes without oxygen.

Three days without water.

Three weeks without food.

It sounded plausible. But then Dad could bullshit with the best of them.

The bit about the water had her doubting the authenticity of his source. If this was only close to a day spent without it, then there was no way she'd manage another two.

Baines knew sticking to the main roads was a particularly bad idea. Creed and his thugs would be up alongside him in a matter of seconds if he didn't change direction soon. Images of being shot at through a lowered car window flooded his mind.

He took a chance and turned a sharp right into the dark opening of an alley. It was too narrow for the BMW to follow, but if it led to nothing more than a dead end, then he'd be done for.

On the left-hand side of the alley was a series of metal doors spaced at unequal intervals along the wall of a nondescript brick building. Opposite was a chain-link fence that leaned into the road like a drunk.

There were no handles to be found on any of the doors, and the close proximity of the person following meant he was in no position to stop and try them.

The man behind him was young. Younger than him, at least. And definitely lighter on his feet than the thick-necked doormen from the Midnight Club.

That meant three assailants Baines knew of. Maybe four.

Creed wouldn't be much of an issue. Not with his ruined knee. Unless, of course, he was the one brandishing the shotgun, or *boomstick*, as fellow inmates had referred to it.

Decisions, decisions.

None of them were without risk.

It was fast becoming clear to him that he couldn't outrun the chaser for much longer.

Stand and fight was his only option.

'Hello rat.' The rodent was back, and thankfully, hadn't brought its mates. Isla wondered if it came at the same time each day. And if it did, then perhaps she could somehow use the creature's visiting habits to keep track of how long she'd been cooped up. It was unlikely, but certainly worth a moment or two's consideration.

The Kosh family had a hot tub in their garden, and a pair of hedgehogs that appeared through a gap in the feather board fence every summer evening at the same time, prompt.

Were rats like hedgehogs?

Did they have a similar time telling ability?

Why the stupid questions?

Was she going mad with a cabin fever sort of ailment?

She swung her leg at the rat when it came within range. '*Fuck off!*' She was swearing again. Mum needed to give her a stern talking to when they next met up.

'Mum.' The word that brought tears every time she let it into her mind.

Isla slapped the chain against the wall more times than she cared to count. To her missing captor, she screamed: 'Why won't you listen to me? Why won't you come and let me go free?' She slumped onto her knees. Exhausted. Crying. And calling for her mother.

Chapter 51

Arvel Baines was deaf to Isla's protests, preoccupied as he was trying to stay alive.

His attacker gripped a handful of his sweatshirt and used it to swing him round. Baines bounced off the wall of the building and planted his forehead slam in the middle of the man's face. Warm blood from a broken nose showered him. The man doubled over with his hands cupped to his face.

That bought Baines some thinking time.

He brought a knee up against the same nose with as much force as he could, pushing the man back onto his haunches. There was the sound of something heavy hitting hard against the ground. A cracking noise that sounded wrong, no matter how he interpreted it. He stood over the man, preparing to let fly with a tirade of kicks if need be.

But there *was* no need. His attacker lay silent and still.

Someone called a name from the other end of the dark alley. It had to be the dead man's name.

Baines considered his options. Retracing his footsteps was a ploy that might have some merit. Creed wouldn't imagine him stupid enough to do that. The gangster would expect him to emerge wherever the alleyway went.

Back it was, then. Past the snooker hall. Fingers and everything else crossed.

'I need to pee. I need to pee. I said I need to *peeee!*' The wall took another hammering from Isla's chain. She was as sure as she could be that she'd landed a toe, at the very least, on the arse of the fleeing rat.

It was out of range now and turned to watch her. A pair of beady eyes married to a whiskered nose. It looked demonic. It's just a rat, she kept telling herself. But the other half of her brain wasn't playing ball. *There's no such thing as JUST a rat*, it teased. *It's here for you.*

'Piss off.'

The rat was attracted to the odour of her urine. Isla could, herself, smell the sodden area at the seat of her joggers. The bucket was tantalisingly close. But not close enough. She shifted on her wet backside until the chain bit at her wrists. When she leaned towards the bucket, her arms were pulled in the opposite direction, away from it. All attempts were futile. And even if she were to succeed and reach it, how then would she use the thing?

She tried something else. Brought her wrists towards the chain's anchor point, stretching every inch of her body. Her toes glanced against the side of the bucket, pushing it away by a fraction of an inch.

'*No!*'

She tried again. Stretched until worried she might come apart at the seams. This time, she got a foot around the side of the bucket and had better leverage. It moved. Thankfully, not away from her. She'd been holding her breath the entire time and was in desperate need of oxygen. For a while she lay there, greedily replenishing low stores. Then she curled the toes of both feet, positioning them on either side of the bucket. Her intention was to tap the thing side to side, and closer each time. It might take a while, but it minimised the risk of her pushing it out of reach altogether.

It was working.

With the bucket close enough for her to hook an ankle behind it, she pulled herself back to her original sitting position.

It was only a small victory, but huge in the sense of achievement it gave her.

Next, she'd have to figure out the logistics of peeing in a bucket while fully clothed and chained to a flaking wall.

Baines made it to the entrance of the alley and waited in the shadows, listening to his heartbeat thump in his head, neck, and chest. He couldn't see or hear Billy Creed. The BMW neither. He was about to step out onto the pavement and go on his way when his phone rang in his back pocket. He grabbed for it, eager to silence the ringer before it pinpointed his position.

Only one man knew that number.

Baines held the phone as though he were about to lob a grenade into an enemy trench. He thought about launching it over the fence and into whatever lay beyond, but didn't. Instead, he pressed *Answer*. There was a silence that lasted for what seemed like forever. Then . . .

'Arvel. I know you're there.'

Baines swallowed. 'Billy.' He immediately wished he'd coughed and cleared his throat before speaking. He could hear the gangster breathing down the line. A raspy sound. He could almost smell the patchouli oil oozing from the angry man's pores.

Creed spoke with an air of calm and was close to believable. 'How's about you and me put this misunderstanding behind us?'

Not a chance. Baines wasn't falling for that one. 'I don't think so.'

'You ain't at liberty to refuse,' Creed told him. 'It's an offer I won't be repeating.'

Baines took a moment to check no one was sneaking up on him. That this wasn't some cheap trick to keep him occupied and in one place. It was best to keep moving, he decided. He turned left and entered the street in the reverse direction to the way he'd earlier travelled.

'Are you listening?' Creed's voice had raised in pitch.

Baines stayed close to the cover of parked cars, his head twitching like that of a ground-feeding bird. 'I've got my own plans, Billy.' He kept moving along the pavement. 'I don't need to make things any more complicated than they already are.'

'And what if I make your plans public?'

Baines laughed. Actually laughed. It did nothing to improve the tense situation. 'You turn grass? Come on, Billy, you'd really go down in people's estimation if you did.' He slunk past the snooker hall. The BMW's parking space was still empty. He increased his pace until well beyond.

It was then he heard the unmistakable grunt of the M-Sport engine. But from where? He thought it might be coming along one of the side streets. He went down on one knee, using a parked car for cover. The engine noise got louder, the BMW growling as it passed on the other side of the Ford he was hiding behind. Creed and his crew were no more than ten feet away.

'Last chance, Arvel. Take it or leave it.'

Baines couldn't speak. Not with them being so close. He pressed his face to the cold glass of the Ford's window and stared through it. If the gangster turned to look, he'd have seen him.

'You just signed your own death warrant,' Creed said, hanging up.

Baines stayed where he was, hanging on the hum of the dead line. The stakes had been raised.

Chapter 52

It was Monday morning, and Reece was attending another crime scene. 'Do we know who this is yet?' he asked, almost straddling the dead man's head.

The victim's right leg was folded beneath him. His arms held wide open and pointing in opposite directions. There was a halo of blood where his head rested in the dirt, but in no way did it make him look saintly. His face was covered in the same blood; most of it coming from what looked like a broken nose. It had dried, leaving scabby areas of reddish-brown on the man's skin. Trickle lines of it spanned from his nose to earlobes, suggesting he'd died while flat on his back.

'Not yet,' Jenkins answered. 'The CSIs have uploaded his prints, and I've got Ginge onto it back at the station. He's going to ring us just as soon as he gets a match.'

Uploaded. Reece couldn't fully get his head around the rapid advancements in forensic technology. Much of it being the stuff of witchcraft, in his opinion. Still, if it sped things up during an investigation, then there could be only one winner. 'Who found him?'

Jenkins pointed to an end-of-terrace paper shop. *The New Deli* introduced itself with gold lettering on a red background set above the glass door. 'A local picking up milk.'

'Did he see anyone? Hear anything?' Reece asked.

Jenkins shook her head. 'Nope. Apart from a few seagulls trying to get an early breakfast off matey-boy, here.'

Reece had initially thought the injuries to the man's eyes had something to do with the fatal assault. But now it was clear the gulls had opted for a light starter before tucking into something more substantial. The crime scene was getting ever busier; a tent going up to hide proceedings from the press and inquisitive public alike. CSIs were taking photographs and numbering things with yellow cones. 'Is Ffion not here?' Reece couldn't see her.

'She's back at the station with Ginge,' Jenkins told him.

'He doesn't need his hand holding anymore,' Reece said, watching people in white bloated coveralls do their thing. Everyone present had a job to do, and all were busy getting on with it.

'I never said he did.' Jenkins stared at the leaning chain-link fence and chewed her cheek. 'It's Ffion I'm more worried about. She's not her herself lately. Something's definitely not right with her.'

'Like what?'

'I don't know. I'll talk to her and see if there's anything she wants to offload.'

'Keep me posted.'

'I will.' Jenkins didn't follow when Reece walked away. 'Where are you going?' she called after him.

'Security camera.' He pointed to the window of the corner shop. 'You never know, they might have one pointing in this direction.'

'It's a long way off from the scene. I can't imagine it being of much use, even if it did record something.'

Reece did a slow pirouette and shrugged on the way round. 'It's gotta be worth a punt.' He started on ahead again, then stopped. 'Remind me to tell you later about my flat tyres.'

When Reece got back to the station a little under an hour later, he was called upstairs to see Chief Superintendent Cable.

'The ACC is up there with her,' George, the desk sergeant, warned. 'Fresh back from his jolly to the States.'

Reece stopped to talk. Harris could wait. 'I wonder if he pissed off the Yanks as much as he does us?'

'Can't help himself, that one.' George leaned on an elbow. 'They're all the same at that level, don't you think?'

'Gobs and egos bigger than their brains,' Reece agreed.

'Have one of these?' The desk sergeant held a half-finished packet of Hobnobs at arm's length. 'Think of it as comfort food.'

Reece took a biscuit and broke it in half. 'Why's it always me they want to see?'

George munched on a biscuit of his own. 'Are you seriously asking me that?'

'Yeah. How many other DIs and DCIs work in this place?' He didn't wait for an answer. 'But it's always me that pair wants to see.'

'True.' George couldn't deny it, given it was usually he who passed on the unwelcome message. Like today, for example.

'I know it's bloody true,' Reece said, coughing on his Hobnob. 'What I want answers to is the *why me,* bit?'

George twisted the packet shut and returned the biscuits to the shelf under his counter. 'It's because you're such good entertainment.' He chuckled to himself. 'Working with you is more fun than having the comedy channel on. Far cheaper too.'

'Thanks for that. I can always count on you to put me straight.' Reece was almost at the door to the stairs when he stopped and came back to the desk. 'I know Brecon's out of area, but you couldn't ask around and find out if there were any incidents involving parked vehicles over the weekend.'

'Incidents. How do you mean?'

Reece told him about the four flat tyres on the Peugeot. 'That's how we found them when we got back from Pen y Fan. It's just as well Yanto had a pump in the boot of his Defender.'

'All four flat?'

'Yep, and none of them punctured.'

'Kids?' George offered.

'Not all the way out where I am.'

'Any damage to the car or cottage?'

'Nope.' Reece scratched his head. 'If I didn't know better, I'd say someone was trying to warn me off.'

George answered the phone after it rung a few times. 'Yes, ma'am. I will, ma'am.' He pointed Reece upstairs and mouthed the word, 'Now.'

Jenkins found Ffion Morgan at her desk, working on her laptop. 'Morning,' she said, crossing the room.

Morgan didn't budge and murmured what might have been 'hello' in reply.

'You busy?'

A brief glance over the shoulder. 'Um, yeah. A bit.'

'Doing what?' Jenkins draped her jacket over her chair and went to get a better look.

Morgan turned the screen away from her approaching colleague. 'Things.'

'Are you okay?'

Morgan tapped the computer keys with a final flourish before giving Jenkins her full attention. 'Yeah, I'm good. Sorry about that. I was doing something.'

'I could see. What were you up to?'

'I wasn't *up* to anything.'

'Steady on. I was just showing an interest, that's all. I won't bloody bother in future.'

Morgan pulled a face. 'Sorry, Jenks, I shouldn't have overreacted.'

'Apology accepted.' Jenkins went back to her desk, where an awkward silence hung in the air for far too long.

'Okay,' Morgan said, getting up. 'I fancy a proper coffee. Do you want one?'

Jenkins shook her head. 'There's plenty in the kitchen. The boss even put some of those filter pods in there, for everyone's use.'

'I fancy some fresh air and a walk,' Morgan said. 'Are you sure I can't get you anything while I'm out?'

Jenkins declined and let her go.

Chapter 53

'Where do you keep the tin hats?' Reece asked, striding past the PA's desk. The woman looked bemused and got to her feet. Reece kept up the pace and didn't knock when he got to Chief Superintendent Cable's office door. He went inside. 'George downstairs said it was important.'

Harris paused mid-sentence and lowered a cup and saucer from chin to belly level. 'Ah, Reece. Just the man. Sit down.'

'I'd rather stand, sir.'

The ACC rolled his eyes. 'Don't start that again.'

Reece took a seat. 'Is there a problem?'

'The chief super tells me you want to bring Billy Creed in for questioning?' Harris squinted, clearly ill at ease with the proposal.

'That's right.' Ginge had found a match for the prints taken from the bloodied victim in the alleyway. The dead man was a known associate of the Cardiff gangster, and an ANPR—Automatic Number Plate Recognition—check in the area had come up trumps for a BMW X5 registered to none other than Billy Creed. 'In connection with the murder of Nicky Zala,' Reece said.

Harris's frown deepened. 'But how do you know the man was murdered? The post-mortem hasn't taken place as yet.' He flicked his head to Cable for confirmation. Then to Reece and said: 'He might have fallen over drunk in that alley, for all we know.'

Reece had made a promise to himself on the way up the stairs to be as civil to the ACC as he possibly could. Harris wasn't making it easy for him to keep that promise. 'Nicky Zala was found on his back, with his face covered in blood. He had a broken nose and what looks to be a fractured skull. This was no drunken fall. He'd taken a beating, sir.'

'But you can't be sure?'

'That's my line of enquiry.'

Harris looked like he might be struggling with something. His eyes narrowed further, giving him his trademark mono-brow look. 'Isn't Creed's snooker club somewhere along that street?'

'It is, sir.'

'Well, then. It's no wonder ANPR spotted him in the area.'

'I still intend to interview him, sir.'

'But why, for God's sake?'

'Because I think he'll know something about it.'

Harris bent at the waist and quickly straightened again. 'This unhealthy obsession has to stop, man.'

'It isn't an obsession.'

'It is, if I say so.'

Sod the promise. Reece rose from his chair. 'And what makes you an expert in what I think?'

Cable forced herself into the conversation: 'ACC Harris has a valid point. If Billy Creed was involved in this, then there's no way he'd have dumped the body so close to home.'

Reece counted backwards. It wasn't working on this occasion. 'I never said Creed did it. I said, he'll know something about it.'

'Like what?' Harris asked, his cup and saucer landing on the desk with a clatter.

Reece got to the door before saying something there'd be no coming back from. 'I'll let you know just as soon as I've interviewed him.'

Jenkins knew that what she was doing was wrong on every level. Snooping on a friend and colleague was bad form in most people's eyes, including her own. But if the sole reason for her doing it was to ensure that the person was okay, *then* . . .

That side of the argument made her feel somewhat better.

It shifted the guilt.

But only marginally.

It still didn't make it right, she knew. She'd already booted up Morgan's laptop and was busy searching through the internet browsing history.

There were searches for expensive shoes and bags. Your typical Ffion Morgan stuff. Makeup and self-tanning products. Short breaks in this country. Longer holidays in sunnier climes. Nothing to cause her colleague to be so secretive or nervy.

There was a link to an online story involving *Maleficent* star, Angelina Jolie. Jenkins wasn't sure why, but she clicked on it and read further.

Jolie had, in 2013, undergone a preventative double mastectomy after discovering she carried the BRCA1 breast cancer gene. Doctors had estimated the actress's risk of developing breast cancer as 87% and ovarian cancer as 50%.

Jolie described how, after surgeries performed over a three-month period, her risk of developing breast cancer had shrunk to just 5%.

Jenkins gulped. 'Not Ffion. Please, not Ffion. She's just reading. She loves all the celebrity gossip. That's all this is. Her keeping up with what's going on in the world.'

But there was more.

Stories of other well-known women who'd undergone similar procedures.

Christina Applegate of *Married with Children*. She'd started with a simple lumpectomy, followed by bilateral mastectomies and full reconstructive surgery.

Giuliana Rancic. Wanda Sykes. Sharon Osbourne . . . The list went on, and Ffion had been checking each individual woman's story.

'What are you doing?'

Jenkins slammed the lid of the laptop shut. 'I was . . . Um . . .' She stood, flustered and red faced.

Morgan was only a few metres away. A paper coffee cup in hand. 'I asked you a question.'

'Ffion. I—'

Morgan marched towards her desk, coffee in hand, her voice shaking. 'That was private.' She slammed the paper cup down next to the laptop. The lid came off, spilling hot coffee. '*Private*, do you hear me?'

Jenkins came closer. 'Your hand.'

'Fuck my hand!' Morgan pointed a finger. 'And fuck you too, Jenks.'

'What the hell's going on?' Reece had arrived. 'I can hear the pair of you from the corridor outside.' He looked from one woman to the other. 'Someone answer me.'

'We were just—' Jenkins got cut off mid-sentence.

'I don't want to talk about it.' Morgan held her scalded fingers in the other hand.

'Tough,' Reece said. 'Office. Both of you.'

Morgan went in the opposite direction. 'Fuck this for a game of soldiers.' It wasn't loud, but it *was* audible.

Reece scratched his head. 'What did you say?'

'Leave her.' Jenkins caught him by the sleeve. 'I've done something pretty stupid, boss. It's my place to put it right.'

Chapter 54

Chief Superintendent Cable and Assistant Chief Constable Harris were on the other side of the one-way glass, watching Reece and Jenkins interview Billy Creed.

Harris was picking at his bottom lip and frowning with increasing frequency. 'I warned him. I bloody warned him.'

'I'm surprised you gave in,' Cable said with a brief sideways look.

Harris bristled. 'I didn't *give in*.'

'You let him do it.'

Harris put his head against the window and mumbled with his shoulders hunched. 'I'm listening to everything he says. Watching everything he does.' For a while, the ACC stood there, true to his word. He took a white handkerchief from his pocket and blew his nose on it. Then he straightened and readjusted the knot of his tie. 'How is Reece doing? Any better than he was?'

'You mean from a mental health perspective?'

A fingerful of handkerchief disappeared up each of the ACC's nostrils in turn. Once done with, he folded the material twice in half and put it away again. 'I've never questioned his policing skills.'

Cable let the claim stand unchallenged. There was some truth in what he'd said. Harris was mostly pleased with Reece's productivity. It was the detective's methods he had more of an issue with. 'There's a noticeable improvement, I'd say.'

'His counselling sessions: he's sticking to those?'

'Yes.' Cable had her fingers crossed and hidden behind her back. 'Things have become rather more complicated since the Wellman case.'

'Complicated. How?' Harris's manner was as brusque as ever.

'There's been a blurring of lines, sir. Reece saving Miranda Beven's life, as he did, complicates things.'

Harris looked to the ceiling and blew air at it. 'Reece being involved in anything complicates things.'

Cable continued. 'What I mean is, in their previous professional relationship, Beven was in charge. Reece needed her, whether he realised it or not. There were clearly defined roles. Clearly defined boundaries. His more recent actions have turned that dynamic on its head. Miranda feels understandably indebted to him.'

Harris was concentrating on what was happening the other side of the glass. 'He's still on the Employee Wellbeing Program?'

'Absolutely.' It wasn't a total lie. Reece would continue his counselling sessions just as soon as they'd worked something out between all parties.

'Good.' Harris couldn't have got himself any closer to the glass, his full attention drawn to something Reece was in the middle of saying.

Cable watched. 'Relax, sir. He promised to be on best behaviour for this one. Even gave me his word.'

Harris's jaw sagged open as Reece shot to his feet. 'Then what the fuck is he doing now?'

'I wasn't talking to you!' Reece told the brief. 'I'm sure Billy's capable of bullshitting for himself.'

When the solicitor went to retaliate, Creed stopped him. 'Let Copper speak. He makes me laugh every time he opens his mouth.'

Reece leaned across the table towards the gangster. 'Copper's got you by the dangly bits this time, Billy, and by Christ, he's gonna squeeze them hard.'

'I didn't have you down as a closet queer.' Creed snorted. 'I suppose without a woman to hold at night, a fella's gonna resort to anything he can. Even *that.*'

Reece stood to his full height with his fists clenched.

Creed offered his tattooed face. 'Raw nerve, Copper?' He sat back, laughing, his sycophantic brief joining in.

Jenkins caught the DCI by the wrist before he could do something he shouldn't. He wouldn't have regretted it, she knew, but she stopped him all the same. 'Boss. Careful.'

Reece's head twitched, Jenkins's warning making all the difference between him calming down and leaping across the table to do Creed some serious bodily harm.

'See what I mean about him having anger issues?' Creed clicked his fingers in the air above him, trying to catch the attention of whoever was watching from behind the glass. He knew someone would be. 'Copper shouldn't be at work. He should be in a hospital for nutters. On *your* heads, be it,' the gangster shouted.

Reece sat down. Slowly. Not because of anything the arsehole opposite had said or done. Jenkins released her grip on him.

The interaction between the two detectives wasn't lost on Creed. 'Cosy, cosy. Maybe Copper's bed ain't that empty after all.' He grinned at Jenkins and blew her a kiss. 'Swing both ways when the itch gets yer, do you, darling?'

Reece felt her catch his wrist again, and heard her whisper: 'Don't.'

'Like a pair of soppy love birds,' Creed told his brief. 'Look at them holding hands.'

'What do you know about Nicky Zala?' Reece asked. He'd come to put the gangster through his paces and wasn't leaving until he had.

'Nicky works for me. Does odd jobs here and there.'

'Doing what, exactly?'

'He's a memory jogger.' The inked face crumpled under the weight of another broad grin. 'Helps people remember when their loan repayments are due.' Creed turned to his brief. 'Nicky's kind-hearted like that.'

'A hired thug, then,' Reece said.

It was the brief who answered. 'Mr Creed only attended today—'

'Because *I* said so,' Reece interrupted. 'So don't flatter yourself trying to dress it up any other way.' He turned his attention to Creed. 'Nicky Zala was found dead last night. Only streets from where your car was caught by three separate cameras.'

The brief and Creed put their heads together, their hands obscuring their mouths. They broke apart. 'My client is genuinely saddened to learn of the death of an employee.'

'I bet he is.'

The brief paused. 'Mr Creed is a respectable businessman, and that involves him travelling back and forth through the areas you've mentioned.'

'Several times a day,' Creed said, nodding.

'And on one of those occasions, a member of your own security detail was getting his face smashed in, in a nearby alley.' Reece saw the look of bubbling anger behind Creed's bloodshot eyes. 'Come on Billy, don't pretend you know nothing about it.'

Creed raised his arms at his sides, causing the brief to duck out of the way. 'I swear on my dear old mother's life, this is news to me.'

'She'll be turning in her grave at that one,' Reece said.

Creed lowered his arms, the brief making sure he was well out of the way. 'On my sister's life then.'

Reece stared. How could anyone in their right mind joke on the memory of a family member gutted by a crazed serial killer? Then again, this was Billy Creed he was talking to.

'I noticed a bit of a commotion round that way last night,' Creed said without prompting. 'Thought it might have something to do with that schoolgirl your lot have been looking for.' He grinned teasingly. 'I thinks she's dead, myself.'

Reece sat up straight. 'Isla Kosh? What do you know about her?'

Creed leaned his elbows on the table. 'Only that it's *Baine* a long time since she was last seen alive.'

Arvel Baines deeply regretted having bought the property in his own name. Doing so meant he could easily be found by anyone with the will or means. Standing impatiently at the front of that queue was going to be Billy *effing* Creed.

He stared into the aluminium bin and the dancing flames that scorched the skin of his hands and face. He was burning potentially incriminating evidence. Notes he'd made while in prison. Cryptic messages detailing the names of intended victims, together with the methods to be used in dispatching them.

But now everything had changed.

He was a fugitive. Not because the police were after him – they had no clue what was going on. It was Billy Creed who'd royally messed things up.

Baines poked the bin, avoiding fireflies of hot ash by ducking and diving like a boxer. He circled it, deep in thought.

There was still the girl to deal with. The bargaining chip that would have John Kosh do exactly as told. If he killed Isla before sentencing day, there would be no reason for Kosh to plead guilty.

Best laid plans and all that.

Billy *effing* Creed!

Reece slumped in his seat once Creed and his brief were gone, his balled fists resting on the table in front of him. Jenkins was standing against the far wall, the sole of her foot pressed against it, her head lowered to the floor. Neither of them spoke. The sound of silence almost deafening.

'What the hell did you think you were doing in here?' ACC Harris prowled in front of the desk, the overhead strip lighting making his Brylcreem'd comb-over shine more than usual. Billy Creed had been released without charge. The team made to look like the 'fools they were,' in Harris's opinion. His wandering came to a halt, but only for a moment. 'Talk to the man, I said. Not go twelve rounds with him.'

'In fairness to DCI Reece—' Cable began.

'Who asked you?' Harris demanded to know. 'I'm talking to the monkey.'

'What did you call me?' Reece twisted in his seat.

Jenkins lowered her foot and looked poised to leap if the need arose.

Cable tried once more. 'Why don't we all—'

Harris turned on her. 'Are you deaf?'

'Leave her alone.' Reece was on his feet, his fists no more relaxed. 'This is between you and me.'

Cable stepped in front of the ACC before he could react, the top of her head not quite reaching the height of his chin. 'With all due respect, sir, I—'

'Respect?' Harris lowered his face to the level of hers. 'There *is* no respect in this department. It's failing woefully and way beyond rescue as far as I'm concerned.' He raised a finger, half-cocked. 'You're going to listen to me.'

'*No!* You'll listen to me for once.' Cable was blushing, but held her ground admirably. 'These are two of the best detectives I've ever worked with.' She pointed at Reece and Jenkins. 'And I will *not* stand by and have you rubbish them.'

Harris scoffed at the comment and collected his hat from the far end of the desk. 'If you want to go down with the ship, then so be it.'

Cable glared at him as he headed towards the door. 'If that means sticking by my team, then count me in.'

Harris paused at the doorway. 'I've decided the Murder Squad is no longer fit for purpose.' He paused and let that hang. 'I'll be speaking with the chief constable first thing in the morning. You're done. All of you.'

Chapter 55

Reece listened to the second-hand make its way around the face of the plastic wall clock. Its ticking sound was somehow soothing. Like his adopted technique of counting from five back to zero. 'You didn't have to do that, ma'am.'

The other chairs were left facing in all directions, the sight obviously too much for Jenkins, who wandered over to straighten them. She'd never fully admitted to being OCD about such things, but Reece would readily wager she was.

'Oh yes, I bloody well did,' Cable said. 'We're in this together and don't you dare forget that.'

Reece smiled. It wasn't much of one, but it was a smile, nonetheless. He dragged his tired eyes away from the clock. He felt old.

Maybe it was time to roll over and let someone else in. Jenkins definitely. With a few more years and a DI promotion behind her, she'd be good to go. But for the time being, he'd steer the ship until she was ready. 'I'm big enough to fight my own battles, you know.'

Cable put her hands on her tiny hips. 'Get over it, Reece. I might be small, but I pack a hell of a punch when I get going.'

He looked to Jenkins. 'I told you she'd turn out to be all right, didn't I?'

Jenkins shook her head. 'Unbelievable.'

'Okay,' Cable said, breaking things up. 'We've a Murder Squad and missing girl to save. Let's get back upstairs and prove ACC Harris wrong.'

'Where's Ffion?' Reece couldn't see the detective constable among the assembled team. He turned to Jenkins and said: 'Haven't you two sorted that out yet?'

Jenkins's shoulders arched defensively. 'When have I had the chance? It's been manic here.'

'Problem?' Cable asked.

Jenkins answered before Reece could. 'A misunderstanding, ma'am. I'm dealing with it on my way home tonight.'

'Make sure you do,' Reece told her. 'We'll need everyone we have on this.' He used his teeth to take the top off a red marker pen and walked the length of a busy evidence board, tapping each bordered section in turn. 'Diric Ali: tortured before killed. Screams gangland. Anyone disagree?' No one did. Run of the mill killers didn't shove plastic bags over their victim's heads and drill holes in their kneecaps. 'That's all we've got so far on this one,' he conceded. 'No evidence. No witness statements. Nothing the CPS would ever entertain taking on.'

'Not so fast, boss.' Ginge waved a few sheets of A4 at him. 'I haven't had a chance to tell you this yet, what with everything that's been going on downstairs.' He came to the front of the room and handed over the updated forensic report for the Diric Ali case, including the evidence items temporarily mislaid first time round. 'And guess who's been in that flat?'

Reece read it for himself. 'You're kidding me?'

Cable pushed between them to get a better look. 'Who, for Christ's sake?'

'I knew it. Nicky Zala. The corpse in the side-street. His prints were found on the tape used to secure Diric Ali to the chair.'

'Not just his.' Ginge leaned over the chief super's head and pressed his finger to a section of text further down the page. 'This guy's as well. A Haydn Davies. And who do you think he's known to?'

Reece was grinning. 'It's like Christmas all over again. Both men, known associates of Billy Creed.'

Jenkins joined in: 'And Creed's already admitted to Zala being one of his debt collectors.'

'What are we thinking?' Cable asked. 'Diric Ali was a collection gone wrong? Zala then made an example of for his violent cock-up?'

The post mortem report on Diric Ali had concluded his heart had given in under the enormous stress his body had experienced. His attackers hadn't, in all probability, meant to kill him. They'd just gone one step too far.

'Corpses can't pay debts,' Reece said. 'Creed would have been pissed off with his goons.'

Jenkins shook her head. 'But he wouldn't have dumped the body so close to home if he was responsible.'

Reece put his hands to his hips. The vents of his suit jacket swept behind him. 'Creed is indirectly responsible for what happened to Diric Ali. I'm comfortable believing that. But for Zala's death, there's another player at large.'

'You think Ali was travelling with an accomplice?' Jenkins asked. 'Someone who caught up with Zala and killed him in retaliation?'

'Anything's possible.'

Ginge looked puzzled. 'Why do you think they were so careful with everything except the tape?'

'You ever try sticking something down with rubber gloves on?' Reece lowered the report. 'Those gloves came off only when they needed to.'

Ginge pieced it together. 'They panicked when they realised they'd killed him and dumped the drill in the wheelie bin on the way out?'

Reece chuckled. 'They were never going to be the brightest. Not working for Billy Creed.'

'It's still not enough for the CPS,' was Jenkins's opinion.

'And that's why we're not bringing Creed in again,' Reece said. 'Not just yet, anyway.' He handed the paperwork back. 'Have you circulated Ali's fingerprints to the relevant overseas agencies yet?' Ginge said he had. 'Good.' Reece tapped the board. 'And what do we have on Haydn Davies's whereabouts?'

'Zilch. He's disappeared, boss.'

'Same fate as Zala, only we haven't found him yet?' Jenkins wondered aloud.

Reece moved along to the section of board kept for the Kosh murder and abduction. 'It's possible. Likely, even.' For a while, he didn't speak. He drew a circle around John Kosh's name and stood there staring at it.

'What?' Cable asked.

'You're not going to like what I'm about to say, ma'am.'

'No change there, then.' She winked.

Reece gave in and smiled. 'Kosh didn't kill his wife. Bear with me a moment, and don't forget that it was *Kosh* himself who presented the CPS with the evidence that convicted him.'

Cable folded her arms. 'But it was our responsibility to find just as much proving otherwise.' She pointed an accusing finger. '*Your* responsibility as SIO.'

That stung. 'There hasn't been a single sensible lead regarding the girl. No sightings. Nothing.'

Cable massaged both temples at once. 'I suppose we should be grateful Kosh is still awaiting sentencing. Let's see if we can't dig ourselves out of this in time for his next court appearance.'

Reece looked across the room. 'Anything else, Ginge, before you go?'

The detective constable lowered his coffee mug and came back to stand next to the chief super, dwarfing her. 'When you were all downstairs earlier, I started going through the statements of the party guests. They're pretty much all in now.'

'Okay,' Reece said, 'let's hear what you've got.'

Ginge lowered his mug. 'The hosts remember a man arriving on his own. Someone who claimed to be living further up the street. Except, he doesn't. They've since checked.'

Reece shut his eyes. 'Why didn't they mention this before?'

'They've only just found out.'

Reece had meant the bit about the lone male being there, not the address, but he let it pass. 'Carry on.'

Ginge did. 'The man helped Kosh's wife get him home. Several people saw him waiting in the front garden, offering his services like the Good Samaritan.'

Reece's head snatched sideways. 'She let him into the house?'

'That's what the witnesses said.'

'We need a description.'

Ginge went through his paperwork. 'Like this one, you mean?' He handed over a composite likeness of the suspect. 'Thought I'd crack on and get it done while I was waiting for you all.'

Reece fought the urge to laugh and just about won that battle. 'Let's get it out there,' he said, after giving the likeness a once-over.

Halfway across the room, Ginge slowed to a halt. 'Can I tell you the bit about the van before I go?'

Reece looked at Jenkins, who appeared no wiser than he was. 'What van?'

'I've been going through CCTV images of all vehicles passing or stopping near the butcher's shop. Cross-referencing them with those seen on Isla's route home from school. If they didn't show in both places, then I put them to one side. And I didn't only do it for the day of the murder. I did for every day of the previous week, as well.'

'That must have been a right balls ache?' Reece said. 'What did you find?'

Ginge went through his paperwork, spilling some of it on the floor. The rest, he held aloft, like a ring-card girl at a boxing match. There were four grainy black and white photographs. 'This first one shows a white van on the school route. The camera's looking downward and the driver's got a hat on, so you can't see his face.' He moved the photograph to the back of the pile. 'This one here shows the same van parked in the street around the corner from the butcher's. You're going to like these next ones, boss. There's our driver in the hat, stood on the road, locking his van. Then this . . .'

Reece took the last photograph from his junior. The driver was on the pavement, a bit further along from the parked vehicle, staring through the butcher's window. 'Ginge, I could kiss you.'

Ginge took a step rearward, much to everyone's amusement. 'That van's registered to a window cleaner in Pontypridd. I've checked.'

'Previous?'

'Nothing I can find on the system.'

That made no difference to Reece. 'Bring him in for questioning. I want every inch of that vehicle gone over by Sioned's team.'

The chief super agreed. 'Shall *I* go make the relevant calls to the people at the Ponty station? We don't want to come across as pissing on anyone's chips.'

'You do that,' Reece told her.

'And the rest of us?' Jenkins wanted to know.

'You're going to lead the team bringing that window cleaner in.'

Checking the time on her phone, Jenkins said, 'I was thinking of calling by Ffion's to get that other thing sorted.'

Reece shook his head. 'It'll have to wait. This is way more important.'

Chapter 56

CREED SHIFTED POSITION IN the front passenger seat of the BMW. Jimmy Chin was at the wheel. The recipient of the gangster's latest outburst was his legal brief, cowering in the back. 'I don't care how you manage it,' Creed said. 'You find out.'

The subject of their conversation was Arvel Baines's current address. Where the ex-con was likely to be holed up and hiding. The place where the '*annoying fucke*r' was soon to be nailed to his own front door and '*gutted like a river trout.*'

'Finding him isn't the difficult bit,' the solicitor replied. 'But not leaving a trail back to us, is.'

'Tough!' Creed snarled. 'We find him before Copper does.' He opened the glovebox and reached inside. Only moments later, he was brandishing a loaded handgun in the moving vehicle. 'I want both of them dead. And I don't give a fuck in which order it happens.'

They'd wasted no time at all. Isla Kosh's life was hanging in the balance. Chief Superintendent Cable had long since made the call to her equivalent at the Pontypridd station – a professional courtesy rather than absolute necessity.

When the *Big Red Key*—the nickname given to the solid steel battering ram—hit just below the letterbox of the door, it had the sole occupant of the property come running down the stairs with a towel wrapped around his pot-belly. 'What the—?'

'Police!' Jenkins pointed a finger at arm's length. 'Stay where you are.'

The window cleaner stepped off the bottom stair. 'Look at my door.' The thing had split up the middle. A small rectangle of coloured glass lying broken on the mat inside.

'I said, stay put.'

'And *I* said, look at my front door.' He tried pushing past. 'You're paying to have that replaced.' Jenkins caught his wrist, spun him round, and drove his arm up his back. '*Aargh!*' he screamed. 'You fuckers must be on drugs?' His face was squashed against the wall, his mouth forced open, baring his teeth. 'I'm running a—'

'Quiet.' Jenkins let the man go once she had a pair of cuffs on him. 'Is there anyone else at home?'

'Just me. Look, what's this all—'

Jenkins turned away before he could finish. 'Go check,' she told the army of uniforms accompanying her. 'Shed and garden as well.' They went off to clear the ground floor first, leaving her with the suspect and one other police officer. She was cautioning the window cleaner when the first drips of water came through the plasterboard ceiling.'

The man shook his head. 'I tried telling you. I was running a bath, you stupid cow.'

'Your lot'll be paying to have that ceiling redone,' the window cleaner said with a snort. 'And the floor.' He turned to the duty solicitor. 'That laminate wasn't cheap crap, you know.'

Reece was busy comparing the CCTV images supplied by Ginge with the man sitting opposite. There must have been a good four or five stones in weight difference between the two of them. 'We'll see.'

The man's eyes bulged. 'I'm a fucking window cleaner, not Rockefeller. You'll do more than *see*, I can tell you.'

'Language,' Jenkins told him.

He banged himself against the back of his seat in protest. 'You smashed down my front door.' He caught hold of the solicitor's forearm and shook it. 'I'd nearly forgotten about that. Put a door on the list. And some compo for PTSD while you're at it.'

'You could have told us you were running a bath,' Jenkins said.

'I tried, but you were too busy throttling me.' The window cleaner rubbed the front of his neck. 'Papers are going to have a field day over this.' He counted them off on his fingers. 'Sun, Star, Daily Shite–'

'Throttle you? It was hardly that.'

'Had me in a choke hold, she did. Put that down as well,' he told the solicitor. 'I'm suing her for assault.'

Reece was on his feet before Jenkins could defend herself.

'Where's *he* going?' the window cleaner asked. 'I'm not finished yet.'

'You're free to go,' Reece said over his shoulder. 'Jenkins. My office. Now.'

Chapter 57

ELAN JENKINS WAS FUMING after being torn a strip by the boss. She marched across the near-empty car park, kicking at small stones whenever she came upon them. So, the window cleaner was bigger than the man in the CCTV footage outside the butcher's shop. Was she supposed to have taken a set of bathroom scales with her? Weigh and measure the chubby sod before cautioning him?

She slammed the car door. Again, when the metal fastener of the seatbelt caught in it. With the aid of an overhead light, she examined the jagged scrape in the paintwork. Lowering her head, she whispered: 'And there's still Ffion to go.'

The car door closed without further mishap; the engine turning over on the first attempt. She sat there, revving it. From her vantage point, she could see a light in Reece's office window. She had no idea for how long he'd stay behind, and given the mood she was in, she didn't give a toss.

Pulling away from the parking space, she reached to put the radio on. Turned a single knob to bring the device to life. No Stubby screwdriver in sight. No Russian newsreader. No hiss of static. Chew on that, Reece.

Mariah Carey had hardly got going when she was rudely interrupted by a shrill ringtone. Jenkins slowed and hit speakerphone. 'Cara. Hi.'

'You're late.' The statement wasn't laced with deep suspicion, nor accusatory innuendo like those spoken by her ex, Belle Gillighan. Still, it made Jenkins shiver with the memories it provoked.

'I've got one more thing to do, then I'm on my way home.' Their shared home. She'd let Cara Frost move in at last, but hadn't yet told anyone at work. She wanted to wait and see how it all panned out first.

'You're working far too hard,' Frost said.

'Says you.'

'It's true.'

'I need to go sort something out with Ffion. I'll tell you about it when I get in.'

'Sounds intriguing.'

'Embarrassing is the word *I'd* use.'

'I want all the gory details.' Frost giggled. 'There's a lasagne browning in the oven. Text me when you're done and I'll put the garlic bread in.'

'Right you are.'

It was getting late. There was little traffic on the roads. Ten minutes tops and she'd be at Ffion Morgan's house.

She pressed the doorbell and waited. No *Big Red Key* required on this occasion. She was nervous.

Morgan opened the door dressed in tartan pyjamas with matching slippers. At first, she said nothing.

'Can I come in?' Jenkins asked.

'It's late.'

'Please.'

The door opened wider, Morgan stepping aside to let her pass.

The place was warm and smelled of toast. 'Thanks,' Jenkins said. It didn't sound right. She stopped, readying herself to say more, but didn't. Morgan hadn't moved. Her head was held in both hands. She was sobbing and sliding down the painted wall to squat on the doormat. Jenkins was there in an instant and got down on her knees. 'Oh, Ffion.'

'I overreacted, Jenks. I'm so sorry.'

'It was my fault. I shouldn't have gone through your search history. You had every right to be pissed off with me.'

'Deep down, I was hoping you would. I had no one else to talk to.'

Jenkins looked along the hallway to the front room. She could hear a TV playing in the background. 'Is Josh in there?'

Morgan's eyes and lips pressed closed.

'He hasn't gone and left you because of this? The *bastard!*'

'I made him go. It was my decision, not his.'

'Ffion, why? Now, of all times?'

'I'm having a double mastectomy . . .'

Jenkins shook her head. 'So?'

'You think he'll still want me after that?'

'I bloody well do. He loves you, Ffi. Don't shut him out.'

Morgan dabbed her eyes with a handful of paper tissues. 'Too late now.'

'It's not. You want me to call him?' Jenkins reached into her jacket pocket.

'Leave it.' Morgan pushed her colleague's hand away. 'Later maybe. Look, my brain is like a scrambled egg right now. I don't know what the hell I'm doing.'

'I'm not surprised.' There was an awkward pause. 'Can I put the kettle on?' Jenkins asked. 'I'm as dry as the boss's wit.'

That brought something of a smile. The early makings of one, at least. 'Go on then. But no mumsy lectures today.'

'Mumsy. *Me?*' Jenkins led Morgan by the damp sleeve of her pyjamas. In the living room, she took hold of the television remote control and muted the sound. 'Sit. I'll do the tea.' With the kettle filled with fresh water, she got the milk from the fridge. 'Where's Josh staying?'

'He's on a mate's sofa. One of the boys he plays rugby with.'

Jenkins could see a kit bag over in the corner of the utility room. A pair of dirty boots poking out of the top of it. Maybe Josh wasn't planning on being away for very long. 'You still not taking sugar in tea?' Jenkins asked, lifting the lid off the tin and reapplying it.

Morgan puffed her cheeks. 'Sod it. Stick a couple in. I'll be losing a few pounds when these come off.' Jenkins thought she heard an attempt at a laugh, but when she re-entered the living room, Morgan was hugging a cushion. Sobbing. 'Why me, Jenks? What have *I* ever done to anyone?'

What was there to say in reply? Jenkins couldn't think of much.

Morgan caught her by the wrists once the mugs of tea were resting safely on a table. 'I didn't mean I wanted someone else to get cancer instead. I just meant—'

They hugged. 'I know what you meant.' There were no words. They rocked gently back and forth together. 'When is the operation?'

'There's a period of counselling first.' Morgan pulled away slowly, dried her eyes, and blew her nose. 'The first phase of that begins next week.'

Chapter 58

JOHN KOSH HAD NO real interest in playing a game of pool before the evening lock down. No matter how much his cellmate Sykes tried persuading him otherwise, he was content to have a *night in* and keep out of harm's way.

'Just one frame,' Sykes promised. 'It'll help pass the time.'

'I'm fine here.'

'Once that judge slaps you with a twenty to thirty stretch, you'll be begging for things to do.'

'He won't send me down,' Kosh said confidently. 'I've got plans on that front.' And he did. But now wasn't the time to share them. Especially with a man he'd only just met.

'That's what everyone in here thinks. You mark my words, you'll be an old codger before you get out of this place.'

'Kosh slapped the newspaper down and rolled onto his side on the bottom bunk. 'Will you leave me alone if I give you one game?'

Sykes clapped his hands and stood one-legged in the doorway. 'You want to play for canteen?' *Canteen* was the term used for additional food items and confectionery bought by a prisoner with their weekly wages. It was the highlight of the prison week, and all hell broke loose whenever it was late, or if any of it got *mislaid* on its way there.

'Who's downstairs?' Kosh asked. It helped to know. Especially with him being a marked man.

'The usual suspects.'

Kosh pushed through the cell doorway and peered over the balcony. It seemed safe enough. There were a couple of screws at the foot of the steps. Stood there chatting. 'Who's turn is it to break?' he asked, leading the way.

Sykes didn't answer.

When Kosh turned, they came at him through one of the cell doors on the landing. Sykes shoved him towards them. Kosh was still shouting for help when the searing-hot fluid soaked his back. He'd been hit with boiling water and sugar—napalmed—and was immediately sent well beyond the realms of any pain he'd previously known.

The scorching fluid went straight through the material of his thin T-shirt, congealing into a scalding paste that clung to his skin, holding in the heat, making his flesh bubble and peel away in sheets. He was gasping for breath and vomiting simultaneously. Bile burned his throat, but was no match for what was happening to his back.

There was shouting. Banging and loud cheering. Most of it drowned out by the wailing noise of an overhead siren. Heavy footfall came up the metal steps and across the landing. What was taking the screws so long?

John Kosh managed to remain conscious only until the first of them appeared. He saw shiny boots and thought he heard their owner say: '*Fuck,* I knew it was gonna be him.' After that, he was aware of nothing else until he woke up in the medical wing some time later.

Kosh was lying on his belly with a paper mâché vomit bowl resting on a low stool on the left-hand side of the examination couch. There was an orange-coloured cannula in the back of his hand, connected to a bag of fluid hanging above his head.

They'd already given him morphine. That's what they kept telling him whenever he complained of pain. Which was pretty much all the time.

They'd also given him medicines to help with the sickness. But those were as useless as the morphine was.

There were people fussing. A doctor and nurse attending to his wounds. He caught snippets of what they were saying, and none of it sounded good. 'Swansea . . . Months . . . Skin grafts . . .' He closed his ears to the rest.

The governor was in there with him, questioning the two screws he'd seen talking at the foot of the stairs.

He heard someone mention 'hospital' for the umpteenth time. It might have been the governor. There was also something about the ambulance being delayed. That was probably the doctor. Could have been the nurse. Kosh didn't know which. The pain, the morphine, and nausea were making it next to impossible for him to focus on what was going on. And there was a lot going on.

Chapter 59

Reece regretted having earlier had a go at Jenkins over the window cleaner thing. He'd ordered her to bring the man in for questioning, and that's exactly what she did. Had she not done so, he'd have chewed her ear for that as well. She couldn't win.

His thoughts wandered to Isla Kosh. It was highly unlikely the girl was still alive. That's what experience told him. Almost a week to the day she'd gone missing and there hadn't been a single sighting, except from the usual nutters reporting witnessed alien abduction.

Nope. There were no leads to a body or living person.

He felt heavy on his feet, pounding the pavement as though wearing working boots and not the expensive running shoes he had on. But at least it was dry for once. Milder too. He'd taken a route through the City of Llandaff. Across the wide expanse of Western Avenue, then a gentle climb past Howell's Independent School. A left turn had him heading down Pen-Hill Road towards the Sport Wales National Centre in Sophia Gardens.

The pavements were getting busier the closer he got to the city. On a few occasions, he was forced out onto the road by groups of people who either didn't or wouldn't get out of his way.

'Brân.'

At first, he didn't recognise it as someone calling his name.

'Brân. I'm over here.'

He stopped and looked back along the pavement towards the Cricketers pub. There was a woman stood in the beer garden waving her arm at him. 'Miranda?' He didn't want to do this, but could see no way out. He walked towards her, his head held low, trying to think of an excuse for letting her down the other night.

She approached, dressed in a long black coat. Even with a minimal application of makeup, she looked stunning. Elegant. 'Apologies for interrupting your run.'

Reece wished she'd let him jog on past. It would have saved them both the awkward moment. 'That's okay. I could do with the rest. It's been one of those days. One of those weeks, in fact.' He was dripping with sweat and added some extra distance between them. 'How are you?'

'Better,' she said. 'I've been following the news. You're still no closer to finding the girl?'

He shook his head. 'You don't need me telling you what the likely outcome of this is going to be.' He thought about sitting on the wooden picnic bench, but decided against leaving a wet patch for others to find. Raising the front of his damp T-shirt, he wiped sweat from his face, exposing a toned abdomen. 'Sorry, I don't carry a towel.'

'That's quite all right.' Beven smiled at him. 'You obviously look after yourself.'

Awkward. What to say next. 'I'm sorry about . . .' That seemed like a fair enough place to start.

'For what?'

Ah, don't drag this out. Please. It's hard enough for me as it is. 'For my no-show the other night.'

'No-show for the show.' Beven forced the giggle, Reece could tell.

'I should have called you back. Given you an explanation for why I couldn't come.'

'Was it something to do with the case?' She put a hand on his forearm. He didn't pull away. 'You probably can't tell me. I shouldn't have asked.'

He thought about lying. Telling her they'd got a lead that went nowhere. He closed his eyes, thinking it might make things easier. It didn't. 'I'm not ready for that yet.' It was out, and he felt better for saying it.

Beven looked confused. 'I thought you'd enjoy the concert?'

'And I would have done. It was a lovely gesture.' He stepped off the path to let someone pass. The man slowed as he approached with a drink in both hands. 'It's just that—'

Beven turned to take a glass. 'Oh, sorry, would you like a drink? Won't you join us for one?'

The newcomer gave Reece a look of apology. 'I didn't realise—'

Reece held his hand up in response, and was already reversing away. 'No problem. I best be going.'

'Brân.'

He could hear Beven calling his name.

'Brân!'

He didn't—couldn't—turn to face her. On the pavement, he broke into a jog. By the time he was crossing the junction with the next street, he was just about sprinting.

Chapter 60

They pulled into the hospital grounds, Reece with one hand on the steering wheel, the other grinding the gears from fourth to second in one awkward movement. 'Look out for the car park,' he said, shifting his gaze left and right. 'They've changed this bit since I last visited.'

They went over a hump in the road, the Peugeot's chassis and suspension making horrible noises as they rose and fell like the riders of a fairground carousel. Jenkins gripped the plastic strap above her head and rocked with the car's momentum. There was no point in fighting it. 'Shit.'

'What?'

'It's broken. Come away on one side.' She lowered her arm to leave the strap hanging like a loose tooth from the sagging roof lining. There was a short screw poking out of the lower end of it. As they watched, it worked itself loose and fell into her lap.

Reece glared at her. 'How the hell did you manage that?'

'It wasn't on purpose. It just happened when I pulled on it.'

'You're not meant to hang from the roof like a bloody chimpanzee.'

'If you weren't driving so fast, I wouldn't have to hang from anything!'

They were in Swansea, not Cardiff on this occasion. At Morriston Hospital and the burns unit for the entire South-West of the United Kingdom.

Reece had earlier got Ginge to ring the prison to arrange a meeting with John Kosh. He wanted to tell the prisoner that they knew about the impostor at the party. The man who'd claimed to live further up the street, but didn't. The man who'd helped Helen get him home before murdering her and kidnapping their daughter, Isla.

As soon as Reece got wind that something wasn't right, he'd snatched the handset from the detective constable and continued the conversation himself. The governor informed him of the head-butt incident involving Meth Mouth. The retaliatory *napalm* assault, including the extent of John Kosh's injuries, and the need to transfer him to Swansea for urgent medical treatment.

Jenkins slapped the dashboard. '*Ambulance!*' she squealed, turning her head away from the impending impact.

'I know!' Reece brought the car to a sliding stop, its front end pulling to the left when he braked hard. They were as close to a string of parked cars as they could have been without contacting them. As the ambulance crawled past, its side window came down, an angry-looking face appearing from within. 'And you, Pal,' Reece said, moving off again. More slowly this time.

Jenkins had her hand held to her mouth. The other one was still glued to the dashboard. 'We haven't got out of the car yet.'

Reece used the rear-view mirror to watch the emergency vehicle recede in size. 'What did you say?' He turned to look at her when he could no longer see it.

'We've only just arrived and already you've almost got yourself into a fight.'

'It wasn't a fight.' Reece's eyes rolled in his head. 'Why do you always have to exaggerate?'

'That paramedic threatened to take you to the Emergency Department in the back of his van.'

'I'd like to see him try.'

'Over there.' Jenkins pointed. 'The car park.'

When Reece first clapped eyes on John Kosh, he didn't expect to glean much in the way of useful information from the man. It looked as though the detectives might have made a wasted journey from the capitol.

That's what Jenkins thought, too. She'd said as much as soon as they'd stepped into the cubicle on the Burns Unit. It smelled in there. Of antiseptic. Stale bandages. And something else. Reece didn't work too hard on trying to imagine what that might be. That's not why he'd come.

The attending nurse told them that Kosh had been in theatre for a large part of the night. To remove bits of T-shirt from the raw wound, and properly clean and dress it. He'd been given a fair amount of morphine-based painkillers and had since been in and out of wakefulness.

'Will he be okay?' Reece asked. Even though he'd warned Kosh about keeping his head down in prison, he couldn't help but feel some responsibility for him being incarcerated in the first place. Chief Superintendent Cable had been right when she'd said they should have done more to prevent it.

He put the awkward thought to one side for the time being and approached the bed. Kosh's eyes were closed, the man mumbling to himself. 'John, it's DCI Reece.' When he got no answer, he glanced at the nurse. She didn't stop him. He tried again. 'John, we know you didn't harm your wife and daughter.' There was a flicker of Kosh's eyelids. The mumbling hadn't stopped, but was quieter. 'John. It's Brân Reece. This is DS Elan Jenkins. Do you remember us?' Reece turned his head to his partner. It was a wasted journey, after all. He was about to come away from the bedside and decide what best to do next, when Kosh said something. 'Can I give him some water?' Reece asked the nurse. 'He says he's thirsty.'

She checked the time on a fob watch and nodded. 'Just wet his mouth for now, he's not long back from surgery.'

'Don't gulp it,' Reece said, holding the plastic glass to one side of John Kosh's mouth. 'You up to talking yet?'

Kosh had his eyes closed. He swallowed. Grimaced, and rolled his head to one side. 'My throat's sore.'

'That'll be the breathing tube,' the nurse said from the other end of the cubicle. She was making entries on observation charts and checking the volumes of various drip fluids. 'It'll get better as the day goes on.'

Kosh asked for more water. Reece didn't check before offering it. 'Do you understand why we're here, John?'

'You've wasted your time,' Kosh croaked. 'There's nothing more to say.'

'You were set up. We know that now.' Reece gave Jenkins a brief glance.

Kosh moved and squealed with pain. 'You don't know what you're talking about.'

Reece perched on the edge of the bed, but only for the time it took the nurse to notice his indiscretion.

'Don't do that,' she said, almost pouncing on him. 'It increases the infection risk.'

Reece got up and didn't dare argue. He repositioned himself a full stride away from the side of the bed. 'It's true I don't know the ins and outs. Not yet. But it's obvious that someone is working overtime to ruin your life.'

Kosh didn't look at him and stared straight ahead. 'There's no one else involved.'

Jenkins handed Reece a large brown envelope. He removed several black and white photographs, and said: 'These suggest otherwise.' He presented each to Kosh in turn. 'This man here has been watching you. He's been driving Isla's school route as well.' He gave Kosh a moment to digest that. 'Why would he be doing such a thing, John? Who is he? Who've you pissed off?'

Kosh's head flopped to its *look away* position on the pillow. 'I've never seen him before.'

Reece slapped the back of his hand against one of the photographs. 'He's watching you through the shop window.' The black and white got another slap. '*Watching you!*'

'He might've been pricing meat.' Kosh attempted a laugh but failed miserably. He swallowed and grimaced simultaneously.

Reece shut his eyes and counted from five back to zero. It was all he had to stop himself throttling the man. 'He was at the party. No one else knew him. He was there for *you*. He spiked your drink and helped Helen take you home. We've got tox reports and written statements to that effect.'

Kosh's head turned towards Reece. 'Helen let him into our home?' That was Kosh's first acknowledgement of there being someone else present.

The chase was on. The prey in Brân Reece's sights. It was now only a matter of lining up the cross hairs and pulling the trigger. 'That's right. Helen let him in.'

'She died because of me?' The whisper was soon a series of sobbing noises. Kosh was moving. So was the nurse. The race unfair; the woman having further to travel.

'Stay where you are, John.' She was trying to reach the bed in time. 'Don't!' Too late, Kosh had ripped the cannula out of the back of his hand, drip fluid and a fair amount of blood soaking into the otherwise white sheets.

Reece put his hands on Kosh's shoulders, pressing him against the mattress.

'Get off me.'

The nurse hit the emergency call bell, and just after that, both detectives were instructed to leave.

Chapter 61

They visited the hospital canteen to await a call telling them that John Kosh and his soiled bed had been dealt with. Reece had his hands in his pockets and wasn't saying much.

'You almost had him then.' Jenkins lifted the lid on her paper cup and blew on her coffee. 'He was going to tell us, I think.'

Reece nodded absentmindedly. 'Maybe I should have trod a little lighter?'

Jenkins's coffee was still giving her cause for concern. 'Bloody scalding, this,' she said, taking the lid off completely.

'Better that than the lukewarm dishwater we get back at the station.'

'At least you can drink that stuff. This, on the other hand . . .' She put the cup on a table. 'I think if you'd gone any easier on him, he'd have carried on with the bullshit.'

'Maybe.' Reece was making his way towards a vending machine against the far wall. 'You want chocolate?' There was a rubber plant on one side of the machine. On the other, a row of bins in varying colours. They were marked: *General Waste, Glass, Plastic, Paper.* He waited for a staff nurse to collect her bag of Quavers and fed coins into the slot once he'd made his choice. 'Nothing for you?'

Jenkins shook her head and gave the lava another try.

'Any better?' he asked when he got back.' Silence and a wafting hand told him it wasn't. 'Have half a Bounty with me.' He offered the bit that was still in the wrapper.

'I wouldn't be able to taste it. This stuff's taken the roof off my mouth.' Jenkins sat down on a moulded plastic seat attached to a bench-like table. 'I saw Ffion yesterday.'

'How was she?' Reece put the whole second half of the chocolate bar in his mouth, rolling the wrapper into a ball when he was done with it. The bins were too far off to give it a try. Besides, they all had lids. He tucked the wrapper away in his trouser pocket. When Jenkins got to the bit about a double mastectomy, she had his full attention. 'Jesus,' he managed, spitting a few flecks of coconut at her. It started him coughing. Washing it down with hot coffee had him swearing again. 'I see what you mean about this stuff.'

'I'm still numb.' Jenkins raised her head to the ceiling. 'I can't imagine how Ffion's feeling.'

'Will she go through with it, do you think?' Reece asked, just managing to bring the coughing under control.

'The operation is at the tail-end of next week.'

'Next *week!*' He lowered his voice. 'That soon?'

'She's going to ring you about sick leave. There's counselling first.'

'Would talking to Miranda Beven help?'

'Ffion's not going to change her mind. She's far too stubborn for that.'

'I meant for the good of her head.'

'And was Miranda good for yours?'

Reece gave that thought. 'She's helped me deal with things. Yes.'

'Any chance of it becoming something more than that?' Jenkins gave him one eye and the makings of a grin.

Reece sat down opposite and got comfortable before answering. 'I never did get round to telling you about my flat tyres, did I?'

After returning to the cubicle on the Burns Unit to finish speaking with John Kosh, Reece and Jenkins had returned to Cardiff. 'Nobody outside these four walls is to get wind of what Kosh told us,' Reece said, sitting at the head of the table in the Cardiff Bay briefing room. 'Isla's life depends on the killer having no clue we know about him.'

'What about the nurse?' One detective asked. 'You said she was in and out of that cubicle the whole time. What if she talks to the newspapers for some extra cash?'

'She wasn't in there when we took Kosh's statement. We made sure of that.'

Jenkins chimed in: 'And she was warned of the consequences of mentioning anything she might have heard before then.'

'We'll need to get that statement off to the CPS, as soon as,' Cable said. 'But they're likely to question the timing of its collection.' She removed her spectacles and put them in her lap. 'You said Kosh was high on morphine.'

'Not high.' Reece looked at Jenkins. 'He was okay, wasn't he?'

'Most of the time.'

Cable nodded. 'I guess we've enough witness statements placing the stranger at his house and at the right time.' She held crossed fingers in the air. 'It'll add validity to his change of story.'

'The CPS will take it,' Reece said confidently. 'They'll have to. There's far too much new evidence to ignore. We've got CCTV footage, witness statements, and—'

'But still no girl.' Cable massaged the bridge of her nose before replacing her spectacles. 'It's been a week since young Isla was taken.'

'We're getting closer,' Reece said. 'And this new information could make all the difference.'

'Do you believe Kosh when he says he's no clue as to the man's identity?'

Reece did. 'Kosh wants Isla found, ma'am. That's not happening if he keeps playing games with us. I'd say he's being straight this time.' Reece looked left and right along the table. 'Where's Ginge? He's supposed to be here. Anyone seen him?'

Jenkins shrugged. 'Not since we got back from Swansea.'

'Ginge.' That usually worked. '*Ginge!*'

'Coming, boss.' There was what sounded like a stampeding horse travelling along the landing outside. The detective constable doubled over in the doorway when he got there, a cardboard box marked **POLICE EVIDENCE** grasped in his sweaty hands. He was panting and smiling at the same time. 'You're gonna love this.'

Chapter 62

It wasn't the sound of a helicopter's engine that caught Arvel Baines's attention. It was the deep throaty grunt of a BMW M-Sport travelling at speed through the winding country lanes.

It was getting louder.

That meant, closer.

They'd found him. Not the police—that would have been the preferred option—but Billy Creed and his band of un-merry men. The long and short of it was, Baines was in trouble and knew he had to get well away from there, and fast. To stay put and bullshit any further was tantamount to suicide.

For a moment, his skittish movements resembled those of a spooked squirrel. Turning in circles. Chasing its tail. Going first left, then right. Repeating the dance once completed. There wasn't time to get across and open the barn door. To start the van and reverse it out of there. Even if there was, he'd then have to drive down the same road the BMW was travelling. There would be no room to get past. It would be suicide, even to try. Simple as.

What was the alternative? What could he do to extend his time alive?

When he ran for the basement, he had little idea why that was. He was wasting time going that way. Risking getting himself caught and killed. He should have been heading out into the forest, making his escape and putting as much distance between himself and a horrible death as he possibly could.

But now he was rattling around in a dark room. Frantic. There for the girl, but with no idea why her safety should matter so much to him.

He'd have killed her himself at some point.

Wouldn't he?

Yes.

No.

The answer to that changed daily and had been a major cause of angst.

He smashed through the closed door with what was a painful shoulder charge. 'Get up! On your feet!' He was shouting and needed to be.

Isla had no time to respond with anything sensible. She rubbed her eyes and did as she was told.

Baines worked a round key in the padlock, his trembling hands causing him to miss on the first few attempts. The chain pulled through the bull-ring attachment with the wall, one end recoiling onto the floor, the other slipping through fastenings on the girl's leather wrist straps. 'Come on. We're getting out of here.'

'Where?' Isla was fully awake now and looking more frightened than usual.

He shoved her towards the broken door without explanation. '*Move!*'

She put a hand to the frame and used it to push against him, unwilling to pass through and experience whatever horrors lay in wait on the other side. 'You're scaring me.'

'I don't come anywhere close to what's out there.' Grabbing her by the scruff of her sweatshirt, he swung her counterclockwise, forcing her against the wall. He put his wet forehead against hers, breathing what should have been her air. 'They've come to kill us.'

'Who has? Oh, my God. My shoes.' Isla bent, swiped, and missed them when he yanked her away.

Baines was on the move again, pushing her on ahead. Up the steps and across the dirty tiled floor. It was slippery, both of them unsure of their footing. Isla more so, jogging on bare skin. Baines stopped to look out of the dirty kitchen window. The BMW was drawing to a halt on a grass verge. There were three men he could see from where he was. Creed, Chin, and someone suitably big and ugly sitting in the back seat.

The passenger door opened, a booted foot reaching for the same patch of earth the wooden butt of a shotgun rested on.

He needed to see no more than that. His next shove almost toppled the girl. Holding her upright, he went through the rest of the house like a Special Forces operative extracting a hostage from a building.

They went out the back way. It made sense. Creed and the hired help were coming from the front.

Isla got little reply to anything she asked.

There was a sudden explosion of loud noise at the front door. Not the discharge of a gunshot, but a heavy boot putting the woodwork through. That would be Jimmy Chin. Not Billy Creed. He no longer had it in him.

Baines could hear voices and thought he heard Creed shout: 'Wendy, I'm home,' up the empty hallway.

Funny, under different circumstances.

But not these.

There was nothing humorous to be had in any of this. 'Run for the forest and don't stop if anything happens to me.' Being truthful with himself, he'd known from the get-go he wouldn't be able to kill her. Had only kidded himself into thinking he might. He wasn't like Sykes. Not a child killer.

And the girl *was* just a kid. She wouldn't thank him for saying so. Wouldn't be at all grateful for anything he'd done. And by God, he'd done enough. All that was left for him now was to stop Billy Creed getting his mucky paws on her.

Isla stumbled. She hadn't been on her feet for any longer than a few minutes each day, other than to use her pee bucket or take the briefest of cold showers. The rest of the time she'd spent lying down. She also bordered on being malnourished. Unlike the rat, who'd likely gone up a full belt size since the girl's arrival. 'I can't go any further,' she said, dropping onto her knees in the dirt.

Baines grabbed handfuls of her clothing and pulled her onto her feet, spittle spraying from his mouth as he screamed: 'Do you want to die like your mother did?' He wasn't wearing his balaclava. Hadn't had time to bring it with him. He could see the girl's eyes travelling every inch of his face. Committing the features to memory. Struggling to comprehend his last words uttered.

She was hanging from the end of his arm, her jaw sagging as she wailed: '*Mum!*' She shook her head. Shook all over. Became a dead weight that refused to budge from where she was.

Baines couldn't see Creed. The gangster must have been lagging behind on his knackered knee. But Chin and Ugly were already out of the cottage. Coming up the broken path in a jog, Chin pointing and shouting in their direction.

'You're lying!' Isla was hysterical and slapped and clawed at Baines with her free hand. 'Not Mum. Not *Mum!*'

'It's true.' He was invading her space again. 'And we're next if you don't pull yourself together.' When she made no effort to move, he contemplated pushing her over and getting out of there. She was slowing him down and now also knew what he looked like. 'Fuck you, Creed. Fuck you for ruining everything I had planned.'

Creed wouldn't have heard him.

But Isla did. She was bent over with her face hovering only inches above the dirt. 'Who's Creed? Is that him? Did he . . .' She was wailing again: '*Muuum!*'

When Baines next looked, the two men were gone. No sign of them anywhere. He scoured the area near the smallholding. Then further afield. Nothing. They'd vanished.

Isla straightened. 'How?' It sounded as though the word had been summoned from deep within her soul. She pushed herself onto feet that were dirty, cold, and marked with the efforts of running more than a hundred metres without shoes. She sniffed and wiped her nose with the back of a hand. Cleared her vision with the fingers of the other one. 'You show me which one of them did it,' she said, grabbing a small rock from the path. 'You *fucking* show me.'

Baines found it next to impossible to look into her eyes. 'I can't.'

'Who are you?'

When he didn't answer, she repeated the question. He knew she was staring, and pointed to where he'd last seen Creed's men. 'They must have gone back for the car.'

'Are you the police?' Isla asked. 'That's some sort of safe house, isn't it? Is dad in trouble with those men?' The questions came thick and fast.

'Ssh.' Baines could hear the BMW's engine growling somewhere off in the distance. 'Yeah, I'm the police. You can trust me.'

Chapter 63

Billy Creed ground his teeth and balled his fists. The BMW's dashboard got another heavy wallop, a sizable chunk of plastic from the air vent snapping free. 'I knew that lying toerag hadn't killed her. The man doesn't have the balls for it.' He leaned in close to Jimmy Chin's ear—considered biting the thing off, he was so angry—and said: 'Neither of them are getting out of these woods alive. You got me?'

Chin's sovereign-ringed fingers gripped the steering wheel as the BMW roared its way into the forest – moss, grass, and grit all spewing out from under its wide rear tyres.

While Baines was trying to run, Isla was doing little more than a hop, skip and jump. 'Come on!' he pleaded. 'They'll be here soon.'

'I can't. My feet.' She got another heavy shove in the back for her protests.

There were several paths through the forest. Baines had walked some of them during quieter times. Most of them converging onto a single route out of there, a mile or two further on.

A stick broke with a loud crack beneath Isla's foot. She screamed and lifted her leg. 'I'm cut,' she said, dusting yellowed pine needles off it to get a better look. There was a jagged bit of splinter poking out of the soft pad of flesh near her toes, a zig-zag of blood trickling along the underside of the bruised foot.

'Let me see.'

She looked unsure and kept her distance. 'Why did you have me chained up, if you're the police?'

'Your foot. We need to get that out.'

'I asked you a question. You had me chained to a *fucking* wall for days.' She lowered her foot. 'What kind of policeman does that?'

Baines was still keeping an eye out for the car. 'We've got minutes at most.'

'Keep away from me.' When he didn't, Isla threw a rock and missed.

He caught hold of her. Went for her leg and gripped it like a farrier shoeing a horse. 'Keep still.' She was wobbling and holding onto him in an attempt to not fall over. The BMW hadn't stopped grunting. It was like a wild bear hunting them through the trees. Fortunately, it couldn't stray far from the rutted woodland paths like a bear might. Baines tightened his grip when Isla struggled to get free. The splinter came away, but he wasn't certain he'd got it all. 'It's time to go.'

'It hurts.'

He was doing the special ops thing again. Pushing her through the trees, ninety degrees to any route the vehicle could take.

'Get off me.' Isla swung an arm and caught him above the left ear. She clawed at it, dragging her nails along his cheek.

'*Bitch!*' He backhanded her and wiped blood from his cheek. It stung. If he was going to kill her, then this was the time he'd most likely do it. He leaned over her and reached for a large rock. Held it above his head, ready to smash it into her face. '*I* killed your mother, not them.' He dropped the rock harmlessly to one side and came away with a hand held to his face. 'I'll leave it to your father to tell you why.'

Isla tried to get up, but lost her footing. She reached for a fallen branch and swiped at him. He was out of range. She missed.

'You're on your own, kid.' And with that, Arvel Baines dusted himself off and fled.

Chapter 64

REECE HAD PEOPLE CLEAR the briefing table to make room for the contents of Ginge's lidded boxes. Coffee mugs and half-eaten sandwiches were temporarily shoved to one side, or binned. 'Is this what you've been up to all day?' Reece asked as the young detective constable arranged the paperwork in orderly piles.

Ginge didn't look up from what he was doing and was quite obviously a man on a mission. 'There was no point in me twiddling my thumbs waiting for you both to get back from the hospital.' Once done, he shoved the empty boxes under the table. 'Thought I'd crack on and get some case files ordered in from Central Records. *This,*' he said, patting a thin, newer looking file, 'is info I downloaded from the internet.

Reece grinned with Cable, though wasn't yet sure if he should. He had no clue what he was about to be presented with. Limited experience of working with the newbie suggested it might be worth the short wait.

Jenkins was frowning. 'How did you get all this brought over here?' She was counting the files. 'Central Records is notorious for not—'

Ginge checked where the chief super was, relative to his own position, and shook his head at Jenkins so imperceptibly that only his eyes moved. Jenkins took the hint and didn't press him on it.

Reece tried not to laugh. Ginge was a chip off the old block, perhaps? He clapped his hands together, and said: 'Come on then, Boy Wonder, you've kept us waiting long enough.'

'Where shall I stand?' Ginge wanted to know. He looked as eager as the rest of them to get started.

'Does it matter?' Reece asked. 'You're going to talk to us, not demonstrate a folk dance.'

Ginge blushed every conceivable shade of red before he began his presentation.

Isla was alone, frightened, and cold. But no longer was she chained to a damp wall in a rat-infested basement. That had to be a positive on any day of the week. That's what she kept telling herself. *Positive thoughts, girl. Keep them going.* She checked the bits of the sky visible above and between the trees and saw it had the makings of getting dark soon. *That's gonna be fun. Not!*

She'd once visited New York. A family holiday while still little more than a toddler. She'd stood on the busy sidewalk, mesmerised by the sheer height of the towering buildings, craning her neck so far back she almost fell over. Dad held onto her, just in case. Everyone laughing. Especially mum.

Isla couldn't imagine ever laughing again. Not if what *he'd* said was true. The only thing that kept her going was the belief it was nothing more than a cruel lie told to control and frighten her.

She had to get her bearings, which wasn't an easy thing to do when surrounded by a mountainous wall of swaying pines.

She could see nothing else. Not unless the blanket of mist descending ominously from above counted for anything. It looked like the forest was smouldering after a fierce fire. But there was no heat. The very opposite, in fact. She was shivering and had to get a move on before the falling temperature really took hold and affected her decision making.

She'd avoid the main path through the forest. That way, she'd steer clear of the men in the car. That's what she hoped, anyway.

She'd gone only a few metres when she stopped again, a thought nagging at her. The men in the car weren't the problem. *They* hadn't killed Mum. *He* had. He'd admitted it himself. The men were after him and not her. That meant they could help.

As the mist chased Isla into the trees, she'd already made the decision to flag down the BMW and ask its occupants for a lift home.

Chapter 65

Reece remembered seeing a missed call from Ginge when he and Jenkins were at the hospital in Swansea. Things had then got busy, and the call wasn't returned.

It had been a hunch on the newbie's part. One that had quickly turned to hard fact. He'd wanted Reece's approval to order the old files from Central Records. Protocol was, it could only be done on the say-so of a senior officer. But with Reece not answering, he'd gone in search of the chief super. Cable's PA had put him somewhere around tenth in a queue of others. What he had couldn't wait that long. 'I told them it was on your orders, boss.' He glanced nervously from Reece to Cable and back again. 'I'm sorry. I know I should have waited.'

'I told you to go get whatever you needed,' Reece said. 'It *was* an order from me.'

Cable agreed with a single nod.

Ginge visibly relaxed. 'The more I've thought about this case, the more likely it was to be something connected with a business deal. Kosh's butcher's shop has been turning a good profit these last few years. I've been through the accounts. Someone else might have wanted a cut of that.' Ginge looked up and smirked. 'Pardon the pun.'

Reece groaned. 'Get on with it.'

Ginge apologised. 'These sorts of killings often happen when there's a business disagreement. Or a love triangle. But in this case, it's the woman who was murdered, and there's no evidence to suggest John Kosh is gay. So, it's a business deal gone pear-shaped, I thought.'

Logical, if not original. Reece didn't interrupt.

'Looking into the purchase of the butcher's shop was simple enough. It changed hands only a few years back, as you already know. There was plenty of paperwork available. Most of it I got from the usual online databases.'

Jenkins folded her arms across her chest. 'And there's nothing you like more than a juicy database, eh, Ginge?'

'That's what I'm good at,' he said defensively.

Reece placed a supportive hand on the younger man's shoulder. 'Ignore her. She's jealous of your expertise with technology.'

Jenkins scoffed. 'Says the man who's outwitted by his phone most days.'

Reece tutted, though accepted it would be unfair to deny the claim. 'You were saying, Ginge.'

'There were no objections to the purchase. Not from any of the other business owners in that area. No disputes with suppliers or customers. No debts. Everything cleared by the end of the month.' Ginge tapped a thin file. 'It's all in there.'

Cable had said nothing until now. 'I'm sensing a *but*.'

'It's the other business that had the issues.' Ginge checked the contents of one of the thicker files. He put it down and opened another. 'There were plenty of disputes logged over the years for Kosh Farm in Radyr.'

Reece scratched his chin, unpleasant memories rising from the paperwork like a toxic gas. The others in the room wouldn't be aware of it as yet.

'There were several issues with sheep straying onto the highways,' Ginge said. 'A couple of chewed-up flowerbeds in the locals' gardens. Warnings and small fines, mostly. The odd appearance in Magistrate's Court for late payments on leased equipment.'

Reece chewed the edge of a fingernail as he listened.

'I haven't had a chance to go through it all as yet,' Ginge said. 'These here came over from Records only a short while ago. But there's plenty of stuff describing feuds relating to land boundaries.' He dragged another file towards him. 'John Kosh's father seems to be involved in the vast majority of them.'

Reece's hand moved to massage the back of his neck.

Ginge continued: 'What if somebody from the neighbouring farm still harboured a big enough grudge to—'

Reece shook his head and shot to his feet. 'It's got nothing to do with anyone being pissed off at John Kosh for selling land he didn't own.'

Ginge looked crestfallen. 'No?'

'I'm a fool for not working it out myself,' Reece said. 'The motive has been staring me in the face all along.' He slapped the young constable's shoulder so hard he almost knocked him off his chair. 'Cheer up. Unlike me, you've done brilliantly.'

Chapter 66

'Dai Kosh was a nasty piece of work,' Reece said, holding a finger to his crooked nose. 'He's responsible for this. A head butt when I was little more than Ginge's age.' Even the memory of that day angered him.

Idris Roberts had laughed when informed of the incident and disagreed when Reece demanded Kosh be charged with assault. Roberts had gone as far as threatening the newbie with an immediate transfer if he hadn't shut up about the farmer being a suspect in a murder investigation.

Reece had known he was right all along. That Dai Kosh was bad to the bone. Shame then, no one at the Radyr police station had been prepared to go down that road and ask awkward questions.

Were they corrupt?

If so, was Idris involved? He might simply have been following orders issued by someone further up the food chain. Reece knew that was a possibility. Please let it be that.

The Old Man Jasper case had shaped Reece as a detective more than he'd ever realised. It was why he often worked outside the box, questioned authority, and had developed a deep suspicion of it.

His thoughts wandered to times of old. He'd always reconciled himself with the view that everything was different back then. SIOs took more risks. Made more assumptions. Required less evidence to secure themselves a conviction.

Excuses. That's all they were.

But then he wasn't naïve enough to believe that modern day policing was perfect in any shape or form. There were rotten eggs in every institution. Even at the Cardiff Bay station.

'Dai and Jasper had been at it for years,' Reece said. Their fathers before them. No surprise then when Jasper turned up dead one day, most of his head missing, courtesy of a shotgun blast.'

'Ouch. That's got to hurt,' Jenkins said.

'Not for very long, I'd imagine.'

'Did Kosh Senior die in prison?' Jenkins asked. She turned to Cable. 'John Kosh mentioned his father having a fatal heart attack, ma'am.'

'Dai never went to prison.' Reece wandered the room, his hands hidden in his pockets. 'He wasn't even treated as a suspect in the case.'

'But you said the farmers had been arguing for years?' Jenkins looked puzzled. 'Wouldn't that have made him the prime suspect?'

'You'd think so, wouldn't you?' Reece told them of Arvel Baines. But what had Yanto said about the landlord at the Druid Inn? 'Shit!' Reece slumped onto a chair, banging the side of his head with his knuckles.

Jenkins went over to him. 'What's wrong? You feeling unwell?'

He looked past her. To Ginge. 'I want you to bring up a recent case file.'

Ginge entered Elgan Collins's name as instructed. He sat back and pointed at his computer screen. 'It was logged as a *death by misadventure.*'

Reece leaned over and read more. 'Scroll down to the bit with the witness statements.'

Ginge rolled the cordless mouse-wheel towards him. 'There were three employees working the night Collins died. They all left together, none of them admitting to going back.'

'Further down,' Reece said. 'What does that say? There.'

Ginge read aloud, skimming the superfluous bits. 'The girl claims to have locked the door on their way out. She was sure of it.' He read the other two statements. 'These guys agree.'

'But the door to the pub was open when they returned the following morning?' Reece took control of the mouse. 'Who was called to go take a look at it?' He read the name of the SIO and buried his face in his hands. 'It had to be him.'

'Who was it?' Jenkins asked, trying to steal a look.

Reece closed the laptop's lid and did a quick calculation of the current date minus thirty years. 'Get onto HMP Cardiff,' he told Ginge. 'I want to know when or if Arvel Baines went free.'

'And where are you going?' Cable called after him.

Reece cracked the knuckles of both fists. 'To bounce that idiot off the four walls of his office.'

Chapter 67

Reece found DI Adams in his office. He marched in without bothering to knock and leaned across the fast-tracked detective's desk. 'A man found dead in his bathtub and three employees insisting that front door was locked when they left.'

Adams told whoever was on the other end of the line that he'd call them back. He put his phone away in his pocket and got up and rounded his desk. 'What are you talking about?'

Reece used his foot to slam the office door hard enough for the slatted blinds to shoot up lopsidedly. 'Yet it was found open the following morning, and you didn't think that odd?'

Adams reached for the blind's pullcord and tried to straighten them. 'How dare you come in here shooting your mouth off,' he said over his shoulder.

It took every ounce of Reece's reserve not to swing a punch at him. He contemplated strangulation instead. That way, he could stare into the idiot's eyes as he slowly died. 'They locked the door when they left. It was unlocked when they got back in the morning. There was a dead man in the bath. Are you catching up yet?'

Adams went back to his seat and rested his hands on the edge of his desk. 'So they made a mistake in their rush to get off home. They *thought* they'd locked up, but hadn't.'

'All three of them?'

'Okay then – Collins let the cat out before going back to finish his bath. Then *kapow!* He never got the chance to go back down and lock up.'

'Kapow?' Reece groaned.

'The post mortem found enough alcohol in his system to put him more than twice over the legal limit for driving.' Adams shrugged. 'He took a tumble and knocked the lamp in with him. It's not rocket science.'

'How much water was there on the bathroom floor?' Reece asked.

'I don't know.'

'You don't know?'

'Some. A bit.'

Reece tried to keep his fists occupied. 'Collins was well over twenty stones in weight. He should have spilled a damn sight more than *a bit* when he fell in.' Something caught Reece's attention on the other side of the glass. Cable and Jenkins were quick-stepping their way towards the office. 'Relax,' he called to them. 'I haven't killed him.' He turned to Adams. *'Not yet!'*

'It might have given us another angle on the Kosh case had we known earlier,' Reece said as he, Cable, and Jenkins made their way back up to the incident room. He'd since apologised to Adams, acknowledging that he'd been just as frustrated with his own shortcomings.

'I'm still unconvinced anyone would have made a link between the cases.' Cable sounded out of breath. 'Including you, after all this time.'

Reece slowed the pace. 'I took my eye off the ball. When Yanto mentioned Elgan Collins's death, I should have made the connection there and then.' He lowered his head. 'If anything happens to that girl because of me . . .'

'It won't be your fault,' Cable assured him.

That wasn't how Reece saw it. He called Ginge's name on entering the incident room.

The detective constable was at his desk, scribbling in his pocketbook. 'Boss.'

'Any news from the prison governor?'

'He's only just got back to me.'

'Are you going to tell us what he said?' Reece asked, massaging his eyeballs.

'Baines is definitely out. He served a full thirty stretch and was released just over a month ago.'

'The timeframe fits Helen Kosh's murder perfectly,' Reece said. 'We should've been notified of the release.'

'I'm sure we were,' Cable replied. 'Standard procedure would have the in-charge shift inspector brief the duty sergeant, who'd then do the same with the junior ranks.'

Reece didn't need a lesson in station procedure. 'Who *was* that inspector?' He mouthed Adams's name in unison with Ginge. 'How many more times?'

'I'll deal with him,' Cable promised.

'Let's move on,' Reece said, leaning against Ginge's desk. 'We have to assume that Baines intends to target everyone involved in setting him up.'

Cable stopped him. 'Are you saying you believe he was innocent all along?'

Reece spent the next ten minutes describing his misgivings over the original investigation and trial. 'It never sat right with me. Not then. Not now. But that didn't matter at the time. No one was listening. Not to a *wet-behind-the-ears* DC like me.'

Cable turned away. 'I can't believe I'm hearing this.'

'What else could I do?' Reece said. 'Believe me, I knocked on everyone's door.' And he had. Not that it did any good.

'Let's refocus,' Cable said, shaking her head at him. 'Those farmhands. Are they at risk, do you think?'

'Without a doubt.'

Ginge referred to his pocketbook. 'Flint and Hodges?'

Reece nodded slowly. 'It won't be easy, but see if you can find contact numbers for both. Ask them to come in for a chat.'

Jenkins tutted. 'It's only just registered with me. When we interviewed Creed, he said something like, "*It's Baine a long time.*" I thought nothing of it. He was being cocky and showing off. He already knew who was behind this.'

Reece had been too angry to pick up on it, but had no reason to doubt what Jenkins claimed to have heard. 'Which means there's a fair chance he knows where the girl is.'

'An accomplice?' Cable asked.

Reece shook his head. 'Creed went to Belmarsh Prison, not Cardiff. Baines and him could never have met and discussed it.'

'They didn't need to,' Ginge said. 'Arvel Baines's cellmate was a Jeffrey Sykes. And guess who *he* worked for before going down for armed robbery and murder?'

'Billy Creed. Sykes will have leaked everything Baines told him.'

'But what would Creed gain from having any part in this?' Jenkins asked. 'He knows he'd have us crawling all over him as a suspect.'

'Bargaining chips over Baines?' Reece suggested. 'Creed would have himself another lackey to do his dirty work whenever the time and circumstance suited.'

'I've found a current address for Baines,' Ginge said, referring to an entry previously made in his pocketbook. 'It's local, if his parole officer hasn't been misled.'

Reece told the team he knew where that was. The minutes that followed consisted of numerous hurried phone calls. To the canine division. *Eye in the Sky.* Even ACC Harris's office. There were people rushing about the room. Grabbing jackets and other personal effects. Knocking over unfinished paper coffee cups in their haste to get going. Jenkins booked a pool car. At last, they were on their way to rescue Isla Kosh.

Chapter 68

Isla had no clue which way she should go. Or how to get back to where she'd been. Everything looked the same in the heart of the forest. There were no landmarks as such, only repeated variants of greens and browns. Rocks and sticks. And pine needles. Plenty of those mean sods.

The mist hadn't followed, and for that, she was eternally grateful. At one point, she'd expected it to unleash an army of bloodsucking vampires. It hadn't. Thank God.

She'd earlier picked out a tree up ahead—one that looked noticeably different to all the others—and walked towards it in an attempt to focus her direction of travel. Her intention was to repeat that for as many times as it took to find her way out of there.

It should work, she'd told herself. But with increasing levels of darkness making it difficult to maintain a straight line, she was beginning to think she might have veered away from her intended course, going somewhere off to the right.

She knew she hadn't meandered in a wide circle, because she'd always been travelling on a downward slope. If all she was doing was walking in circles, then she'd surely have gone uphill in places.

She hadn't done that. Not yet, anyway.

Her bare feet were raw—like a pair of unkempt hedgehogs stuck to the ends of her legs—yellowed pine needles protruding in all directions. She sat on the mossy trunk of a fallen tree and began removing them one by one. But there wasn't enough time for that. She swiped her hands across each foot in turn, shifting as many as she could while crying out with the pain of it.

'It smells like Christmas in here,' she kept telling herself in an attempt to remain positive. 'And the pine needles are like the ones Mum's still vacuuming out of the carpet several months later. *Mum.*' Isla whispered the word. It hurt far more than any of the splinters did.

Reece pulled out of the station car park with a show of blue lights and some *kangaroo petrol* – the vehicle lurching forward a couple of times before he selected a more appropriate gear.

There were no arguments. No swearing. Just out onto the road and away at an increasing rate of speed.

Jenkins opened the passenger glovebox and searched for something she didn't find. 'Damn, we've got the one without the screwdriver,' she said, closing the lid with a loud bang. She reached above her left shoulder and caught hold of a short strap. 'But it does have one of these. Da-*da*.'

'Shut up.' When Reece caught her eye, the pair of them shared the joke with raptures of belly laughter. They were at ease with one another. A perfect working-partnership. Like buttered scones and strawberry jam.

Ginge hadn't been on the recent trip to the hospital in Swansea and didn't get the joke, and so managed a bemused smile only. His head was squashed so far forward between the front seats, that if Reece braked hard, it'd likely snap the younger man's neck. 'No sign of Billy Creed, then. You think he knows we're onto him?'

'Course he does,' Reece said. There had been simultaneous raids on the Midnight Club, Green Baize snooker hall, and other shady businesses dotted in and around the city. The detectives had been listening to radio transmissions, none of which had yet reported finding, or taking the gangster into custody. 'That's why he's nowhere to be found,' Reece said, crossing the busy junction when the traffic gave way to another blast of the siren.

'Do you think he's shacked up at Baines's place?' Jenkins asked.

'If he is, then he won't be talking his way out of this one.' Reece gripped the steering wheel and grinned ear to ear. 'Oh, Billy Boy – Copper's coming to get you.'

Chapter 69

Arvel Baines had the urge to kill again. Not just anyone. Someone in particular.

Running about the forest with needle-spiked branches whipping his exposed flesh was making him angrier by the second. Billy Creed was now top of his death-list. Not the farmhands. Not his useless defence lawyer. Certainly not the detective. But Billy *fucking* Creed.

Baines could hear the BMW searching for him. 'Persistent sons of bitches.' It wasn't that far away. Even so, it would have to be a lucky strike for its headlights to catch him in their beams. And he'd see it before its occupants saw him.

He had the upper hand. The darkness and extra mobility of being on foot was a welcome advantage. He was outnumbered, but unlike his time at the snooker hall, he was no longer playing with a fistful of jokers.

His new plan was to keep the growling BMW within earshot. Get a visual on it, if he could. Get alongside and then . . . And then, what?

He hadn't thought that far ahead and was still mulling it over when he caught a glimpse of blueish-white halogen lights in the middle-distance. They appeared to be strobing as the vehicle travelled adjacent to the stout, upright trunks of the trees. When he couldn't keep up, he began a cautious jog. When that wasn't fast enough, he ran hard. Hurdling rotting logs in order to keep it in sight. He was breathing hard. His feet slipping on moss-covered rocks. Once or twice, he took a blow to the face from a low-hanging branch. More often than that, his clothing got snagged and slowed him down.

He wouldn't let up any more than the trees would. He pushed on and was almost sprinting. Not looking where he was going. More interested in keeping the BMW in his sights. When he realised there was no longer anything underfoot, it was already too late.

Arvel Baines was falling through the air.

'Pull over. Stop!' Creed lowered the window and stuck his head out into the night. He wouldn't as yet have seen the red and green navigation lights of the approaching helicopter, but could hear its engine and slap of its rotor-blades cutting through the early evening air. It was a fair distance away, still. That wouldn't be the case in only a few minutes' time. 'Copper's onto us.' He brought his head back inside and closed the window.

'What we gonna do, Billy?' Jimmy Chin waited for instructions.

Creed caught the bigger man by the knee and squeezed until Chin was squealing and writhing in his seat. 'What did I tell you earlier?'

Chin massaged an area of lower thigh once Creed had let go of him. '"No one gets out of these woods alive."'

The gangster leaned across the front of Chin and popped the door locks. 'So why the fuck are you two still here?'

Chapter 70

REECE AND THE TROOPS weren't the first to arrive at Arvel Baines's smallholding. When they pulled up in front of the main house, there was already a dog team present, the back doors of the canine van left wide open.

'Where are the stars of the show?' Reece called to one of the handlers.

Not a moment later, two English Springer Spaniels appeared, running in circles with their noses glued to the ground. 'They're familiarising themselves with the area,' the handler said, bringing both dogs to her side.

There were armed response officers [AFOs] present. All of them wearing visored helmets with Tac vests and body armour. Reece went over and spoke with their Team Leader; a plan of action quickly agreed between both professionals.

The *Eye in the Sky* was hovering low above them, its engines making standard voice communication difficult without shouting. A downdraught blew like a gale.

The AFOs split into two teams. One group going to clear the barn and other outbuildings. The second, to make ingress into the house from the front and back. Both locations would be hit simultaneously.

Everyone else, including Reece and his murder squad, stayed put until told the immediate area was safe to enter. 'Okay, let's go,' he said, responding to a call to approach the barn. Jenkins and Ginge went with him.

'That's the van from the CCTV footage,' Ginge said as they approached the open door. He pointed to areas inside the barn. 'Spray gun just there.' He followed the others in. 'And rolls of paper for masking off the wheels and windows.'

'I want the contents of that bin gone through,' Reece told a uniform.

Jenkins hovered her head over the top of it. 'Someone's been having a right little bonfire.' She took a piece of dowel-rod from the top of the workbench and poked at the burned contents. 'I don't think we'll get much out of this, boss.'

'Do it anyway.' Reece approached the Team Leader. 'How long before we get access to the house?' The man spoke into a shoulder radio and told him they were good to go. 'Any sign the girl's been in there?' Reece asked. The AFO walked with him and asked the same question of one of his officers on guard at the doorstep.

'Can't say for sure it was the girl, sir, but it looks like someone's been held captive in the basement.' The officer held onto the front door and checked with his senior before letting Reece pass.

Chapter 71

Something moved nearby. The unmistakable sound of the push and pull of branches. Sticks snapping underfoot.

But who's feet?

Isla thought she heard someone cough. She definitely heard voices. There was no doubt about that.

A conversation was being had between two men she couldn't yet see. They were coming her way.

Then there was the sound of a helicopter drowning out everything else in the area – a wide beam of bright light playing on the tops of the trees.

It was searching.

They were searching.

And this time, for her.

She screamed at it and waved her arms in the air. The helicopter and its light moved on; its crew unable to hear her cries for help.

Unlike the two men on foot. They knew exactly where she was and were now only a few metres away.

Arvel Baines swayed in the canopy of a tall tree. Landing there had been a feat of good fortune. That and much grabbing at the passing air as he'd gone over the side of the cliff, or whatever it was.

He'd seen Sylvester Stallone do something similar in the film *First Blood*. Or was it *Rambo?* Stallone had badly lacerated his arm in the fall and closed the wound with a needle and thread.

Baines had also cut himself. His right side was soaked and warm. Just above the hip. He put a hand to it and felt a soft lump. Exploring beneath his clothing, he was horrified to discover he'd been stabbed by a length of snapped branch – some of his innards now turned to *outards*. He was making up words. Trying not to think the worst. Anything to avoid dwelling on the fact he'd likely be bleeding internally. How ironic was it to have been shanked when a free man?

Below him was a good thirty, if not more, feet of vertical drop. He could tell only because of the foaming white surface water of what sounded to be a fast-flowing river.

When the helicopter arrived overhead, fixing him in its search beam, Baines took the opportunity to eyeball his surroundings. There were trees to his right. The drop to the river a lot higher than he'd first calculated. In front of him was a vertical rock face peppered with patches of silvery lichen, cracked and dripping with water draining off the land above it. To his left, and not very far away, was a grass bank covered with ferns and sapling trees.

The drop to the bank was no more than ten feet. It had to be worth a punt.

The downdraught from the aircraft's rotors risked sending him to a watery death. It backed off a little, but not by much.

That gave him an idea. Moving in time with the motion of the swaying tree, he built momentum, letting go only when he believed he had enough of a spring to land on the grass bank. His immediate problem after that was to stop himself from falling backwards into the void below.

Chapter 72

'Get off me!' Isla aimed a handful of broken fingernails at Jimmy Chin, narrowly missing his face when she struck out. She screamed as loudly as her sore throat would allow, but with the helicopter hovering only fifty metres or so ahead of her current position, its crew had no chance of hearing her.

Chin grabbed Isla's wrist and pulled her awkwardly to the floor. He fell on top, pinning her to the ground with his heavy hulk. 'I likes them with a bit of fight,' he said, nuzzling into her neck.

He smelled of stale sweat and far too much aftershave. Isla forced her knee hard into his groin. 'Just as well,' she said, hitting him with it a second time. 'Coz, you're going to get yourself a right fucking tear-up if you think you can try it on with me.' She was on her feet, searching for something heavy enough to whack him with.

'Don't let her get away,' Chin told the other man between episodes of noisy vomiting. He rolled over onto his knees and took a knife from his pocket. 'I'll be the one to kill her.'

While her attackers had strength and better numbers, Isla had youthful agility on her side. She ducked beneath an outstretched arm. And again – this time in the reverse direction. She grabbed for a branch, drew it back like the string of a bow, and let go. It hit Jimmy Chin smack in the face, making his nose bleed. She didn't hang about to witness what happened next. She was off. Racing through the trees. This time in the direction of the beam of bright light.

The crew of the *Eye in the Sky* had reported contact—male, not female—giving precise coordinates for the ground team to close in on what they expected to be Arvel Baines.

Reece, Jenkins and Ginge were among that ground team, beating their way through the forest using batons and their booted feet.

The dogs were further ahead. Sniffing. Barking. Following the scent provided by the school shoes found in the basement of the abandoned cottage.

'There was no sign of any spilled blood in the basement,' Reece said at the top of his voice. 'We have to be thankful for that.'

'How do you think she got away?' Jenkins asked just as loudly.

'No idea.' They were almost at the sighting point, the helicopter hovering directly above them. Reece put an arm out in warning. 'Remember what they said about there being a shear drop nearby.' He was breathing heavily, and only partly with the exertion of the chase.

One of the search dogs barked and pulled in the opposite direction, the second one adopting similar behaviour not a moment later. 'They're onto something,' the handler said. 'It'll be the girl.'

Reece stood still. There was a decision to make. Which way to go now? Twisting at the waist, he checked behind them. Then up at the empty treetops where Baines had last been sighted. Next, he stared somewhere beyond. 'There he is,' Reece shouted. 'Over there on the bank.' When he went to move off again, Jenkins grabbed at his coat sleave and pulled him back.

She used her extended baton to poke at the air near their feet. 'We're right on the edge of that drop. You can hear the river now that the helicopter has moved a bit further on.'

'Get me away from it.' Reece couldn't budge. 'Quickly, for Christ's sake.'

'Come towards me,' Jenkins told him. 'Slowly.'

'I can't.' Reece's eyes were screwed closed. 'My legs aren't listening to what I'm telling them.'

'Take my hand.' She tapped him when he didn't respond. 'Boss. My hand.'

He curled his fingers so tightly around hers, that he worried he might break her bones. But try as he did, he couldn't loosen his grip.

'Step towards me.' Jenkins pulled gently at first. 'Trust me,' she said, pulling more firmly when she had him. 'That's it, you're almost there.'

Reece lurched forward and threw himself to the ground, face down in the wet grass. He couldn't speak. Couldn't open his eyes.

Jenkins knelt beside him, her hand on his shoulder. 'It's okay, boss. You're safe.'

All but one of the AFOs had remained at the smallholding. A rapid safety assessment between Reece and their Team Leader deeming it unsafe to have that many firearms in the dark woods with *friendlies* and Isla still at large. They'd put one marksman in the helicopter; to be utilised only if presented with a clear shot at the target.

'What do you want me to do?' asked the woman with the excited dogs. 'They're onto a strong scent this time.'

Jenkins got to her feet. 'Boss. The dogs?'

Reece sat up slowly and leaned away from the drop. His response was a simple one. 'Go find the girl.'

Chapter 73

Arvel Baines gripped a short length of sapling, winded by the impact of hitting the ground from such a height. He was in terrible pain with the stab injury to his side, his jeans and lower part of his sweatshirt soaked with warm blood.

There was shouting coming from the other side of the drop. Indistinct silhouettes of people skirting the edge of it. He'd only moments earlier heard the barking of dogs. That was receding now, as the group disappeared into the trees.

He shifted himself away from the drop to the river below, using the toes of his boots to dig into the soft soil. He grabbed for another sapling and heaved himself towards what he hoped might be a place of safety.

He had to get away from the helicopter and escape the deafening roar of its engine as much as he did its blinding searchlight. The crew must have read his thoughts and taken pity on him, the aircraft pulling away and following in the direction of the dogs. There was no one to be seen on the clifftop. If they were trying to get to where he currently was, then they'd first have to travel in a northerly direction for a good ten minutes before cutting west and then almost back on themselves again.

By using individual saplings for hand-holds, Baines crawled up the slope under cover of the trees. He welcomed the respite from the helicopter and its intrusive beam of white light. Resting his back against the trunk of a tree, he lifted his T-shirt to examine the wound. He wiped the slimy mess and put his fingers to his nose. 'Shit.' Literally. He'd punctured his bowel – a death sentence without urgent surgery and access to powerful antibiotics.

He got to his feet. Ahead of him was an open patch of ground that had undergone recent logging activity. Felled trees were scattered here and there. He staggered towards it, knowing he was more exposed. But with the helicopter busy with other things, the open ground made it far easier for him to make his escape.

It was when he got almost two-thirds of the way across it, he made a startling discovery. There was a car—a BMW X5 to be precise—parked on the dirt track a little further ahead. The interior lights were on, obscuring the sole occupant's view of the outside.

Billy Creed was smoking a cigar, and for once, was minding his own business. There was no sign of Jimmy Chin or Ugly.

Baines shuffled his way round to the driver's side of the vehicle, knowing he'd never get a better chance to punish Creed. When he opened and then slammed the door shut behind him, the gangster couldn't have looked any more surprised. 'Evening, Billy. I bet you didn't expect this?'

'What the fuck?'

Baines popped the door locks and got the engine going with a single tap of the Start/Stop button. He revved it hard while bleeding and leaking liquid shit onto the leather seats. 'Couldn't keep your nose out of my affairs, could you, Billy?' The interior lights went off, throwing them into darkness.

Creed swung a fistful of sovereign rings, opening an area of flesh above Baines's left eye, the smouldering cigar lost to the carpeted wheel well.

Baines selected reverse on the automatic gearbox, releasing the electronic parking brake while subjected to a deluge of heavy punches. Luckily for him, the cramped conditions and close proximity made it next to impossible for Creed to land a good one.

When the car pulled off the grass banking, Creed was reaching for the glovebox, and struck his head against the dashboard. As he recoiled from the impact, Baines returned the compliment, smashing his clenched knuckles against the gangster's nose.

Creed pushed back in his seat, screaming obscenities. Twisting his upper body, he cocked a handgun and let off the first shot. It missed. The bullet exiting the vehicle through its roof, leaving a black hole smoking in the cream lining.

The noise was deafening, leaving Baines convinced his left eardrum had been shredded. He kept one hand gripped on the steering wheel and used the other to fend off a flurry of pistol whips. He knew exactly where he was taking them and steered the BMW off the rutted dirt track and into the clearing left by the loggers.

Isla was past caring about her feet. She had bigger things to worry about. There were two men chasing her. At least one of them carrying a knife and a hefty grudge.

But why had they wanted to harm her?

Why kill Mum?

What had Dad done to get the family into this?

Why, why, why?

There were still no answers. Only questions.

The trees tore at her clothing as she smashed through them. She stripped off her school cardigan and tossed it to one side.

'There she is!'

Ugly had somehow got in front of her and blocked the way. He grabbed. She ducked. Turned, and ran no further than a few more metres before the man with the knife caught hold of her.

'You're gonna wish you were never born.' Chin undid the buckle of his leather belt, pushing Isla to the floor with his free hand. 'Hold her down,' he told the other man. 'You get sloppy seconds.' As he slid his jeans down his thighs, the only thing louder than Isla's screaming was the crack of a gunshot coming from somewhere behind them.

Chapter 74

EVERYONE IN THE FOREST would have heard the gunshot. The unmistakable calls for help from a young female were not lost on them either. 'Get that helicopter over here,' Reece told Jenkins, pointing to where he wanted the light.

It took only seconds for the crew to fix Isla, Jimmy Chin and Ugly in the snare of its searchlight. Chin rolled off the girl and pulled at the waistband of his jeans. When he got up, he stumbled and fell over.

'*Jimmy!*' Reece snarled the name.

'Boss!' Jenkins went after him. 'They could be armed.'

'You stay put,' Reece said above the din of the helicopter's engine. 'That's an order.'

Ugly ran into the forest and beat a path through trees. Jimmy Chin, on the other hand, stayed where he was, brandishing a knife in front of Isla Kosh's neck. 'I'll cut her fucking head off,' he warned, reversing them both out of there. 'She's coming with me.'

'Let her go.' Reece went closer, albeit more slowly. 'It's over, Jimmy.'

'I'll do it. Stay the fuck away.'

Even from where he stood, Reece could see how perilously close the blade was to slicing through the flesh of Isla's neck. He knew he couldn't let Chin disappear into the trees. There'd be no guarantee of keeping the girl safe were that to happen. Reece dropped to his knees, adopting the surrender pose he and the marksman had earlier agreed on as the *sign*. 'You're in charge,' he told Chin. 'I'm staying put.'

Isla was crying and no longer trying to fight her attacker off.

'It's going to be all right,' Reece said, his hands held behind his back, the index finger of the right one pointing towards the ground. It was a simple enough gesture. As clear as it was concise. It meant *one shot: one target.*

Chin looked as though he was about to say something before he was interrupted by the sound of a solitary gunshot. He fell onto his back with little drama, a neatly placed hole between his eyes, oozing blood and brain tissue.

Reece got up and reached an arm. 'Isla, come to me.' The girl hesitated and was close to hysterical. He went to her instead. 'I'm Brân,' he said, taking her into his arms and hugging her like she was his own child. She didn't object. When they broke apart, his smile was warm and genuine. 'I'm one of the good guys. We're here to take you home.'

Chapter 75

Arvel Baines wasn't going home. He'd long since resigned himself to that fact. He wasn't going back to prison either.

He was going to hell.

Still fending off Creed, he drove one-handed. The gun discharged a second time. Once more after that. The first bullet took out the side window next to his head. An inch more to the right and it would have killed him. The other hit the infotainment console in the centre of the dashboard, rendering it useless.

When Ugly came out of nowhere—fixed in the BMW's headlights—he looked like a zombie lurching towards them with open arms. The wing of the SUV collided with his pelvis, spinning him around and sending him under the front wheel. Neither occupant turned to check out of the rear window.

Baines knew he couldn't continue for much longer. He was fighting to stay conscious, his vision narrowing down to only seeing what was directly in front of the car. He was blinded to everything else. The fourth gunshot had little effect on him.

Billy Creed was pulling at a door handle that wouldn't let him out. He turned the gun towards it. It recoiled in his hand as he let off another volley of shots. When at last he got the door open, he couldn't lift his leg. He'd been sitting in one position for longer than his knackered knee could manage.

Baines grabbed hold of him, but had no real strength left. He wedged his foot against the accelerator pedal, the back end of the BMW twitching violently. He needed both hands on the steering wheel as he directed them towards the cliff's edge.

Creed couldn't have known what was looming up ahead. Even if he did, there was no time to get out. He pressed the gun to Baines's chest and let off one last shot.

As the bullet ripped through him, Baines had a feeling of weightlessness for the second time that evening. On this occasion, the trees parted and let him through to the river below.

The BMW didn't explode on impact. Instead, it concertinaed. White airbags bloating on all sides. The horn blared with a monotonous note that accompanied the noise of metal scraping on rock as the vehicle sought a resting place.

The only sound after that came from fast flowing water and the wind in the trees.

Chapter 76

THORNHILL CREMATORIUM. ONE WEEK LATER.

A PAIR OF WELL-BEHAVED black Friesian horses walked ahead of Billy Creed's carriage, their shod hooves clip-clopping on the damp tarmac. Wiggley-Jones, the undertaker, held onto the reins, steering them along the winding road towards the crematorium building.

There was a Cardiff City football shirt draped over the gangster's casket. A display of white roses spelled *Billy*. Another was shaped like a thick cigar and brandy glass.

'It's like a who's who of the criminal underworld,' Reece said, watching the usual culprits pass by. He and Jenkins were trying to look inconspicuous, standing next to a tree on the sidelines. It was taking every ounce of Reece's self-control not to get himself positioned in front of the hearse and bare his arse at it.

There were two unmarked police cars bringing up the rear of the funeral line, there to issue an alert should things turn *tasty*.

'That's ACC Harris, isn't it?' Jenkins stooped to get a better look inside the jag.

Reece did the same. 'What's *he* doing here?' Once the last of the vehicles were past, they both stepped out onto the road and followed behind.

One of the unmarked cars stopped almost immediately. The one carrying Harris.

'Here we go.' Reece said. 'Let me do the talking.'

Jenkins glanced at him. 'Do you think that's wise?'

He ignored her. 'Sir. What brings you to a place like this?'

Harris squinted. 'I could ask you the same thing. What the hell are you up to, Reece?'

'Why do I always have to be up to something?'

'Because . . .' Harris marched him off to the safety of the side of the road. He checked the surroundings and lowered his voice, even though there was no one else about. 'Because you can't *fucking* help yourself.'

Reece grinned. Provocatively. 'I'm a detective.' He shoved his hands in his trouser pockets and shrugged. 'It's what I do.'

'You go nowhere near that main building. Do you hear me?' Harris was reversing away. Heading for his car. 'Reece?'

'Okay, sir.' Reece raised a hand. 'One more thing before you go.'

Harris waited next to the open rear door of the Jag. 'What is it?'

'I don't suppose we'll be hearing from the chief constable? Not now we've wrapped this up.'

Harris went bright red.

Jenkins tapped her foot against Reece's. 'Don't go there, boss. Don't go there.'

He wasn't listening. 'You'd have looked a bit daft asking him to disband the Murder Squad – what with the press and family singing our praises to anyone willing to listen.'

Harris turned away and got in the car.

'Why?' Jenkins asked. 'Why do you always have to deliberately wind people up?'

Reece pointed after the car. 'Because his lot are clueless. That's why they've spent an entire career locked away in offices. You can't rely on them to get anything right in the real world.'

'He's our superior, whether you like it or not.'

'*Senior*. Not superior.' Reece was walking towards the crematorium.

Jenkins stayed where she was. 'You promised Harris you wouldn't go anywhere near there.'

'No, I didn't.'

'Yes, you did. I heard you.'

Reece gave her a cheeky grin. 'Well, I didn't mean it.'

She lowered her head. 'A transfer. That's what I'll do. Put in for a sodding transfer.'

'No, you won't.'

'Just watch me.'

Reece held an arm out in front of him. 'Come on. Off you go. I'll give you a head start.'

'Why the head start?'

He dangled two fingers and wriggled them. 'To compensate for your little legs.'

Jenkins checked. 'Who said they're little?'

'You did. At the hospital.'

'I said they're shorter than yours, that's all.'

He gave her a quick once over. 'How tall are you, anyway?'

'About five-five. Five-six, maybe.'

'There you go, then. A short-arse.' He twisted out of range before she could wallop him.

'What do you think about Ffion not going through with the operation?' Jenkins asked as they walked together.

'It's a good thing, isn't it?'

'I don't know. I've done some reading of my own. That gene is a shitty thing to have. I only hope . . .' She let the rest remain unsaid. 'Tomorrow's funeral is going to be a right tearjerker, don't you think?'

Reece used a finger to make room between his shirt collar and neck. 'Isla's going to be in bits.'

'She'll never be the same again.'

'She's strong,' Reece said. 'And there's her dad to concentrate on once he's discharged from hospital.'

'Thank God she wasn't raped.' Jenkins looped her arm in Reece's and rested her head against his shoulder. 'What's wrong with the world?'

Reece needed the physical contact as much as she did. 'Fighting for people like Isla and her family is what gets me out of bed in the morning. The world would be a damn sight worse if people like us didn't bother.'

They waited outside the crematorium building, Reece threatening to sneak around the back – unwilling to accept that Billy Creed was gone until he'd personally witnessed the council hitting him with temperatures of up to 1800 degrees Fahrenheit.

'I wonder what hymn they'll play during the committal?' Jenkins went to the window to listen.

'*I Shot the Sheriff*, knowing that lot.'

'That's not a bloody hymn.' When she turned to give Reece a telling off, he was preoccupied. 'What's the matter?' she asked.

The first of the family had appeared from a doorway in the side of the building. Reece was staring open-mouthed as a woman walked towards them. She was tall and athletically built, and wore a long fur coat. One side of her head was shaved completely bald. The other covered in shoulder-length black hair.

'Boss, who is she?' Jenkins repeated when Reece didn't answer the first time.

'Huh?'

'I asked if you knew her?'

'That's Creed's younger sister.'

'How come I don't know of her?'

'She's been away. Prison. Abroad. I'm not sure which.'

The woman must have heard them. She came and stood as close as she possibly could without making physical contact. 'Marma Creed's come home,' she said, putting a finger to Reece's lips when he tried to speak. 'Copper had better watch his p's and q's.'

About the Author

Liam Hanson is the crime and thriller pen name of author Andy Roberts. Andy lives in a small rural village in South Wales and is married with two grown-up children. Now the proud owners of a camper van nicknamed 'Griff', Andy and his wife spend most days on the road, searching for new locations to walk Walter, their New Zealand Huntaway.

If you enjoy Andy's work and would like to support him, then please leave a review in the usual places.

To learn of new releases and special offers, you can sign up for his no-spam newsletter, found on his Facebook page:
www.facebook.com/liamhansonauthor

Printed in Great Britain
by Amazon